The Stranger in the Dark

* * * *

Eight stories up, the stranger had jumped to another roof across the narrow alleyway.

Travis followed.

The impact was brutal, jarring the breath from his tortured lungs in a quick gasp, scraping the length of his body against the roof, rolling. Stunned, disbelieving, Travis watched as his weapon cracked against the asphalt and flew from his grasp, skidding to a whirling halt some four feet beyond his reach.

Travis turned his head, and time stopped as he stared at the stunned figure of the stranger stretched out less than ten feet away. Suddenly, shocked, he met steady green eyes. They were piercing, cool.

Breaking contact in the same instant, they looked quickly at the weapon positioned just ahead, then looked back again. There was an amused recognition of purpose in the green eyes as they shared the same thought, the same challenge. They both lunged...

ATTENTION: SCHOOLS AND CORPORATIONS

WARNER books are available at quantity discounts with bulk purchase for educational, business, or sales promotional use. For information, please write to SPECIAL SALES DEPARTMENT, WARNER BOOKS, 666 FIFTH AVENUE, NEW YORK, N.Y. 10103

**ARE THERE WARNER BOOKS
YOU WANT BUT CANNOT FIND IN YOUR LOCAL STORES?**

You can get any WARNER BOOKS title in print. Simply send title and retail price, plus 50¢ per order and 50¢ per copy to cover mailing and handling costs for each book desired. New York State and California residents add applicable sales tax. Enclose check or money order only, no cash please, to: WARNER BOOKS, P.O. BOX 690, NEW YORK, N.Y. 10019

DEATH WARRANT

A GARRICK TRAVIS NOVEL

GARY HUNTER

WARNER BOOKS

A Time Warner Company

WARNER BOOKS EDITION

Copyright © 1990 by Gwen Hunter and Gary Leveille
All rights reserved.

Cover illustration by Jim Bandsuh
Cover design by Mike Stromberg

Warner Books, Inc.
666 Fifth Avenue
New York, N.Y. 10103

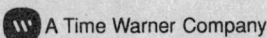 A Time Warner Company

Printed in the United States of America

First Printing: October, 1990

10 9 8 7 6 5 4 3 2 1

Acknowledgments

Earl Jenkins, Jr., M.D., of Rock Hill, South Carolina, for advice on forensic procedures.

Col Isom Lowman, M.D., for his ability to recognize talent, among other things.

Jean Morse of Rock Hill, South Carolina, for helping us to meet deadlines and for correcting our awful spelling.

Mike Prater and Joyce Turner for proofreading and support. Rod Hunter for patience and time. Our families for their enthusiasm.

Bob Bristow for training. Edna Ann Belk for her French help. Ken D. Cruse of Cruse Vineyards in Chester, South Carolina, for computer assistance and chemical know-how.

Officers Diedrich and Matticks for allowing us to share our friendship on paper.

Dewey Stokes, National President of the Fraternal Order of Police, Washington, D.C. Gary Hankins at F.O.P. Lodge Number One, and Detective David Myers, D.C.

Edward J. Krueger for the inspiration to go for it.

Jeff Gerecke for doing what an agent does best and for having a thick hide.

Charles Conrad of Warner Books for taking a chance on a couple of unknowns.

Author's Note

To protect the men who protect society, the author has taken certain liberties with fact. Police codes, location names, street names, and business names of places frequented by police officers have all been changed. Admittedly the author also has an eye to the nuisance of liability.

Catcher Joe's is a composite of the best cop bars in this cop's drinking history. Gertie's, alas, is no more nor has been for many years. But the woman upon whom Gertie is based lives on in the memories of those she touched. To place Gertie in today's D.C. is but a bit of poetic license and wistfulness.

A special thanks to the Fraternal Order of Police. Without the help of National President Dewey Stokes, and Gary, and the rest of the family at F.O.P. Lodge Number One, this book would have lacked some authenticity. For all the assistance rendered as specialists of the D.C. underworld and for warnings about the city's special dangers, we thank you.

Lastly, the author wishes to thank those officers whose likenesses are rendered herein for permission to plagiarize their personalities and characters. You know who you are.

—Gary Hunter

PROLOGUE

April 12, 1980
11:00 P.M.

HIS little finger shook slightly as he dipped Vaseline and smeared it into his nostrils. It was a particularly fine grade of coke Simpson had offered. And a particularly fine girl.

Polynesian, her dusky skin depilated and oiled, her almond eyes showing a hint of the Orient, she had danced a slow hula as the grasses fell one by one from her skirt. It had been a jungle scene. A tiger-painted man had crouched on a ledge before the black mouth of a cave; slit-eyed, he'd followed her dance. The stealth with which the tiger-man pursued the girl, the curving ploy when he captured her, the way he toyed with her before their mating, before the blood ran. . . . It had been exquisite. The reenactment of some legend. The tiger-god and his sacrifice. Their coupling had been exotic. Intense. Spectacular. He closed his eyes against the memory of pleasure.

The moment passed, his pulse slowed. Gratefully he breathed in the damp air. He placed the Vaseline back into the glove compartment, sliding it next to an old Colt .45. He really should see about oiling the Colt. A man's life was only as safe as the condition of his weapon. Yes, he would do that this evening.

Calm, the memories safely banked away like coals for a long night, he turned the key in the ignition. The low hum of the Mercedes soothed him. Checking his rearview mirror, he pulled into the deserted street.

CHAPTER 1

The Present—Day One

IT had been a monotonous night, deadly boring and deep cold in a room full of holes and slow-moving roaches, and with a stink of age and slum that only a razing could cure. Seven and a half hours of sitting on uneven crate slats had left bruised imprints on his thighs; the wall at his back had never warmed and his muscles were stiff and numb as he shrugged his shoulders to relieve the strain. His thoughts had become as morbid as his surroundings. He glanced out the window.

Condon Terrace in southeast D.C. had once been a blue-collar neighborhood, the streets clean and the sidewalks lined with grass. Now it was just one of the city's forty-five known hellholes, a haven for winos, cocaine whores, dopers, street punks, and the dealers who tormented the remaining residents with terrorist tactics and automatic-weapon fire. A drab, dirty place, it was strewn with garbage, abandoned cars, broken concrete, decrepit buildings, violence, and ruined lives.

The building the Narcotic Task Force was using had once been a tenement. Now condemned, it was a shooting gallery where street addicts and dopers retired after their buys to inject or inhale their purchases. It was also a refuge for the homeless; a half-dozen men, two families—one with young children—and a few women slept, cooked, and lived in its squalid halls and empty rooms.

The tenement across the street was dirty and crumbling as well, but was still in use. The residents had begun to move out as drug traffickers slowly took over the entire building. Soloman Davis, a man with connections to most dealers on the eastern seaboard, now ran one of D.C.'s best-protected and most profitable crack-processing plants in the back. An efficient distribution center was located up front. The drug den was so well camouflaged and managed that the city's Narcotic Task Force had discovered it only three weeks earlier. According to street sources, the outfit had been in operation for over a year.

Garrick Travis looked at the den and returned his gaze to the gray room. Wet, frigid air blew across the floor, aimlessly sweeping aged, wrinkled leaves, a cigarette butt, and the exoskeleton of a long-dead insect. There was graffiti scrawled in black spray paint across one wall, arched to pass around and over a hole fresher than the others. The wind died momentarily and the incessant scratching of a rat nesting in the wall caught his attention.

He turned his head slightly, the gray light outside catching his face. It was a strong face, lightly tanned, the skin taut across wide cheekbones and the long, slightly curved nose. The face could once have been called refined, but it was now simply bleak, shadowed, a frozen mask of conflict and cynicism. A passing stranger, had he been able to see into the cracked fourth-story window, would have taken him for a neighborhood tough. Experienced. Dangerous. Possibly deadly.

Though he never liked to think of himself in those terms, it was this expression as much as his expertise and training that had put him to work as an undercover cop in drugs and vice in the D.C. city streets. And it was all of the above and his own peculiar history that kept him there. For some there was no other place to go.

He turned his wrist, not really surprised that it had been only ten minutes since he last looked. From down the adjacent alley came the dull sounds of a half-hearted cat fight, the loser overturning a trash can on its way out into the street. Except for police radio traffic, the meanderings of three cocaine whores, and two street punks who had entered the den and not yet come out, it was the only activity he had heard in over an hour.

The team was using Tactical Communications Channel three, screening out most police communications traffic. Only the special dispatcher and the team members had access to Tac three during the course of this operation. It wasn't much entertainment, but it was all he had to keep him awake.

Travis listened to the voice of the rookie, Rojowski, as he checked off and headed back to the Task Force Headquarters at Fourth and K streets. He remembered how eager the boy's pale blue eyes were the day they took him out of uniform and put him in the streets. Rojo's chance to join the Task Force had been based solely on Travis's recommendation. Travis was justifiably proud of the kid's progress within the department. Rojo had a strong belief in the ideals of law enforcement and had established a stable position in the Task Force.

Travis angled his head and looked out the window once more as the wind again found its way into the room, blowing up his pants leg and through the toe of one of his dirty Pumas. The skyline was slightly grayer than the last time he'd looked, and what sunrise there might have been was hidden behind the leaden clouds and further dispersed by the cold mist that enveloped the city. On the street, a dog, his backbone standing several inches above the surrounding flesh, rummaged through the trash from the overturned can. A horn blared.

He shrugged his shoulders again, aware that by now he did it out of habit, not because of any real benefit. The wind shifted and carried with it a different smell this time, of wet, rotten wood, old urine from a wino's stupefied night, the tell-tale odor of disuse, decay, and mildew, and the distant stench of a decomposing rat.

The smell was familiar and its odor had been working on Travis's mind for weeks. It was the smell of Nam. It left him feeling deadened and slightly nauseated, haunted by memories that were beginning to mingle in his mind, demanding recognition. The memories reminded him of his private theories about this case and made him wonder if they were as real as his mind insisted they were, or as tenuous as his fears suggested. It made him uneasy.

In Vietnam Travis had been a Military Police Investigator, a member of the MPI's Special Drug Operations, stationed on the docks of Da Nang, a major port city in the war-torn country. The South China Sea brought a living and food to the Vietnamese, supplies to the Allied troops, and drugs to feed the addictions of both. The Drug Op's job was to disrupt and destroy the drug shipments into the country. Methods were not specified. Only results counted.

Travis and his associates had traced the drug traffickers to a man named Alain Brevard, a man who had got away and whom Travis had never forgotten. Travis still stalked Brevard at night in his dreams, and by day on the streets of the nation's capital.

Brevard had once been in D.C., and Travis believed he was still in the city, hiding in the gutters of the underworld or parading as one of the city's beautiful people. It had been years since Travis first found clues suggesting the presence of his old target. Then, Brevard had been placed in close proximity to a known drug dealer, acting as the dealer's supplier and backer on the streets.

Travis looked at his watch again. This time almost five minutes had elapsed, and his relief should have been here by now. Wilson was a good man, but he was always late. Until he checked in, Travis was both the Bravo senior man and Wilson's replacement in the event of problems, not that anyone expected any action at this time of the morning.

Mentally, Travis reviewed the last few minutes of half-heard radio communications. Bravo three five had just checked off; Travis was the last Bravo team member still on duty. The other members of the night shift had all been relieved. By the time Wilson finally got here and Travis gave his report, it would be full daylight outside. Not that there was anything to report, just as there had been nothing to tell his replacement any morning for the last three weeks.

The team was composed of thirty men on three staggered shifts, each shift pulling ten-hour days. Travis's team was Bravo, the graveyard shift, a five man team working from nine P.M. till seven A.M. Bravo's job was to mesh with team Charlie between nine and midnight, the hours when a go-ahead was most likely, and more men were called for. Between one A.M. and six A.M., Bravo was for surveillance only, and worked without a lieutenant.

The morning shift was Team Kilo, a twelve-man shift consisting of two sharpshooters, a coordinator, and nine actives. In the event of a go-ahead on day shift, the Task Force would move in two stages. In the first stage, a cover team of four officers would move from their concealed locations to their firing lanes. Once their field of fire was set and the street was cleared of pedestrians, the second stage would receive a go-ahead. An entry team, composed of four officers, would open an access in the well-secured den, by use of either a battering ram or plastic explosives. Both the ram and the explosives were on the first floor of the old tenement, watched over by Josey and Sanderlin, who posed as drinking buddies loitering in a front room.

Once the den was accessed, the two teams would combine and penetrate the building. The cover team consisted of Amy Winston, Josey, Sanderlin, and Jack Smith. The access team consisted of Lamont Lucas, Jane Randall, Ed Manning, and Wilson. Everyone carried a 9mm, and Manning and Lucas were also armed with folding-stock shotguns. The only other access was a back door used for deliveries. A single man, Drew Thomas, covered this exit, armed with a standard-issue 9mm and an M-16 assault rifle.

Timing was essential, the crucial seconds counted down by the team coordinator, Jarvis. Harshel and Powell, the sharpshooters, were strategically placed on the roofs of the tallest buildings. Armed with .380 Winchester rifles, they were the team's final backup, should there be any problems. In such an event, and on Jarvis's authority, the sharpshooters would eliminate the designated targets.

Travis, like all the team's members, had been fully briefed on the workings of the other shifts. Any member could fill in for another to cover for days off or sickness, with the exception of the sharpshooters. They were specialists, secluded in their own little world.

The stakeout had lasted far longer than expected. Travis didn't like it when things took too long; men got jumpy, reacting too soon or too late, reflexes responded out of sync, and mistakes were too often the norm. But his superiors hadn't asked his opinion and wouldn't have listened in any case. They just wanted results, the more spectacular the better, as long as no civilians got killed in the process. Innocent bystanders were bad press. Travis grimaced cynically. Dead cops were a different story and always had been. Even in the military.

To the high-ranking officials of both civilian and military police forces the dead were little more than numbers. Danger was part of the job for a civilian law officer, a simple reality that called for bulletproof Kevlar and widow's funds. The black expanse of the Vietnam Memorial was mute testimony to the government's viewpoint. MPs who had gone undercover with Travis in Vietnam had spaces reserved on the black rock. David Moss's name had already been carved. For Jack Delane, though he was technically still alive, it was only a matter of time before his name too would be added.

Instantly, out of long habit, Travis's mind shut out the cluttered memories of the war, closing him off from the past and its rotten smell, snapping him back to the present and the dark room. Travis heard rat sounds again, and if the skin on his face had not been so cold, he might have smiled. Rats found the most unusual places to mate. He checked his watch again, bored and half-angry now at the time and no replacement. His empty Styrofoam cup was seized by the icy dawn wind, and it danced across the room, vanishing down the stairs. He leaned his head against the wall and closed his eyes, craving a fresh cup of coffee.

Seconds later static sounded on the radio.

"Kilo four five. We got company." It was Ed Manning, the day-shift lookout on the roof of the warehouse one building over.

"Kilo one five, I see him." Harshel responded.

Travis whirled and looked out the smeared glass, but the street was empty. Pivoting his tall frame quickly off the crate, he crouched at the far side of the window, ignoring the stiffness of the long night, his radio already secured in his left hand.

This was what he wanted, even needed. A little excitement, few results after all the weeks of sitting and waiting.

A Cadillac Brougham approached slowly from the west, its pearl-white paint job, white walls, and polished chrome glistening even in the dull light. As it approached the tenement, the driver cut its headlights. It was the car they'd been waiting for, the one they'd been expecting for the last three and a half weeks: Soloman's car.

Gliding smoothly on the uneven surface, it slowed, its silver-spoked wheels reflecting debris from the gutters. Smoked glass windows, so dark they were illegal, obscured the occupants, but Travis knew who was inside: Abdullah, six feet two and two hundred sixty pounds of concentrated black death, and Cooch, the driver, just as big and almost as mean—bodyguards, collectors, and professional killers, skilled in a variety of methods. This time, if the team was lucky, Soloman would be with them, there to check on his den, to make his presence felt, his gold teeth smiling hugely in a face that was all cherubic innocence. Travis remembered looking at that face from the safe side of a one-way glass on several occasions, the most recent only one year ago, during their latest attempt to take him.

Soloman Davis was as big time as street dealers went, heading an organization which supplied ninety percent of the product on the streets in D.C., and distributing maybe forty percent of the entire eastern seaboard's. DEA wanted him, but with their agents strung out all over Central and South America they simply didn't have the manpower needed to devote to a local operation, even one this big. Condescendingly, they turned the investigation over to local law enforcement. In return all they wanted was information leading to Soloman's upline man, the man who supplied the suppliers. The man Travis privately believed was Alain Brevard.

If Soloman was in the Cadillac, then the waiting would be over. This time they would take him and his network. And this time, when they took Soloman, there would be no mistakes. The minute the three walked into the dope lab where the "cook rock" was made, Travis and the others would take them—Soloman, the bodyguards, the dope, the money. And then maybe Travis could sleep easily, the ghost of Marlow finally banished from his dreams.

Marlow had been Soloman's best working girl, a call girl who routinely made a thousand dollars a night catering to the desires of high-rolling clients, most of whom were Soloman's business associates. She had been a trusted confidant, until Travis turned her. And now, because of Travis, she was dead. Soloman had made sure of that.

"It's Howdy Doody time," Kilo two six sang over the radio. Josey was ass-deep now. Travis grinned. Richard Joseph, aka Josey, was a damned fine amateur comedian, but his sense of timing needed work.

"Cut it out, clowns. Maintain proper radio procedure." It was Lieutenant Jarvis's nasal twang, already rising to falsetto with tension.

Travis chuckled harshly, shaking his head, looking away from the street momentarily. Lieutenant Jarvis, aka Fuzzballs, was a panicky communications major from Idaho, the ideal man to run this show, Travis thought sardonically. Jarvis had botched so many stakeouts, rumor had it he would be promoted just to get him off the streets if there was one more. Some of the men had their fingers crossed.

The radio was still crackling. Travis figured that Jarvis

must be checking his index cards. The man couldn't find the john without his notes.

"Kilo one five, are you in position?" The voice squelched on the last word. Eventually, Jarvis remembered to remove his finger and the radio went silent.

"Too bad abortion wasn't legal forty years ago," Travis muttered to the floor. "Too bad your mother didn't have one anyway."

"That's a big ten-four, Lie-u-tenant," Kilo one five mimicked back shrilly. Harshel, the sharpshooter on the roof two stories above Travis, was trying to take some of the heat off Josey.

Travis laughed, returning his gaze to the street. The Caddy was coming even with the condemned building that housed the den. Crackling with each acknowledgment, the radio counted down the call signs, Travis wincing slightly each time Jarvis spoke.

Jarvis and Harshel were in Travis's own building, Harshel on the roof with his .380, Jarvis at a nice, safe, fourth-floor window behind a reinforced wall. Amy Winston was out front, her displaced-person outfit making her one of the homeless refugees who lived in the building. Winston was the only member of the team who had been inside the den. Thirty-six hours ago she had entered and made a controlled buy with marked bills. Unlike some of the other men on the team, Travis didn't mind working with a woman as long as she did the job, and Winston was good at it. She had a good eye for detail. When she sketched out the interior of the den, she had detailed it down to the size of the doorways and the color of the flooring. More important, she knew weapons and had given a fair estimate of the opposition's firepower.

Josey and Sanderlin were already moving, preparing the battering ram and the C4 on the ground floor, ready to move in. Powell checked in from his position on the roof.

Steve was a fine shot, but he lived in a world of his own making. Some claimed it was Vietnam that had made him so strange. Travis believed Steve was just plain strange, Vietnam or not.

Finally. "Kilo two five." It was Wilson's call sign, but Wilson still hadn't arrived.

Pressing the transmission button Travis drawled slowly, sounding bored. Deliberately provoking.

"Bravo two five. I'm here. Wilson hasn't shown yet. As usual."

"Well, where is he?" Jarvis asked.

"Could still be humping Glenda, L. T. Oh, I'm sorry. Glenda is your wife's name, isn't it?"

It accomplished nothing, yet somehow, being sarcastic always helped. And it drove Jarvis crazy to have a snide person around when he was getting hysterical. Travis made it a point to drive Jarvis crazy as often as possible.

"Well, get ready." Strain sounded in Jarvis's voice.

"No shit, Sherlock," Travis breathed noiselessly. Then he said into the radio, "O-Tay, L. T.," and smiled with a perverse satisfaction.

The car glided to a stop and the radio broke silence again.

"Kilo two one, can you see in?"

"Jesus Christ, Jarvis," Amy Winston responded. "Anybody knows you can't see through that kind of smoked glass. You think I'm Wonder Woman?"

Travis's grin widened. Amy's ass would be in a sling for that crack. At this rate the whole day shift would be on report.

The front passenger door opened, and Abdullah emerged, his tan suit stretched uncomfortably across a massive frame. He scanned the street slowly, joined from the other side by the driver, Cooch, flexing his shoulders.

Satisfied with the empty street, Abdullah reached for the rear door.

A half smile touching his face, Travis exhaled, relaxing. It was starting. The King was here. The man never left his bed before noon—the whole operation had been planned with that fact in mind. Travis had chosen his shift knowing that the hours from nine to midnight were the most likely hours to catch Soloman. Luck and fate had decided to pull a fast one, but Travis had had a little luck of his own. Silently, Travis thanked Wilson for sleeping in.

With agonizing slowness, almost gracefully, a third body stepped from the backseat of the Brougham. Travis froze. The radio ground with too many transmissions.

"Who is this guy?"

"Anybody recognize him?"

They had spent three and a half weeks watching this car, this den, and a half-dozen other locations. They knew all about Soloman, where he ate dinner, where he bought his clothes, who he slept with, even who did his laundry. There could be no surprises. Yet this stranger was a surprise. Tall, even taller than Abdullah, but slender, fluid, slow moving with the grace of a stalking cat. He looked young, maybe twenty-five or twenty-six, and his dusky face was angular, with a high forehead and perfectly straight nose. He could have been Arabic or Jamaican or Colombian. Travis weighed the implications of that possibility and smiled. It might mean they were now one step closer to the man at the top of Soloman's supply network.

Soloman got out of the car and stood beside the stranger, his stout body clumsy by comparison. The younger man spoke to Soloman and smiled. He seemed calm and confident, yet intent, on guard, like the drug runners and black marketeers Travis had investigated and infiltrated on the docks of Da Nang. The thought brought back memories he had buried only moments before, as well as his theory that there was a connection between Soloman and Brevard. Maybe, Travis thought, this stranger was the connection.

Abdullah scanned the area once again, looking into the alleyways, then headed toward the door of the condemned building. The others moved with him, except for the stranger, who stood poised and still, watching the windows of the abandoned building concealing the team. Travis pulled back, feeling exposed as the stranger's eyes scanned the fourth floor. Still smiling, the stranger turned and followed Soloman.

"They're entering the building. Teams get ready."

Travis didn't respond. For once he felt the lieutenant's ordinarily useless command was necessary. The four men vanished into the building.

Amy Winston's voice, garbled by a burst of static, acknowledged, "They're inside."

"Move in," the lieutenant ordered.

"Lieutenant. They're not in the back room yet. We need them in the processing plant," Winston said.

Jarvis, shouting, responded, "I said move in. Go."

From his fourth floor window Travis watched the cover team clear the street of two loitering whores and then move into their firing positions.

"Damn." Travis said to the empty room. "Three and a half weeks and all we'll get them for is B and E." Travis waited for the entry team's go-ahead in an operation he felt had already begun to go sour.

Suddenly a firecracker sound echoed into the street from inside the den. There was a momentary silence followed by a short, distinct burst of automatic-weapon fire.

"Shots fired. Shots fired," Winston shouted into the radio.

"Hold your positions. Everyone hold your positions," answered the lieutenant.

Cooch and Abdullah staggered into the street, Cooch supporting the bigger man, who wielded an Uzi with his right hand. Smoke was still steaming from the barrel of the weapon. Blood stained Abdullah's left thigh.

Jarvis's voice, magnified by a megaphone, announced into the street, "This is the police. Place your weapons on the sidewalk in front of you."

Abdullah, startled, released a quick burst of gunfire in the direction of the sound. Travis, kneeling at the corner of a window, hit the floor as shards of glass and wood fell around him. Instantly, he heard the cover team return fire.

Jarvis, his voice shrill with fear, again shouted into the street, his amplified voice lost in the sound of gunfire. Travis pulled his weapon and, rising, crouched at the shattered window; the weapon fire from below was concentrated at the ground floor and the officers positioned there. Abdullah fired from behind the hood of the Cadillac, while Cooch had taken a position at the trunk.

Travis shoved the useless radio into the back pocket of his pants, and, ignoring Jarvis's last order to stay put, he bolted from the room. The sharpshooters would take care of the bodyguards. Soloman and the stranger had not been seen, and might take the delivery door out back, where Thomas was positioned. Travis instantly knew he had to be there.

Travis was running down the last flight of stairs, his weapon held before him, when a nearby wall exploded into splinters. He froze and saw that Sanderlin and Winston were pinned down just inside the doorway. Josey lay sprawled in the street outside. The noise of the weapons in the street was deafening as two Uzis fired and rested in tandem.

"Travis," a voice called from the room below. Travis turned to his right. Wilson stuck his head out from behind a partition. "Over here. We're not supposed to leave our posts."

"Fuck that. Soloman's getting away." Travis switched the weapon to his left hand and, pivoting with his right hand on the rail, leaped over and landed on the floor below. Turning, he sped to the back of the building, Wilson close behind.

They passed a room where a family cowered on the floor, the man's body covering the woman's. Pairs of small legs stuck out from beneath. Blood pooled around them. Shots pierced the wall before them, showering the family with plaster dust. Travis almost paused to help but knew there was nothing he could do while they were pinned down. He raced on.

Bursting through the back door of the tenement, Travis leaped over the prostrate form of a wino and raced to the left down the alley. Wilson stumbled over the sleeping man and cursed. Piles of garbage and a rusted-out auto barred their way. Leaping and twisting past the debris, the two men reached the end of the alley and turned left again, running toward the street. Travis and Wilson were in a blind spot, partially protected by the walls to their sides as they moved up the service alley. Police sirens wailed as uniformed backups answered the emergency call.

At the front corner of the building, Travis slammed his body against the wall and ducked his head back and forth into the open, gathering a picture of the action in front of the den. Josey and Sanderlin were sprawled in the street, their bodies still. Winston pulled herself out of the doorway, blood streaming down her arm. The Cadillac's once-sparkling finish was riddled with bullet holes. Cooch lay sprawled behind the car, his arms above his head; the Uzi lay on the sidewalk nearby. Sharpshooters had finally been allowed to take him out. Abdullah was behind the Cadillac, firing over the hood, his body shielded from Travis by what was left of the opaque windows. Travis had no clear shot at him and felt a rising tide of fury at Jarvis and the idiots in charge downtown.

Shaking, he looked across the street, away from the action, into the service alley beside the den. A swift movement caught his eye. Boards fell from the wall, their clatter lost in the noise of the battle. The lithe form of the stranger emerged from the concealed window, his gray silk suit almost iridescent in the darkness. The short fat frame of Soloman was right behind him. They moved toward the back of the building.

Travis looked toward the action at his left. Abdullah was still firing into the tenement, but the bodyguard would not have time to turn from his firing stance and get off a shot in the split second Travis would be exposed to him. Travis's eyes met Wilson's and agreement was reached. Wilson would cover.

Inhaling sharply, Travis darted into the street, toward the opposite alley. He was halfway across, highlighted in the quickly dispelling gloom, when Soloman turned and spotted him, instantly reaching beneath his jacket for his weapon. Instinctively, Travis threw himself down and to the right, rolling onto his right shoulder and coming at once to his feet. He heard the unmistakable firecracker pop of a .32 as he flattened himself against the wall of the building to the right of the den.

A moment later, Wilson was by his side. For a moment they were exposed to the firing lane of Abdullah, but someone in the task force building had spotted the two officers and set up a punishing barrage of cover fire, keeping the bleeding bodyguard busy. Ducking into the alley, Travis and Wilson took cover behind a dumpster.

"Close," Wilson said. They exchanged a grin.

Travis edged his head around the dumpster and peered down the length of the dim alley. The two shadowy figures were flying toward the back of the building, the taller form to the right of Soloman, almost pushing the slower man. Travis hurled himself after, his weapon before him like an extension of his arm.

Suddenly, ahead, a third form swung into the dark alley and assumed the point-shoulder firing position. Everything seemed to slow in sharp, cold focus as Travis heard the words "Freeze Poli . . ." interrupted by the pop of the .32. The officer, his face in shadow, snapped back into the light, his throat a leisurely explosion of blood and flesh. Slowly his arms flew out and, gently, like a dancer, he fell. It was Rojowski.

Something in Travis snapped, something old and primeval. Something familiar. "No," he screamed, his words roaring in the echo of the shot.

Soloman, gold teeth bared, weapon ready, whirled.

Travis fired three times; Soloman caught the impact of the rounds in his upper right chest. Chips of tissue and scarlet flew into the alley as Soloman was thrown up and against the wall. His head cracked loosely into the brick and left a bloody trail as he slowly slumped to the ground.

Travis reached Soloman's body in time to hear a groan exhaled in a last bubbling breath before the dealer went still. "Shit," Travis said. He turned and saw Wilson bending over Rojo, trying to find a place on the kid's ruined throat to check for a pulse. Travis had never seen so much blood. It puddled beneath Rojowski's body and ran thinly, steaming, down the alley. Wilson looked up and shook his head; Travis turned and took off after the stranger.

Travis felt hard and empty. Useless. It was a familiar feeling. There was nothing he could do for Rojo.

His weapon low, horizontal with his hip. Travis sprinted down the alley, certain Wilson would follow. Travis calculated the stranger had at least a hundred yards on him by now, and was sure he had lost him. Yet, when Travis burst out into the street, he glimpsed a gray-suited figure moving smoothly north on Eighth Street. Glancing back to be sure Wilson was following, Travis sprinted after the stranger.

Travis's hearing returned as he ran. The stranger was pulling ahead. Wilson waved Travis on and pulled out his radio to call for backup. For now, Travis was on his own.

A bag lady pushing a shopping cart was watching him, her thin voice raised in "If I had a hammer." The words "danger" and "justice" followed him down the street. Three kids reeking of wine jeered from a stoop and threw a bottle after him.

Minutes passed as Travis and the stranger raced the numbered streets, still heading northeast. They crossed intersections and turned down Southern Avenue. He knew Wilson's backup call was useless, for Wilson was now nowhere in sight.

Gradually, Travis gained, only to lose sight of the suspect when he veered into another alley. This one was narrower than most and, still cast into shadow, was darker than the one in which Rojowski lay. Travis ducked in, his vision quickly adjusting. The alley ended in a brick wall, spray-painted with graffiti. He advanced slowly, cautiously. To the left he heard a door creak on unused hinges and the sound of soft-soled shoes taking wooden stairs. It was no gamble. The stranger had no other choice. And neither did Travis.

His breath wheezed as he entered the building, following the sounds. One floor above him, the footsteps paused, then seemed to retrace their steps and change direction. Travis slowed, his eyes becoming adjusted to the darkness. The ill-lit building had once been a mid-priced hotel. It was one of several similar structures that lined the blocks in southeast D.C.

Travis's lungs ached and his heart pounded painfully as he climbed the stairs. He paused at each landing and swung out, assuming point-shoulder, his weapon raised to sweep the next flight up. There were nine flights, each long and narrow, and the stranger out-paced him. But Travis refused to surrender caution for speed.

He paused at the foot of the last flight of stairs as the door to the roof banged shut, then dashed up to it before the short echo had died. Sweat trickled into his eyes, ignored. Lashing out, his foot caught the door and crashed it open. He paused and, reminded of Rojowski, swung out onto the rooftop and assumed point-shoulder. Crouched, his weapon extended in both hands, Travis moved around the small enclosure that housed the stairs. Sweat blurred his vision and his heart hammered. He blinked rapidly.

Ahead and to the side, his eye caught movement. Whirling, he saw only a strip of gray cloth, the tail of the silk suit, flying over the short wall off the roof. Eight stories up, the stranger had jumped to another roof across the narrow alleyway, and, without looking to gauge the distance first, Travis followed, calculating in the last instant the necessary thrust to cross the space. He caught a glimpse of the blackness beneath him and felt his scrotum tighten, tensing him just before he hit.

The impact was brutal, jarring the breath from him and knocking loose his 9mm. Stunned, disbelieving, Travis rolled and watched as the weapon skidded to a halt some four feet beyond his reach.

Travis turned his head, and time stopped as he stared at the stunned form of the stranger stretched out less than ten feet away. And suddenly, shocked, he met steady green eyes. They were piercing, cool, yet somehow amused. Their color was odd in the chiseled, even face. Without breaking the hypnotic stare, Travis saw the taut, smooth skin, the rich almond color of mixed parentage. The stranger's high forehead was plastered with fine, damp, black hair. Sweat trickled down his face. A fist lying at his cheek dripped blood. He and Travis exhaled together, the rhythm hoarse between them.

Breaking contact in the same instant, they both looked quickly at the weapon positioned just ahead, between them, and back again. There was an amused recognition of purpose in the green eyes as the stranger and Travis shared the same thought. The same challenge. They both lunged. Travis fell short. Long fingers cradled the weapon. Brown fingers. And they held it comfortably, securely. Like an old friend.

Travis turned his head away, letting the asphalt roof paving fill his field of vision. He saw clearly, distinctly, each stone, each rough edge, every line of color variation in each rock. His mind was empty, waiting for the shot and the emptiness.

Cops share a similar nightmare, where they are helpless and a laughing suspect has a loaded weapon trained on them. Travis felt he had waited all his life for this moment, this vacant horror. The moment stretched on, pulled shrilly against nerves already shredded with tension. His fingers curled into the rough roof surface like claws. Strange memories flooded his mind. Not the memories he would have expected to flash before his eyes when he faced death. Not the soothing memories of a good life. Rather the violent memories of failure and pain.

A murderer, laughing as he walked out a courtroom door, released on a technicality.... A young black woman, brutally gang raped, treated as a criminal rather than a victim by a prejudiced elderly judge. All six defendants set free.... Marlow ... bloated, stinking.... Alain Brevard, his cultured face saturnine in the evening lights.... The two MPs Travis had worked undercover with in Nam: Jack, gibbering, saliva dribbling, incontinent.... and David, the rhythm of his head against the hull of a boat.

Then strangely, amid the horror, there was a crisp, clean scent of youthful patriotism. In a single violent leap, he had signed away the easy out of a college deferment and volunteered for the Army. He had done it for the training and the excitement and the need to be doing something. Anything. He had landed a job as a Military Police Investigator.

The flickering memory snapped into an image. Hoehne.

Sergeant First Class Hoehne, his first instructor at Military Police Investigator school, first and undoubtedly the best. He stood in front of the class, flat-footed and steady, probing and violating as he spoke. His piercing hazel eyes ferreted out each man's weakness, each man's fear. The epitome of the military law enforcement officer, he was austere, grim, his mouth a stern slash above a square chin that was almost cleft, but not quite, as though held back by a determined effort of will. Never hiding behind the podium, Hoehne was always moving, though not with restless energy. Rather, each movement was precise, clipped, sharp, like the click of the silver pointer he telescoped open to tap the board behind him, then snapped shut to drive the point home.

Somehow the fresh memories Travis always associated

with MPI school suddenly seemed intense and solid. Even the smells had been clean and sharp there, with the outdoor smell of Pine-Sol tinted with a hint of ammonia that made windows sparkle and even the beige walls shine. And it all contrasted with Hoehne's darkness as he talked about the victim when the victim was a Military Police Investigator. Statistics were Hoehne's specialty, all backed up by full-color photos showing tape measurements and white chalk lines...

And with that memory the horror returned. A sordid angry pain.

Jack.

David.

Marlow.

...Brevard....

All this in less than a second.

Slowly, Travis raised his head from the gray-black surface and met, full on, the gaze of cool green eyes and the barrel of his own weapon. The eyes were calm, deliberate, as if they measured the man before him. And then curious, as if he wondered how Travis would react to his next move.

In a quick sure motion he hit the spring release and slid the magazine from the weapon. Disbelieving, Travis watched the green-eyed man toss the clip behind him over the low roof wall and then eject the round already in the chamber. He tossed the useless weapon away but held onto the round—the round meant for Travis—rolling it between his thumb and forefinger a moment before he slid it into his pocket.

Travis pulled his legs beneath him, preparing to rise. The stranger flashed a quick smile, took two steps, and leaped over the low wall. When Travis reached the edge of the roof, the gray suit was gone.

Over the pounding in his ears and his own ragged

breathing, Travis could again hear Sergeant Hoehne's voice, brisk and sharp as he spat out statistics.

"The average shooting incident occurs within seven to twelve feet. It is a quick-draw, shoot-from-the-hip type of action, and the whole shooting incident takes place in about two and one half seconds. The officer does not expect to be shot. In two and one half seconds the unaware law officer is drawn upon, shot, and killed."

Travis had beat the averages. He was still alive. It never occurred to him to leap the wall and resume the chase. Somehow, in those two and one half seconds a bargain had been struck, an understanding had been reached: the green-eyed man hadn't killed Travis, therefore Travis wouldn't follow the green-eyed man. But the memory of the clear green eyes was a part of him now. With Soloman dead, there was no one to lead him to Brevard. The smooth-skinned stranger could be his last trail.

An hour later, back at the station, Travis sat at his desk feeling fatigued, nauseated, and achy from the chase. The Narcotic Task Force's headquarters was a mad house. Officers were running and shouting; phones were ringing and being ignored; a detective interviewing a suspect banged repeatedly on his desk, driving home a point to the apprehensive man. Hollow-eyed, unshaven men and lank-haired women stared out windows or into half-finished reports, postures and faces etched with defeat and fatigue. The bedlam would have made anyone sick, but Travis's gut was wracked by more than the office frenzy.

The memory of Rojo's bloody throat was fresh and intense in his mind, overlaid with a pair of amused green eyes of a suspect he had failed to bring in. The sensation was strange, and Travis knew he'd never be able to justify his failure to the team. Yet, faced with the same set of circumstances, Travis knew he would duplicate his decision.

Proper procedure required careful handling of the 9mm marked with the green-eyed man's prints. Travis went down to the property room and instructed a lab technician stationed there to dust the weapon before running ballistics later, downtown. The weapon was tagged, suspended on a wooden dowel in an evidence box on the third shelf, and the Chain of Custody Form was signed and immediately filed. Within twenty-four to seventy-two hours, with any luck, Travis would at least have a decent set of latents for the green-eyed man.

Suddenly cold, Travis shivered. The feeling of nausea intensified. Adrenaline breakdown left the system full of toxins which acted on the digestive tract and nervous system like a drug. He needed sugar and caffeine to counteract the effects, so he bought a Pepsi and went to his desk cubicle. He was so tired that even the hard desk chair felt good.

"Goddamn it, Travis," shouted Captain Hammit as he stormed up to Travis's desk. "Where were you? We looked for you at the scene. We need your weapon for ballistics. You know the Goddamn procedure." Red-faced and bellicose, Hammit loomed over the desk, a coffee stain displayed prominently on his tie.

"Good morning to you too, Cap'n," Travis said wearily.

"Your weapon," Hammit said, glaring.

"It's already been dropped off in property to be dusted and tagged. I wanted to make sure we got the prints on it."

"What prints?" Hammit grunted.

"You'll hear about it at the debriefing."

"Well, where were you? We tried to reach you on the radio for over half an hour."

Travis stood and reached into his back pocket for his

radio. The case came apart in pieces, several landing on the floor.

"I don't think it's working," Travis smiled, surprised he still knew how.

"What the fuck happened?"

"I guess I landed on it when Soloman got off his first shot. I dove and rolled in the street." Travis tossed the few remaining intact pieces on the desk top. They separated and scattered on impact. "I'll get some Elmer's," he said.

"Funny. But I'll tell you one thing Travis. You better get your story straight about Soloman. I've got everyone from the corner newspaper seller to the NAACP to Saint Peter calling me about this fiasco, and half of them think we executed three law-abiding citizens today. Your previous run-in with Soloman is part of it. The Shooting Review Board is tomorrow. The brass on Indiana Avenue are going to be looking hard at this one."

"Don't worry, Cap'n. It was a legit shoot."

"Yeah, well, sorry you didn't get him before he got Rojowski."

Travis saw a flash of pain in Hammit's eyes as he turned away and strode back to his office. Travis leaned back in his chair, trying to remember why he ever thought he belonged in law enforcement.

The debriefing was called almost immediately, with nearly thirty men and women attending, crowding into the windowless, stifling squad room, sitting at the few school desks, squatting on the floor, or leaning against the walls. There were uniformed officers, crime-scene technicians, and all the plainclothes street cops who had been on duty at the Condon Terrace location. Travis saw Ed Manning, his usually bland face pale and dirt-streaked. There was blood on Ed's jacket where the sleeves rested on the floor. Amy Winston, her arm in a sling and her hair still damp from a shower, was wearing fresh clothes, her eyes puffy and red. She kept looking down and squeezing her eyes shut to stop fresh tears. Travis knew she had been close to the men on her team and wondered which of the still bodies at the shooting scene hadn't made it. He couldn't bring himself to ask.

Obermier, from the night shift, sat near Harshel, the two talking in low tones. Obermier wasn't the only one from the night shift still at the scene after signing off. Travis wondered how many of the others had taken part in the operation after they had signed off. Travis leaned against the wall at the front of the room and guzzled Pepsi, trying not to think of Rojo lying in an alley, his throat blown away. If the kid had come back to Fourth and K when he signed off, like the regulations required, or if he had shielded himself by standing behind the wall when he tried to stop Soloman, he would still be alive. Travis felt the responsibility of Rojo's death settle on him like a shroud.

Adrenaline breakdown always made him edgy. Travis popped the top on a second Pepsi he had brought into the squad room and drank half, hoping the sugar and caffeine would dissipate the effects of the toxins in his blood stream. The toxins had broken down now to the point where he felt removed from the activity in the room, and a headache was beginning in the back of his skull. He was still in the danger zone though, where his reflexes and reactions were governed more by the primitive brain than by the rational brain of modern man. Travis looked around the room and noted the doughnuts, pastries, and coffee cups as others tried to relieve their own discomfort.

The reaction to adrenaline breakdown was taught in police academy, and then learned firsthand on the streets. It was something every active street officer had to deal with at some time.

Captain Hammit chaired the debriefing, his voice clipped and angry as he laid down the parameters of the operation as it had been intended to proceed. He sketched out the scene on the blackboard, placed each officer in his assigned place by writing in the call signs, and then called on Jarvis to recount each officer's part in the operation.

It went smoothly at first, and Travis paid scant attention, trying to filter out the worst of Jarvis's nasal tones. Jarvis explained the events leading up to the arrival of the Cadillac, and recounted the countdown to the go-ahead for the cover and access teams. Travis felt like a spectator at his own funeral.

Suddenly Jarvis turned to him. "You moved after being ordered to maintain your position," he accused. "If you had stayed put we might have Soloman alive in custody."

Travis, his body wired on caffeine and full of breakdown toxins, was brittle and close to the edge. He lunged, grabbed the front of Jarvis's white shirt, and threw him against the wall.

"You son of a bitch," Travis yelled. "It was you that gave a go-ahead too soon. If you had done one fucking thing right, just one, Rojo wouldn't be lying in a morgue right now." He struggled against hands that grabbed at his shoulders and clothes, trying to pull him off. The room was pandemonium as arguments broke out and officers took one side or another.

"That's enough, Travis," Hammit said, his voice rising over the room's uproar.

"But I—"

"I said, that's enough," Hammit roared.

"Okay. Okay," Travis said. He threw his leg across the back of a suddenly vacant desk, shrugging off a hand that rested on his shoulder. His stomach was a single burning pain.

Wilson, his voice carrying from the back of the room, told about Rojowski and Soloman in the alley, described the sequence of shots, even diagrammed the location and positions on the blackboard. And, then, for the first time, Travis heard the names of all the dead officers.

Joseph, Richard. Sanderlin, David. Rojowski, Samuel. Six others were being treated in the hospitals. There was a moment of silence, and finally Travis was asked to give his version of the events.

Suddenly drained, he told it in a monotone, ignoring the gasps and whispers when he described his green-eyed man and the events on the rooftop.

"You let him go? You let him get up and walk away?" Jarvis whined.

Travis shrugged. "I guess I could have gone after him bare-handed, but he was long gone when I got to the edge of the roof. You think you could have done any better, Fuzzballs?"

Jarvis ignored him and the meeting broke up. Travis wrote up his report, went home, and fell into bed. He didn't even remember taking off his clothes.

He woke with a start, his heart throbbing and his sweaty palms holding bunched blankets. Thinking for a moment that he was still dreaming, he remembered green eyes and dropped his head back to the steaming pillow. He knew he would not get back to sleep. The clock read 3:00 P.M., and the afternoon sunlight made a bright frame for the "blackout" window shade and the terry towel that did duty as a curtain. He was off today and had no court cases. He could sleep on if he wished, but knew instead he would lie there for another hour, thoughts turning. Then he would get up for an hour of basketball, a quick shower, and a trip down to Catcher Joe's to drink beer with the other guys. They would go over for the hundredth time the fiasco that had blown three weeks of careful watching and planning, in an operation where timing was the key element and Jarvis had jumped too soon.

He tried not to think of Rojowski and the others.

It was only then that Travis remembered the full magazine tossed carelessly away by the green-eyed man that morning. He'd have to fill out more forms to explain the missing clip. Basketball would be out today. He had an alley to search.

CHAPTER 2

February 1, 1975

THE figure ahead moved into deeper shadows.

The footsteps of the man following him were muffled by the sound of the water below lapping against the deck pilings. The lights were dim on the poorly patrolled docks. Pausing in the shadow of a building, the figure turned and scanned the docks in each direction, listening. The man in black who stalked so closely waited. He was indistinguishable in the nebulous moonlight. Eventually the figure moved ahead.

Behind, cautiously, the black form followed, his body slipping from shadow to shadow. Slowly, effortlessly, he closed the gap.

Moments later he struck, and three shots echoed among the docks, sending a dozen bats wheeling and keening. The victim, writhing in gurgling agony, died, and the only sound left was the soft plink of his blood on the water below. The man in black slipped a playing card beneath the body and moved quickly away.

Only then did the man the victim was to meet step from the shadows. Alain Brevard was a distinguished-looking man, his expensive suit out of place on the decrepit docks. It was attire more fitting his role as liaison between the drug-running, intelligence-gathering guerrillas in the North and the CIA operatives who ran him. He bent and plucked the card, bloodied and almost unrecognizable, from beneath the still, silent form of the former drug runner, one of dozens who worked for Brevard's organization.

It was the ace of spades.

The killer was getting too close, Brevard thought. Too silent. Too good. He would have to be eliminated. If they could catch him.

Minutes later, the man in black stood before a cracked, rippled mirror cleaning the black and green camouflage grease from his face. Smooth-skinned and youthful, he had the eyes of a much older man, eyes that had lost their youth, their idealism, eyes that retained only their sense of purpose.

Military Police Investigator Sergeant Garrick Travis turned away from the mirror, stripped the sweat-soaked, sour, black-cotton clothes from his too-lean frame and fell across the thinly padded mattress in the corner. Absently, he considered moving to another location, then discarded the idea. At the moment he still felt safe here. But the real reason he stayed put was simply that moving meant finding another safe place, and that would mean time lost from his pursuit.

For an American to hide out in the heart of a city of millions of Vietnamese, undetected, unrecognized, was a thing few attempted. Only a handful of deserters, drug addicts, and AWOL cowards and drunkards tried hiding here. Only those running from the system . . . and him. Of the American servicemen tucked away in the Vietnamese slums, he alone was still following orders.

Although he was cut off from the U.S. sector, cut off from support, he was still doing his job—still stalking the quarry assigned him by his commanding officer, still on duty, though the Army might not agree. He hadn't gotten around to notifying the U.S. command about those orders yet. And what wasn't in writing in triplicate wasn't fact. Not to the Army.

After four months alone, perhaps it was too late. Travis didn't really care. The only thing Travis cared about any more was his quarry—Alain Brevard. The man who had killed David. The man responsible for Jack's living death. Now, after four months, he was close to Brevard. So close he could taste it. And Brevard had to know it. After tonight he would surely know it. Travis grinned fiercely into the darkness.

January 2, 1985

The man slid behind the wheel of the silver-blue Mercedes and sank into the slightly worn, sueded-leather upholstery. It molded instantly to his muscular form. The specially designed back curved around and supported, gently, almost sensually, the lower lumbar vertebrae, just as its creator had promised. The superbly tuned engine turned over with a muted growl, coughed, then caught. At the smooth sound he smiled at his reflection in the rearview mirror and adjusted its tilt. It was the only thing the Germans were any good at, he thought—low, boxy beauties. Both varieties.

Hands encased in black leather gloves gripped the polished wood wheel lovingly and directed the car down the drive past low, manicured shrubs. They were dark, almost black, in the murky light of early evening, outlined with the harsh straight angles and detailed precision of an English gardener's clippers against the remaining patches of snow at their bases. At the gate the guard saluted, his posture as precise as the well-trimmed hedge. The man in the car ignored the guard and pulled into the street.

Glinting under the thousand reflected lights on the public buildings, the Mercedes glided smoothly onto Constitution Avenue and then quickly off again at Twenty-first Street. He passed Kelly Park and the State Department building, his attention for once on the streets behind him rather than on the seats of power to the sides. He wove through the campus of George Washington University and then, certain at last that he hadn't been followed, he pressed the accelerator.

He passed swiftly from the orderly, building-lined streets of central D.C. into the northeast section of the district, where the buildings underwent a change, subtle at first, and then sudden as he made a turn onto Florida Ave. Garish neon lights and flashing signs hid the decrepit, crumbling façades, and as the buildings changed, so did the people. Hookers now lined the streets, painted and sequined, bodies outlined in clinging fabric, and they smiled at the darkened windows of the silver-blue automobile. At an intersection at Florida and T streets a man in drag tapped at the driver's window and asked huskily for a light. Several turns later the driver passed through the last of the porn theaters and adult bookstores into a darkened industrial area, cut his lights, and slowed, pulling into the alley beside a warehouse. Moments later, a sliding door in the building was raised and he drove in. The door quickly slid shut behind the car.

He got out, a medium-sized man in well-tailored, crisply laundered clothes, his back ramrod straight, his gait measured in black-leather shoes that sounded a sharp, bright clip in the vacant building. The man's breath suddenly caught in his throat. It was beginning. It had been fifteen months since he had been here. Fifteen months of abstinence. Fifteen months of penance and mourning. Fifteen months of shaking with a desperate need no one saw or suspected.

Suddenly, eagerly, he stepped forward and tapped on a door. Standing in front of the security peephole so that the dim light would catch his face, he allowed his identification by the person beyond. A metal slot on the face of the scarred door slid noiselessly back, and after a moment he lowered his head to the grate, his lips even with the darkness within. He swallowed, then spoke, his voice rough with mounting excitement.

"I have an invitation," he said.

"What color?"

"White."

Instantly two bolts slid, and the heavy steel-reinforced door opened slowly. A man just inside looked surprised, then smiled and spoke.

"Well, what have we here?"

The man outside felt a sudden rush of anger at the odd tone of the welcome. It was as much triumphant as gracious.

"Don't push it, Simpson," he said, swallowing again. "I got the invitation and I'm here, so don't push it. Don't push *me*."

"Hey, calm down, friend," Simpson said, and smiled placatingly. "I'm just delighted to see you is all. After all, old friends are special, some more so than others. And it has been quite a while since you responded to one of my special invitations. Come in. Come in." Simpson waved him through the door into a small parlor, ornately decorated with fine antiques and richly sculptured oriental rugs in strange hues that somehow melted into one another and cast reflected light on the honey-colored walls. A fire crackled in the hearth, throwing out warmth and a heady hickory scent. The room radiated an easy peaceful ambience not lost on the newcomer.

"Sit down. Relax. Brandy?" Simpson asked in his soft, slightly foreign accent.

The man nodded, and, trying to recapture the fleeting sense of excitement, sat stiffly in a plush armchair. He watched Simpson across the room at a seventeenth-century communion table pouring dark amber liquid into a crystal snifter.

Tonight Simpson wore a white dressing gown made of heavy woven silk that tied at the waist. His black hair was sleekly brushed, his freshly buffed nails gleamed. He was the picture of a cultured gentleman, which he had perhaps been once upon a time. Gracious, warm, Simpson smiled and held out the snifter. The man relaxed into the plush chair.

"It's your favorite," Simpson said, "from Colombia."

Unprepared for the word and for his own reaction, the man gulped the pungent liquid and choked, his eyes reddening from the pain. "Don't talk to me about Colombia," he whispered when he could. "Not now. Not ever. Colombia was a mistake. My job . . . my security . . . the security of this country," he gasped.

"Sorry. An error," Simpson said solicitously, handing him a soft, neat handkerchief. Then, as though the exchange hadn't taken place, he said, "I put a little something in the drink. It should have you relaxed soon. You do seem a bit edgy. And tonight is no time to be edgy. Think about the show. It's special tonight. Very special."

Before the man could reply, Simpson was gone and he was alone. The drug in the liquor worked quickly and soon the ramrod posture eased a bit, the trembling subsided, and the man, his eyes closed, smiled as he took Simpson's advice and thought about the show. Last time had been the best. She had been tiny and fiery. Hot, with small breasts that tilted up and no body hair. She had been good, the best ever. But it had cost him—more than he ever thought he would pay. He'd never let *that* happen again. If it was discovered what he had done, how he had used his position, his authority, he would be ruined. And the scandal to the service would be irreparable.

The drug Simpson had placed in his drink muddled his thought processes, dulled his fears. The picture of the girl, small and dark, with innocent eyes and perfect skin, her smile piquant, reappeared in his mind and he smiled.

"We're ready." Simpson's words interrupted him and, smiling, his mind empty and burning, he followed the swishing white silk robe. The hallway was stark in contrast to the opulence of the small parlor, but he scarcely noticed, concentrating instead on the rush of blood and heat throughout his body. A door opened and he stepped through, leaving Simpson in the hallway, a smile pasted on his bland features. The door closed silently.

He was standing in a booth some five feet square, its forward wall a one-way mirror. Though one of four similar booths, this one was decorated just for him. He was its only occupant, the only man who ever sat in the deep, charcoal-gray armchair before the Plexiglas wall. It was his.

He removed his clothes and put on a burgundy velour dressing gown, its folds soft against his skin. He slid into the welcoming deep armchair. His posture was lax with the drug and the expectancy, bearing no relation to the tight military bearing of less than an hour past. The snifter was empty, and with a steady hand he replenished it from a bottle on a low glass-topped table beside his chair, his hand scraping against the carpeted gray wall. He sipped. It was the same brandy, spiced with lemons and exotic herbs. He never drank it at home. It was too precious. It belonged in this booth. Low music, its strands sweet, wafted over the speakers recessed in the shadows of the dark ceiling. It was Mozart.

The drug Simpson had placed in the drink had faded, and, smiling, the man leaned over the low table, lifted a glass rod, and sniffed deeply. Two of five lines of cocaine, arranged neatly on the tabletop, vanished. The effect was instantaneous, and he fell back into the chair, sloshing the brandy. The music took on a rich quality, the bass notes sounding smoother, beating with a pulse in his head, hands, and groin. The room beyond him was still dark. The waiting was good. Simpson always timed it right, just long enough to build the need. He downed the last of the brandy and set the snifter beside the pile of plush gray towels, taking one.

The music grew louder, then softer. Time ceased to have meaning. As the second line of coke went to work the lights came on slowly in the room beyond.

The music increased in intensity as a door, obscured in a mirrored wall, opened. When she stepped into the room he inhaled, gripping the arms of the chair.

Dressed in a white, sheer robe, the sheen of her bare skin lustrous beneath, she was perfect. Swaying, her hips moved, bringing the smooth pubic skin close to the front of her robe and away again in an unconscious dance. She opened her robe slowly, languorously, as if it too were following the music, and it slid to the floor. Her nude body gleamed. She touched herself, a look of surprise on her face as if she were discovering her body for the first time. She touched her breast with a feather-light caress, her fingers lingering on the rapidly hardening nipple. A slow smile touched her lips.

He sighed, leaned over, and inhaled another line of cocaine.

The dance, though as yet it was nothing more than a hypnotic sway, continued. She danced as if she were alone, unobserved. And yet she danced for him. The pace of the music increased.

At last, his breathing rapid, he allowed his fingers to touch himself in the darkness of the booth. Gently at first, then faster, following the music.

Her hands touched and fluttered, the movements languid, teasing. Her nipples stood erect and swollen. The dance became heated, pulsing. Her movements were fluid and the expression on her face changed from passionate to feverish as she twisted and writhed her body to the music. Rolling her body from booth to booth, she teased herself at the glass and left her mark damply.

The mirrored door opened slowly and the girl turned, faint surprise registering on her reflected face as a tall man entered and strode toward her. Naked, he was erect and breathing raggedly through his open mouth. Without preamble he turned her and entered her from behind. Above the sound of the music she groaned, grinding into him, her thighs taut bands sheened with exertion. Their hands moved together across her breasts and down and she screamed hoarsely as he touched the moist fold of flesh and she came.

Suddenly there was a flash of silver as he exposed the blade he had concealed in his right fist. He slashed, and a red streak opened diagonally across her chest and abdomen, splitting her unevenly from left breast to right hip. Her eyes opened wide with slow, stunned disbelief as a second and third slash painted her pale smooth skin with her own blood. She screamed, her voice a high-pitched response of pain and fear, her eyes bulging and glassy.

The man in the booth moved his hands to the pace of the macabre dance.

The slashing continued until the woman fell, the scarlet reflected brilliantly again and again from a thousand angles on mirrored walls. As her body went still, the killer left the room.

In the charcoal-gray cavern of the darkened booth, the man moaned in ecstasy, waiting for the painful irregularity in his chest to slow. Then he smiled and reached for the towels, mentally disassociating himself from the scene.

Later, a pleasantly smiling Simpson, now dressed in a suit, led him from the booth and into a parlor in the carefully orchestrated order that prohibited the four booth's occupants from sight and contact. A fresh brandy awaited him. He drank in silence, alone, and let himself out of the parlor, leaving a neat stack of hundred dollar bills on the table beside his empty glass.

The Present
Day One, P.M.

The door to Catcher Joe's banged shut behind Travis with a childish petulance that was as embarrassing a finale as he could have wished. Exactly the right finishing touch, he thought irritably, to a night when he had made a total ass of himself. That the slamming door was an accident didn't alter things. He was still an ass, a fact his two closest friends had just explained in kind, if blunt, terms.

It had started out a dull, lifeless evening in the crowded bar, where spirits were down and consumption was up. He sat alone at the bar, served by a morose Mitch who ignored him but for precognitive refills and change he made under the counter, keeping track of tips and drinks out of a twenty Travis had tossed him on entering. It was a longstanding arrangement, one usually accompanied by an easy banter and "Have you heard the one . . ." Not tonight. Rojowski and Jack Smith had been regulars. Rojowski wasn't coming back. And Jack would be laid up for months—if he lived.

Travis, after a fruitless search in the alley for the clip he knew he would never find, had arrived early. He had since lost track of both time and beers. But instead of easing his dark mood, he found himself reliving the events of the day with an alcoholic's memory for the harshest details. Each time he blinked he saw Rojowski's throat in a scarlet explosion superimposed by a pair of amused green eyes in a serene face. And even the cigar-laced air of the bar couldn't erase the scent that clung to him, the smell of the condemned building in which he'd sat. The smell of the past, of failure.

Behind him he heard a shuffle, which he ignored.

"Yes, ladies and gentlemen, here we have the hero of the day, the famous—some say infamous—Trav Travis." It was familiar, a soft-pitched voice schooled like an easy-listening FM announcer's, which originally it had been, before Dan Matthews decided to turn cop. "Just today, my friends, this very morning, this fine looking, highly trained, and skilled law enforcement officer blew the bloody fuck out of Soloman."

Travis's mouth twitched. Mitch replaced his empty with a full mug and Travis focused on the amber liquid as he drank. There were further shuffles behind him, and peripherally he saw the stools on either side of him fill.

"I don't know, Dietrick," the soft voice continued. "Maybe it ain't him. He's drinking real beer. I thought the good guys only drank milk."

"Warm," a laconic voice from Travis's right answered.

DEATH WARRANT

"Right. Warm milk. And he's drinking beer."

"Maybe it ain't real beer." A pinky finger slid slowly into his mug and out. A distinct smacking sound followed. "Nope, it's the real stuff."

"Shameful. Ladies and gentlemen, our hero is drinking real beer."

Travis's mouth twitched again.

"Barkeep, for our listening audience—and the private titillation of Officer Dietrick and myself—would you please—for the record—state the number of beers consumed by Officer Travis this evening."

Mitch, for the first time in hours remembering to smile, walked over and again replaced Travis's empty. "Private titillation, huh? They let you say things like that on the air?"

"Our editing crew will use its usual discretion I assure you, sir," Matthews said, grinning.

Travis almost smiled.

"Well then, if you're going to have *discreet* tits, this mug right here is Travis's eleventh."

"Whew," Dietrick said, "I was afraid for a minute that he'd got a head start on us. Bring us a couple of pitchers, Mitch."

Travis laughed and the tension in his face eased somewhat as he looked back and forth between his friends.

"I've been saving your seats."

"So I see. Guarding them with your life," said Matthews.

"And that shit-eating-go-to-hell expression."

"Please, Dietrick. Remember our audience."

"Oh, yeah. The discreet tits."

"Right." Matthew's voice changed suddenly, and Travis knew from long experience this part wasn't for fun. "So. About that expression, Officer Travis. It's extremely familiar and brings back some, shall we say, unpleasant, best-forgotten memories."

Travis didn't answer, and the seconds ticked by.

"Travis?"

Dietrick downed his mug, refilled his glass.

Travis swallowed. For a moment the memories surfaced full force. Not just those of today, but those of eight years ago, when Marlow was a part of his life, a big part. That was when Soloman, as an up-and-coming young underworld lieutenant in an old organization, had neutralized the only witness to a half-dozen federal offenses. When Travis had busted Soloman then, Dan Matthews had literally sat on Travis for almost a week, preventing a retaliation that was as natural to Travis as breathing, but that would have landed him in the state pen for murder one. But that had been a younger Travis. The memories faded and Travis met Dan's calm steady gaze.

"I'm okay, Dan."

"No private wars?"

"No. No private wars. Besides, there's no one left to fight." Travis deliberately did not mention the green-eyed stranger. And not even his friends knew about Brevard.

Dan nodded slowly and drank down his beer. "Good. Let's get polluted."

"Sounds good by me," Dietrick drawled and drained his second mug.

But the effects of a dozen solitary beers and powerfully stimulated memories continued to work on Travis's mind and, even with Matthew's and Dietrick's company, the vivid flashes of violence continued. The roar in the bar grew, and a heated argument started, ran its course into alcoholic illogic, and faded away. Closer still, a typical policeman's argument was in progress concerning how one or two enterprising cops could clean out the drug dealers. One of the more vivid suggestions involved administering a beta blocker to any highly placed asthmatics and holding them down till they suffocated. Behind them in the nearest booth was a discussion of the rapture, and just beyond that an even louder voice detailed the gyrations of a monumentally proportioned exotic dancer. Occasionally Travis heard a voice he half-recognized mention Rojowski or Jarvis or Sanderlin. Half the bar's patrons were cops, and most of those had been on his shift at the stakeout.

Travis began to feel claustrophobic, the half-buried sensation growing and climbing into his throat to mingle with the onions of an earlier pizza and quick flashes of green eyes and steaming corpses and an alley where garbage pickup had occurred a day early. Travis swallowed against the nausea and caught the last few words of a nearby conversation.

". . . lung and rib halfway across the alley. Blew a hole this big out his other side."

The voice was Harshel's. Harshel was young, only thirty-two, a big, beefy, brainwashed ex-Marine, who, when he changed uniforms, forgot to change attitudes. He had a big mouth, a big body, a big head, and a brain too small to work either one properly.

"Always had it for Soloman. Glad he got the fucker."

"Heard there was some trouble once with a girl and Soloman." The voice held a faint trace of Yiddish staccato. Obermier.

"Yeah. One of Soloman's girls. He was hot for her. Soloman got to her first."

Travis felt himself grow cold and instinctively knew Matthews was listening too.

"Too fucking bad he didn't finish the job then instead of now. Three good men would still be sitting here tonight."

Travis reacted so quickly Matthews was left unprepared. Travis had a glimpse of his arm rising just before he grabbed Harshel and threw him against the booth back. Harshel, a good five inches shorter and forty pounds heavier, smacked solidly into the wood. The bar fell silent.

"At least one of those three men would still be alive right now if you had done your job, you son of a bitch. If you had taken out the Uzi at the front when the shooting started, Soloman would never have made it to the alley and Rojowski wouldn't be lying on a slab right now." Travis's voice was low and hard, and carried easily in the still bar. He felt a hand on his shoulder, shrugged it off. "Abdullah got Josey and Sanderlin in the first fifteen seconds of action. He was an easy target. What the fuck took you so long?" He ended on a hiss.

Harshel's face drained white.

"Departmental policy—" Obermier started.

"Fuck departmental policy. Once the shooting starts, it doesn't fucking matter what some chair-bound captain thought when he was safe at his typewriter."

Harshel slowly slid back down to his seat and looked at the table. His breathing was ragged and his eyes were hollow.

Obermier looked past Travis to Matthews. "You tell him."

Firmly Travis was led, stiff and resisting, away from the front booths to the back of the room. As they walked, the noise level resumed and an interrupted game of pool continued. Travis's head ached and the lights at the back seemed too bright.

Dietrick sat at a booth Mitch had already seen to, and poured fresh mugs from an icy pitcher.

"Tell me what?" Travis could hear the gruff anger in his voice.

Matthews slid into the booth, lifted his mug, and drank. He patted the seat next to him.

"Have a seat. Nice of Mitch to get this ready," he said, indicating the pitcher. "I always wonder how he does it so fast."

"The man has second sight. Probably had the table wiped and the mugs out before Harshel opened his mouth." Dietrick looked up at Travis. "You look real bright just standing there, Travis." Then in the same breath he continued to Matthews, "You see 'Star Trek' today? It was the one where Spock went back to Vulcan to get married. Ugly-looking woman to get so upset over."

Matthews lifted a brow. Matthews hated "Star Trek."

Travis exhaled and sat.

"No. I was far too busy flossing my teeth. I'm afraid I missed it today. What a shame. You see it, Travis?"

"No," he answered, his voice calmer. "I didn't know they showed 'Star Trek' anymore."

"Sacrilege," Dietrick said, only half in jest.

Travis drank, and for the first time tonight he tasted the beer. It was cold and refreshing, washing away the acid taste left by anger. He drained the mug, and set himself to being patient. He knew from years past that Matthews and Dietrick wouldn't talk until they were ready, and even then they might talk all around what they wanted to say, letting him pick out the meaning by inference. Or they might be brutally honest. A ten-year friendship allows a man certain privileges. After half an hour of drinking and small talk, they applied that privilege.

"Thought you might want to know," Matthews said, "Harshel is being brought up on charges for his action today."

"You mean inaction," Travis corrected softly. But even as he spoke he knew somehow what was coming next, and he grew cold and still inside.

"No. His action. He took out Cooch on his own,

without orders. And then left his position and went after Abdullah."

"I heard him call Jarvis three times for the go-ahead," added Dietrick. "Now the scuttlebutt is, Jarvis is recommending termination. He'll probably be brought before the Civil Service Board in the next couple of weeks."

"Obermier finally got Abdullah, but only because Harshel drew his fire long enough for Obermier to get in a clean shot. And you might as well know. Rojowski just got engaged to Harshel's little sister. She's in the hospital right now. Couldn't take it."

Travis looked at Matthews, whose eyes were watching the slow twirl of his mug in its water ring. Dietrick's eyes met Travis's over the rim of his beer, and he shrugged with his brows in a gesture that was half apologetic but not conciliatory.

Slowly Travis's eyes traveled the length of the room, past the line of booths to the bar and beyond. Harshel was standing in the aisle, weaving, shouting for another round and trying to stick his hand down Amy Winston's blouse. Until now Travis hadn't even seen her. She was staring at Harshel with helpless concern, easily fending off his hands and half holding him up. From the look of him, Harshel needed it. Travis knew Harshel wanted sergeant more than anything else in life.

The feeling of uncontrolled, impotent anger overcame Travis again, and the room closed in on him.

"Shit."

"That's one way of putting it," Dietrick said, pronouncing it "puddin it."

"I feel like an ass."

"Acted like one too."

"Thanks, Dietrick."

"Welcome."

"I guess I should apologize."

"I wouldn't. Not now," Matthews said. "Later. When he can appreciate it more."

"Um," Dietrick agreed, nodding.

Travis felt like a twelve-year-old getting advice from mommy and daddy. Excusing himself, he left the bar. But the feelings followed, intensified by the slamming of the door.

He felt sick standing in the icy mist, listening to the occasional ping of sleet around him. He hated sleet. He found his car and two pot holes with his left foot. Dampness soaked through to his sock. The engine responded and, wheeling out into the street, he felt a slight easing of tension.

Later he found himself on Interstate 95, doing almost that, and forced himself to slow down until he could turn off. Near Springfield, down a freshly blacktopped, poorly lit back road, he pressed the accelerator. The Trans Am shot forward, dark in the mist. For over an hour he drove, his hands firm on the wheel until the claustrophobia passed and he could roll up the windows. The heat felt good on his wet foot. He pulled off his shoe to let it warm.

It wasn't that he had any guilt about letting the stranger go, and he wasn't confused. He understood perfectly well why he had allowed the man to get away: He had seen respect in those eyes, respect from a criminal. And that was strangling him. All his life he had found the deepest satisfaction in shoving the guilty against a wall, kicking their feet apart, and slapping on the handcuffs. That was justice. But not this time.

Travis sighed and punched on the radio. The sound was soothing for a few moments, but the announcer's voice was an intrusion and Travis turned it off, preferring the silence. He adjusted the rearview mirror slightly, overcompensated, and got a glimpse of his own reflection. Most of his face was in shadow—only his eyes were highlighted. They stared back at him with an intensity, hollowed, pained. He grinned at himself, a cool cynical expression that never softened his eyes. Shocked, Travis recognized them as the ones that had littered his thoughts all day. Green as old jade, clear, banded round the outside with a darker ring of green, they could have been the stranger's. The expression was the same. Exactly the same. Quickly he readjusted the mirror again, bringing the blacktop into line behind him. He passed an all-night gas station and, slowing, wheeled in, paying cash for five-dollar's worth and checking the oil. The attendant was a syphilitic blonde with bad teeth, and she wanted to talk. Travis didn't want to be bothered with manners and left silently, yet, back on the road, he no longer felt good in his own company. After a few miles, he turned the car and went back. Finding a quarter, he used the pay phone outside and called Chris, the woman he'd been seeing off and on for two years. He couldn't remember how long it had been since he had called her, but the number came back easily. And with a tired desperation he would never have admitted, he listened to the rings.

The silence between the tiny sounds seemed ominous and his mind filled the spaces with transparent overlays of memories, none of them good.

She answered on the fourth ring. He had awakened her, and though she sounded hoarse from sleep, she insisted he come over. Perhaps the desperation showed in his voice. Perhaps she was lonely. It never had occurred to him that it was too late to call or that she might not have been alone.

He found his way back to the city and to her brownstone by instinct, not bothering with street signs or stoplights, the sleet whispering unpleasantly against the windshield.

She heard the peculiar rhythm of her buzzer and without bothering to confirm it was him, released the apartment-building door. Only he used that particular rhythm when he buzzed her.

Chris stretched and groaned at the pull of tight shoulder muscles. She had overdone her workout on the lateral arm pulley the day before, leaving the muscle fatigued, bunched, and hot.

She walked to the door, her slipper socks sliding on the carpet. The tap sounded, the lock slid back, and she opened the door, holding it back with one hand, the other against the jamb. It wasn't a sexy pose. She knew how she looked. From her checkerboard slipper socks to her loose-fitting nightgown to her elaborately tousled chestnut braid, she was a picture of anything but the appealing lover.

Chris grinned as she surveyed Travis. He looked miserable.

"You look horrible," he said.

"So do you, thank you."

"So can I come in or what?"

"I don't know. Let me think about it."

Travis walked in and headed straight for the kitchen.

"Very funny. Got any coffee?"

"Of course, Travis. I always keep a fresh pot on the stove in the middle of the night. It helps me sleep."

"Cute, where's the cups?"

"Oh, I rearranged the kitchen cabinets two months ago. They're on the right now."

He removed a single cup and saucer.

"Two months? Has it been that long since I was here?"

"Longer. I got bored waiting for your call, so I rearranged the kitchen in revenge." She pulled two frozen croissants from the freezer and put them into the microwave.

"Where's the sugar?"

"In the sugar cannister." She pointed. "It's new."

A spoon tinkled against the cup. Chris grinned. Deftly she plucked the coffee cup from his hands. "Thank you, Travis. That looks good.

"Oh, and feel free to fix yourself a cup, too."

Travis grinned slowly, relaxing.

"I guess you're trying to tell me I walked in and took over again, huh?" he said, reaching for a second cup. "Got anything to eat?"

"In the microwave, and after you've stuffed your face and drunk all my coffee, you might consider kissing me hello."

"Oh. Sorry."

He slid an arm around her and pulled her close. He smelled like a cigar factory and tasted like stale beer, but it had been a long time since she had been kissed quite so thoroughly. Her outfit had paid off.

"I shouldn't have stayed away so long." Travis's voice was suddenly husky.

"Not to worry. I've found someone to keep me in practice." Travis lifted a brow, but she pretended not to notice. It was none if his business anyway. He picked at the cheese croissants, waiting for them to cool.

"Oh, you want one of these things, too?"

"No. You can have both of them. From the way you're staring at them, you probably haven't eaten in hours. And when you did, I'd lay odds it was pizza or tacos."

"Think you got me pegged, don't you?"

"Yeah. I just haven't decided what to do with the information yet."

"Well, when you decide, how 'bout letting me in on the secret."

"You'll be the first to know, and you won't know what hit you."

"You gonna hit me?"

"Maybe. If you're lucky."

Travis ate quietly, devouring the first croissant and dunking the second into the coffee. A greasy cheese and sugar film settled on top between bites, but must have added flavor, because he finished that cup and poured a second. The whole enterprise lasted less than three minutes. He washed his fingers at the sink.

"You should go to your mom's for a good meal. How is she?"

"A good meal at mom's always gives me indigestion. She's fine. And why don't you fix me a good meal?"

"Freeloader."

"Admit it. You've missed me." He picked up his coffee, dropped in more cream, and headed for the sofa.

Chris sighed. She *had* missed him, but not the skipped dates, the late arrivals, the casual attitude toward their intermittent relationship, or the constant long absences.

They talked for an hour, curled up on the couch beneath a blanket.

"I'm sorry about Rojo," she said. "I know he was special to you."

A lump formed in Travis's throat as he tried to swallow past the pain. He didn't look at her—his gaze was faraway, focused on his own internal replay.

"I saw it on the news," she continued.

Travis swallowed. "Yeah. I'm the killer cop who shot the 'innocent citizen' in the back alley. Channel 7." His voice was dispassionate, removed.

"Soloman Davis."

Travis nodded slowly. "He'd just got Rojo. Wilson and I saw it. Some innocent citizen." His voice broke.

Suddenly there weren't words enough to tell her all that had happened. It poured out in disjointed half-whispers, the anguish scarcely controlled. He finished with the description of a green-eyed stranger and a macabre scene on a roof.

After a moment Chris said softly, "I can understand the situation. But do you feel guilty because he beat you to your gun, because you didn't chase him, or because he let you live while Rojo died?"

Travis sucked air in a sharp hiss. "You don't mince words, do you?"

She smiled again.

Chris tucked her feet beneath his thigh and snuggled deeper into the blanket. He looked away and let his eyes fall out of focus. He massaged his head briefly and closed his eyes. Chris watched for a while, trying to ignore the pull of sleep, her eyelids heavy.

The conversation with Chris got Travis thinking about Soloman's drug ring. He was so positive that the capture of Soloman would have led him to Brevard. But with Soloman out of the picture, he'd have to find Brevard alone, without turning the investigation over to the Drug Enforcement Agency. Brevard was *his* target, and he was determined not to let DEA have him.

Brevard had been his obsession for so many years that everything else in his life had been shadowed and tainted by the compulsion to locate the man responsible for so much death and suffering half a world away, and now, it appeared, in D.C.

Though he'd only met the man twice, he knew how Brevard thought, the way he lived, the way he did business. Travis knew Brevard's extensive CIA contacts in Southeast Asia had helped him escape the violent aftermath of the U.S. pullout from Vietnam. The man was too good, too perceptive to have been caught unprepared by the U.S. abandonment of that war-torn country. And his claws were too deeply buried in too many people for him to have been left behind. Even before Travis had confirmed Brevard's escape, he had known it. So for years Travis had been searching, tying bits and pieces of the man's past to events in the present.

A long series of murders in D.C., beginning over ten years ago, was why he had left Wisconsin—where he had settled after the war—and started over as a rookie cop in the nation's capital. The murders had Brevard's signature all over them. They matched murders in Vietnam that Travis had linked to Brevard before the war's end. And Travis was sure Brevard had been Soloman's supplier. Ten years of working the streets, listening, questioning, had assured him of that. And once upon a time he'd even had a witness to confirm it: Marlow.

Then the green-eyed stranger had appeared, and the balance between the past and the present had been lost. Now some on the force were suggesting the stranger at Soloman's side the day he had died was the man no one had ever been able to identify or locate, the man only Travis knew was Brevard. But the green-eyed man was not Brevard.

The heater pinged and hissed, battling with the sleet for recognition. Its sound was soothing.

Perhaps he went to sleep, but he didn't remember waking. He remembered nothing until he focused slowly on her face, solemn in sleep, and was surprised. Had the silence stretched so long between them? It must have, for the rattle of sleet had vanished and there was only the sound of the city trucks outside the window, grinding their way up the streets as they deposited salt and sand on heavily traveled intersections.

He felt a sudden curious delight in her. Another woman faced with his withdrawal would have pestered him with questions or tried to make him laugh, or, worse, would have become angry. This one went to sleep. He felt his mouth relax, and the tightness began to leave his eyes. She was the only woman he had ever known who would allow him to withdraw into silence and sit brooding in the dark. Not even his mother had permitted that. She had always been fearful, watching him. Suddenly he grinned. He hated men who compared their women to their mothers.

He reached out and brushed a strand of hair away from her face. She wasn't his type at all, he decided, as he gathered her into his arms, sighing and pliant, and carried her into the bedroom. Not his type at all. Too easy. Too gentle.

Morning was still only a shadowy possibility when Travis gently nudged Chris in the back.

"God," she rasped. "Don't you ever sleep?" Her face was buried in the pillow, her back to him.

"Seldom. Especially when I'm in bed with you. Come here."

"Go brush your teeth."

"Not now."

"Why? Aren't you afraid to leave me with memories of bad breath? I'll have two months to reminisce on the odor."

"You're awful sweet-tempered this morning. Could I convince you to turn over if I promised you a night of my homemade lasagne, Chopin, candlelight . . . a champagne bubble bath. . . ." When she didn't answer he added,

"And a hot-oil massage." He could almost feel her smiling into the pillow.

"Your place or mine," she temporized.

"Here."

"Good. I don't think I could handle an attempt to be romantic in the dump you laughingly call an apartment."

"Cute. Real cute. Now come here."

Day Two, A.M.

The library was shadowed, lit by a single lamp whose pale gold glow was limited to the disarray on an antique Spanish desk. The desk top was strewn with papers—original files, computer printouts, photostats, manila envelopes. With a soft plop a final folder was added to the clutter. It was a personnel file, designated METROPOLITAN POLICE, WASHINGTON, D.C.

The man behind the desk shifted, his silk suit slithering softly. He stared at the folder for several silent seconds, his fingers steepled before him, positioned below his opaque green eyes. The shadows turned his café au lait skin a burnished mahogany. His face was composed, almost serene, as a clock, lost in the shadows, chimed the quarter hour.

Finally he sat forward, unfolded his hands, and sorted the papers, binding them chronologically into a manuscript box. Taking an ebony pen and a single sheet of heavy writing paper, he composed a letter, which began, simply, "Honored Sirs." The letter was in three parts—a summary, a conclusion, and a recommendation. He wrote with swift, sure strokes, pausing only once near the end, where he chose his words with care. As usual, it was left unsigned.

Folded once, the letter joined the bound papers in the box, which he wrapped with a plain brown wrapper and sealed. To the right of the address label he added a small figure. The secretary who intercepted the messenger-delivered package would see that it never reached the bureaucrat to whom it was addressed. Rather, she would hand deliver it, unopened, to an executive office in the Justice Department. From there it would reach the Honored Sirs for whom it was intended. Within thirty-six hours he would have an answer delivered by a prearranged second route.

The subterfuge was almost a waste of time, for already he knew what their response would be. It had been easy at first to keep the police officer separate, in place yet not activated. But by his own action, Garrick Travis had become marked. Yesterday morning's fiasco had condemned him. Officer Garrick Travis had to be stopped.

Rising with a grace better suited to a jungle war than a library, the dark-skinned man scanned the desk and floor for stray scraps, crossed the room, and flicked off the light. Instantly the room was bathed in a soft glow from the security lights outside the tall windows. Something about the darkened room with its rich yet austere Spanish air touched a memory, deeply buried, and suddenly he paused. A hint of sadness brushed past his features, and for a moment he remembered to pity the man whose life he was about to transform. Then he stepped out, and the door closed quietly on the empty room.

CHAPTER 3

Day Two, A.M.

TRAVIS again awoke before sunrise, rolled over, and pulled Chris against him. She mumbled protestingly in her sleep, frowned slightly, and relaxed against him. Her face, its outlines blurred in the dim light, looked soft, inviting. She smiled softly. Lightly, with one long forefinger, he touched her lips and brushed a strand of hair back from her face, then silently slid from between the warm flannel sheets and stepped into the bathroom. Later, dressed, his keys held quietly in his palm, he stared down at her again, surprised at his acute reaction to her. He smiled, reached out once more, and touched the curve of her hip, rounded beneath the comforter. He had never been the type to analyze or question his own emotions, and simply enjoyed the easy warmth he felt as he let himself out of the apartment.

The clouds overhead raced with a strong wind, and Travis pulled his jacket closed against the chill. It was going to be a blustery, icy day. Travis smiled again, found his car, and drove to K Street.

The feeling at the station today was different, subdued, no longer clouded over with frantic activity and strange faces as it had been the previous morning. It was quieter, expressions were less grim with anger, bodies moved more slowly, as though weighted. Travis clocked in and paused to read the sole memo on the cork surface above the clock; it listed times and places of the funerals. The memory of Rojowski as he last saw him shadowed Travis's mind, and he left the bulletin board rapidly, his left Puma squeaking on the freshly waxed floor. He wondered how the mortician would disguise the boy's lack of a throat.

Travis's desk was littered with paperwork, some of it his, and he settled into the stack of reports, welcoming its dulling effect on his suddenly unruly thoughts. In less than an hour he was caught up, and a measure of his earlier fragile peace had rejoined him. He got a cup of coffee. It was bitter, and he knew it would sit heavy on his stomach, but he drank it anyway.

By seven-thirty the big room, crowded with desks, was bustling with the sound of typewriters, small talk, and voices giving and taking reports. Travis watched as a woman clocked in, her mouth turning down as she scanned the memo. It was the same reaction the next three made. Travis felt the ache in his jaw and loosened his pressure on the muscles grinding his molars together. Instantly the vision of Rojowski lying in his own steaming blood returned to his mind. Travis cursed silently and drained the last swallow of his coffee.

The phone buzzed, the interoffice light bright in the dull gray plastic. Travis decided he hated gray phones. It buzzed again and Travis, knowing the intrusion would spoil the quiet of his morning, crumpled the Styrofoam cup into the metal can at the side of his desk and reached for the receiver.

"Travis," he said.

"Captain Hammit wants you, Travis," a soft voice

said. "He said whenever you can make it as long as it's now. And, Trav?"

"Yeah."

"He's a real bear this morning."

Travis smiled. It was her standard estimation.

"Thanks, Jessie. I'll keep it in mind." A bear was mild compared to Hammit some days.

When Travis walked into Hammit's office, smiling at Jessie on his way in, Hammit didn't bother to look up. His face was tired and pale, pasty, as he bent over a stack of reports and files.

"Close the door behind you, Travis."

"Morning, Captain."

Hammit looked up, a ghost of an answering smile on his features.

"Sorry. Is it morning yet? Yeah, I guess it is," he said, answering his own question with a flick of his wrist to check the time. Hammit's shirt was crumpled and open at the collar, his tie thrown across the back of the worn leather desk chair. His hair, prematurely gray and thinning on top, was mussed and slightly oily, as though he had run his fingers repeatedly across his scalp, a common gesture when tired. Travis thought he recognized the clothes from two mornings past, though then they had been fresher.

"I take it you haven't been home yet."

"Home? What's that? My wife and kids haven't seen me in so long they may sue me for desertion."

Travis's smile widened. "I'll be a character witness at the divorce proceedings."

"On whose side?" Hammit grunted. "Speaking of proceedings, the shooting board convenes at nine, you go up at ten, room 102. I got your reports here, want to add anything?"

"No, nothing. Why? Anything irregular in what I said?"

"No, just a routine question, but what about the clip?"

"No luck. It's in a landfill by now."

"Shit. Be there at ten."

Knowing he was dismissed, Travis left the room. He had over two hours to kill and decided on breakfast, first pausing at the duty schedule. He would be reassigned now that Soloman was finished, but there was nothing there for him. In fact, his name wasn't even on the new schedule, an oversight he cheerfully pointed out to Jessie. She looked confused, then irritated, but didn't swear, and he admired her control, wondering if it gave her ulcers. Later he would remember the schedule and wonder if it was part of the puzzle, an odd-shaped piece similar to all the other odd-shaped pieces, none of them having similar sides.

Breakfast was good, hot and filling, and he ate alone, recovering from the leftover feeling he had carried away from Chris. He tried to phone her, but she'd already left for work.

At ten-thirty Travis sat in the hall outside room 102, his hands tucked beneath opposite armpits in a characteristic pose, his right big toe jumping irritably against the loose leather of his shoe. The murmur of voices within the room penetrated into the hall, indistinguishable except for Hammit's, which was raised, sounding angry. The last man, Wilson, had left almost fifteen minutes earlier, his lips tight against Travis's questions, a wary look in his eyes. All he would say was something about an Adam Larkin and certain references to the man's lineage. Finally the door opened a crack, and Hammit's face and hand motioned him in. He looked grim.

The smell of cigarettes hung fresh in the smoky room,

though none of the men sitting at the disordered table were smoking. Travis sat down in the chair indicated to him and stretched out his legs. This was his first time before a Shooting Review Board. He knew the procedures and he knew the protocol. He knew Soloman was a legitimate kill. Yet, suddenly he felt inept, overwhelmed by the same disastrous feeling he'd had when he leaned over Rojowski's body in the alleyway. Suddenly he wished it were all over or had never happened and that he was back with Chris, holding her, making her miss work. He remembered with a sharp clarity how peaceful she had looked, curled into the patterned comforter. But none of this showed on his face. It was even and unreadable, delivering the impression he wanted to the men in the room—calm professionalism. It was a sharp contrast to his feelings.

"Officer Garrick T. Travis?" The question came from a steel-haired man at the center of the long table, who spoke without raising his eyes off the paper in his hands. He was a heavyset man with a strong chin and loose jowls, and thin lips drawn slightly down at the corners. Whether this was an act of nature or from years of frowning, Travis had never been able to determine. Travis had a fleeting thought, wondering what Deputy Chief Burrell had looked like as a child. He fought a smile at the picture his thoughts conjured.

"Yes, sir."

"Do you understand this Shooting Review Board was convened pursuant to Chapter 12, Section 35 of the *Police Manual* to determine if the shooting that occurred yesterday at approximately six A.M. was a lawful and legitimate act?"

For the first time Deputy Chief Burrell looked up, his eyes resting on Travis. Travis could read nothing in their expressionless depths, and Burrell looked down again, continuing his monotonous reading, his gravelly voice hoarser than usual this morning. "This is not a legal proceeding. If the shooting is decided an irresponsible act, possible criminal charges could be involved. Should this occur, all information and conclusions gathered by this board would be forwarded to Internal Affairs and the district attorney. Is that clear, Officer Travis?"

"Yes, sir," Travis said, but the reading reminded him curiously of being read his rights. Travis was instantly wary.

"Officer Travis, let me introduce the members of this board to you first, then we'll get down to business."

He introduced District 7's captain, Captain Donaldson, and his immediate supervisor, Captain Hammit. Travis acknowledged both men with a nod. Burrell then turned and gestured to his right.

"In keeping with this department's open-door policy, representing the public interest, we have Professor Ronald Holstein from Washington University and Mr. Adam Larkin, chief executive of Aztec Systems."

Travis studied the two men, recognized the plump, bald, watery-eyed man with soft pink fingers as the professor, and dismissed him instantly. The second man was a different matter. Adam Larkin sat reared back in his chair, one arm draped behind it. Larkin had heavy-lidded eyes and an uneven brow in a thin face—underlined by a mouth that had no lips. Travis had a sudden, acute sense of being analyzed carefully, and then the man's expression changed so quickly and completely Travis wasn't certain what he had seen. The man smiled, reached inside his business jacket for a pack of cigarettes, and lit one with a lighter from the tabletop, holding the Kool 100 casually in his left hand.

He had smoky gray eyes, and the kind of face easily missed in a crowd—yet, for that one instant before he smiled, his eyes had been hard and calculating, piercing with a volatile energy and determination. And something else. Somewhere in the depths was a strong sense of animosity. Travis wondered if he'd once given the man a ticket or something.

Larkin, drawing on his cigarette, looked up, cocking a brow. The man seemed amused, the kind of amusement a parent might display toward a recalcitrant child. Superior. Travis recalled his predecessor's assessment of Larkin's strange and unusual parentage. Larkin looked like he was aching for a fight and hiding it poorly—that same look Travis had seen too often on the faces of weary officers in Nam, while they waited for the order to begin the next search and destroy. His feeling of unease grew. Travis turned his attention to the deputy chief, who was still speaking.

". . . And I am Chief Burrell.

"Officer Travis, we have reviewed your report as well as all the reports of the other officers involved. Now, if you will, in your own words, please tell us what transpired on the day in question."

Slowly at first, then more quickly as the events unfolded, Travis told what had happened, feeling himself tense as he described once, and then again for the benefit of the professor, the exact sequence of shots fired in the alley where Rojowski and Soloman were killed. With the aid of a city map, Travis showed the route the fourth man had followed during their chase through the city to the rooftops, and he offered a detailed description of the man, especially his strange green eyes. Some twenty minutes later he finished, and, glancing around the room, he noticed Larkin, the man from Aztec Systems, whatever that was, relax. It was nothing overt, no more than a slight movement of the shoulders as he sat back more easily in his chair. Thinking back, Travis realized the tension had appeared in the man just as suddenly, at the exact moment Travis had begun to describe in minute detail what the stranger had looked like.

Travis pulled away from the map and sat back feeling tired, thinking of Chris, wondering if he should leave, questioning this last part with his eyes to Hammit. Hammit shook his head and glanced at the deputy chief, who seemed once again burrowed in the reports.

"Questions, gentlemen?" Hammit asked.

Travis sighed. His part wasn't finished yet. Larkin leaned forward, lit another cigarette, and exhaled. "I have a question. Speaking strictly for the private sector, of course, and apologizing for my lack of knowledge of police procedure, but why did you leave your assigned place? It is my understanding that you were not to move."

"Yes, sir," Travis said. "But my friends were being killed." He smiled coolly. "I never have liked men who hide behind orders and regulations while people die. It's just another word for cowardice."

Larkin lifted a brow, knocked ashes from his cigarette, and sat back.

"Officer Travis, why did you not pursue this individual?" Burrell's voice was worsening, his hoarseness growing scratchier with each word.

"As I stated in my report, I was stunned from my fall and was unable to give chase at that time. By the time I was able to walk, the suspect had vanished."

"You have never seen this individual before?" It was the voice of Adam Larkin, a soft voice with a hard Bronx accent. The words were short and clipped. Travis looked at the man, meeting his dark, almost expressionless eyes. Almost. They were still amused.

"No."

"Well, Officer Travis," Larkin said smiling. "Don't

you think you should have made an attempt to locate him? Even though he was out of sight he didn't simply evaporate."

"Yes, sir, Mr. Larkin, that might have been possible. But I didn't know how long I had been stunned and I didn't know if the individual was armed or not. When I did come to I thought of the weapon, of his handling the gun—his prints would be all over it. I decided I could get an easy ID off of that."

"Where is the weapon now, Officer Travis?" It was Larkin again, one brow cocked. "And the clip this mysterious stranger handled."

"I turned it in to the lab for fingerprints and ballistics testing. That is the usual procedure . . . sir." Travis deliberately paused before the last word, the insult a matter of timing rather than content. "The clip is missing. I couldn't find it immediately after the encounter. By the time I returned to continue the search, city crews had cleaned the alley. A day early, by the way. You'll see all that information in my follow-up report."

"Ah . . ." Larkin said, his tone ambiguous.

"And have you seen the results of those tests?" asked Burrell, his black eyes boring into Travis.

Travis paused, then associated the question with ballistics. There was a sudden increase of tension in the room. Travis, instantly on guard, could feel the heat of it, and he looked from man to man.

All were staring at him strangely except Hammit, who seemed engrossed in the movement of his little finger tracing circles on a blank page before him. Hammit was angry, uncomfortable. Perhaps embarrassed.

"No, sir," Travis said slowly. "Not as yet."

"Officer Travis, according to the lab there were no prints on the gun." Burrell looked at him hard. Travis was stunned. He looked at Hammit for confirmation. The captain's lips tightened.

"No. That's impossible. I saw the man handle the weapon myself, he grabbed the..." Travis was smoothly interrupted.

"Perhaps, Officer Travis, the man simply wore gloves." A smile was beginning to broaden across Larkin's face. The man was baiting him, and he seemed to be enjoying the exchange. Travis felt a surge of anger and clamped down on it, lifting a brow himself.

"No, sir. I saw brown ungloved hands holding the weapon, sir." Travis drawled on the last word, his voice slightly sarcastic. "And blood. Gloves don't have buffed fingernails and gloves certainly don't bleed."

"Are you sure? It isn't too late to amend your report." Larkin's voice was sweeter now. Patronizing. Almost pitying.

"The report stands. I know what I saw and did." Travis felt his anger mounting, felt a flush deepen on his cheeks. Larkin reminded him of his elementary school principal. "Besides," he said, suddenly realizing the fact, "my own prints were on the gun, too. What happened to those?"

"No prints, Officer Travis." Larkin leaned forward, smiling. "None. Not one. Not even a smudge. Here, read it yourself." He pushed the lab report across the table at Travis.

Travis resisted the urge to knock the shit out of him and closed his hands around the table edge to keep them from forming fists as he pulled himself to his feet.

"That's impossible. There's just no way..."

Deputy Chief Burrell cut him off in mid sentence.

"Officer Travis, we've heard enough about this matter. And about this *mystery* man no one has ever seen before.

Please let us turn our attention to the matter of the actual shooting."

"But..."

"Sit down, Travis." Hammit's voice cut into the exchange, just as unyielding as on the day of the debriefing. "It must have been a lab error. Someone must have wiped the gun by mistake. If so, we'll find out."

"Someone went to a lot of trouble by mistake," Travis said harshly.

"Sit down, Travis," Hammit said softly.

Slowly Travis sank back into the chair, fighting the anger that threatened to force him back to his feet. It was absurd! Impossibly inept. The timing the day of the shooting fouled up, now the prints wiped off the gun, and a pompous ass named Larkin smirking as if it were all a joke. Travis felt slightly ill at the stupidity of it all.

Burrell flipped through a stack of papers before glaring up once again. Businesslike. "Thank you for regaining your seat, Officer Travis. Now, about the shooting. We understand that this was not the first time you've had a run-in with the man known as Soloman. If you'll tell us about the previous occasions."

In a monotone Travis answered, fixing his eyes on a spot in the wall behind Burrell's head, his hands clutched tighter on the arms of the chair.

"I first had... contact"—he let the word slide over his tongue—"with Soloman eight years ago, I think. It was when he was a suspect in a prostitution ring being run on the lower east side."

"What happened then?" Hammit encouraged.

Travis felt Hammit's eyes on him but kept his gaze firmly on the spot he had chosen, kept his voice thoroughly calm. Only Hammit knew what this part would cost him. And Hammit hadn't warned him it would even be brought up.

"We could never pin anything on him. One of the witnesses was found with her throat slit. As I recall, we arrested him on a minor weapons violation."

"The second time was about the same year." Travis paused, swallowed, and breathed evenly, forcing away the bitter taste that always appeared when he remembered. "We got word he was trying to eliminate the only witness to several felonies. We picked her up at one of his warehouses. And once again the witness was found dead. But this time..." Travis's mind shied away from the memory and then back again. "This time she had been tortured first—before she was executed with a .45 slug in the back of the head. That was Soloman's trademark for a snitch."

Travis focused hard on his chosen spot, concentrating on the slight discoloration as though to blot away the memory of Marlow's face and body when he finally found her.

It had been his fault, his error. He should never have left her, not even to pick up a pizza. It had been his idea to cultivate Soloman's best girl. His idea to set up the operation that had left her frightened and running from a suddenly angry Soloman bent on revenge. His idea, his plan. And it had worked. Except for the part about his own reaction to Marlow. That had been a surprise as much to her as to him. The passion that flared between them had been scorching, intense. It had blinded him to everything, even simple procedure, and so he had left her for half an hour and gone after pizza. And when he returned, the apartment had been a shambles, with a trace of blood on the back of the door as if they had thrown her there, shattering her face against the sharp wood.

Marlow had been his best—his only—lead to Brevard. She had pulled a trick with a rich Middle Eastern client.

A trick which nearly cost her life. A trick set up by Soloman for his upline man. His boss man.

Blindfolded, she had been taken to meet Brevard. She had thought him a gracious, cultured gentleman. And then Brevard had turned her over to the john. The man had beaten the hell out of her while they watched a girl being murdered. A live show. Marlow had survived— until a damned-fool cop had turned Soloman against her and then gone out for pizza.

They had searched for two days before he, working alone, located her body stuffed into an empty washing-machine box in an alley five blocks from the so-called safe apartment he had rented her. Temperatures had been in the nineties for both of the two days he had searched. And the odor... He had never forgotten the odor.

"Snitch?" The question brought him back to the smoky room. It was the baby-soft voice of the professor.

As the term was explained, Travis allowed his burning mind to cool. That day had almost seen the end of his career as a law enforcement officer. The sight of Marlow's rotting flesh had snapped something inside him. He had gone out after Soloman and his two best boys, the associates who had followed orders, carrying them out on Marlow's lovely body, and he had gone alone, except for enough firepower to stage a small war. Only the intervention of Matthews had held him back. He could still hear Dan's mellow, low-pitched voice, smooth in the angry air of the room to which he had tracked Travis. Somehow Dan had brought him down from the Nam-induced reaction, pulled him away from the killer heat that possessed him so fully. Travis had slipped back then—the only time since Nam—to the days when he had changed for a few brief weeks into something predatory and rabid, delivering justice where no one else would. He had been his own law then, violent without conscience, a cold, icy killer, a long vigilante—an animal on the scent of Brevard.

It was a memory of himself that he hated. Travis had confined that part of himself well, up until Marlow, managing to bury the instincts that Nam had bred even as he still tracked the man responsible for their formation. But with Marlow's death, something inside him had cracked, thrusting him back in time. Travis had wondered ever since—whenever the memories overcame him—who he really was. What he really was. But when control was restored and the past safely buried in his mind, the question never arose. Only when something reminded him or someone mentioned Marlow. . . .

Travis closed his eyes, swallowing hard to force down the memories.

"Officer Travis." Donaldson spoke for the first time. "Did you have a personal relationship with this last witness. I believe she called herself," he flipped through reports on his desk, "Marlow."

"Yeah," Travis answered tonelessly, ignoring the reaction of his mind at the sound of her name.

"She was a friend. A good friend. So what?"

"I believe you know what Captain Donaldson means." It was Larkin's voice, amused, his quirky brow lifted.

Travis looked hard at the man, and the extent of his sudden rage must have shown in his eyes, because the expression on Larkin's face wavered and he sat back quickly in his chair.

"Just what are you trying to imply, sir?" Travis asked softly, leaning forward.

The mask of civility dropped over Larkin's features as he explained.

"I'm not trying to imply anything, Officer Travis. It just appears that you have had a run-in with Soloman on two previous occasions in which witnesses have been killed. This last time a friend," he said, stressing the word only slightly, "was involved. That sounds to me like a motive for... well..."

"Revenge," Travis finished for him softly. "Conspiracy. You've got to be kidding. I had no reason to kill Soloman and every reason to bring him in alive. Information, sir."

"That will be all, Officer Travis," a gravelly voice rasped. "You will be notified of the findings of this board. You are excused."

Somehow, later, Travis found himself in the hallway, the hot, dry air of an overhead vent blowing down into his hair. Around him were long splinters of wood and two or three casters still spinning. In his hands was the spindled back of a chair in two parts. He didn't remember busting it against the wall, but the scarred place on the smooth, beige semigloss paint, and the jarred feeling in his shoulders, left no other explanation. Slowly he bent and laid the chair back on the floor with the rest of the pieces.

His head began to clear and certain points of the interview suddenly stood out. The first, most obvious point was that someone had wiped off the fingerprints. Travis was going to find out who.

Travis spent the next two hours with the stub of the property tag in his hands, chasing clerks and technicians, but he got nowhere. The moment when the clerk took the weapon, tagged it, and put it on the wood dowel was the last time anyone remembered seeing the 9mm. Six hours later a technician looked for the gun and found it sitting on the shelf, shining clean. There was no wood dowel through the trigger guard, no protective carton. In the intervening hours, ten to twenty unidentified people had been in and out of the room where it and all the hundreds of other items were kept. Any one of those people could have cleaned the weapon. But that would mean that someone in the department was either incredibly stupid or was... protecting the fourth man at the scene—the green-eyed stranger. The claustrophobic feeling closed in on Travis again.

The well-fingered property tag still in his hands, Travis was sitting behind his desk when Hammit found him early that afternoon. The anger of the morning had burned away, leaving only a dull feeling, a poor substitute for the peace of being with Chris.

Hammit had showered and shaved and looked, if not quite fresh, then at least more alive. "Got a minute?"

"Yeah. Come on in." Travis pulled his feet off the desk top and pushed a chair over.

Hammit dropped a file on the desk, sat slowly with a small groan, and rubbed his forehead with his fingers. "Well," he sighed, "I've been getting complaints from clerks and lab technicians for half an hour. It seems someone has been bashing heads and rapping knuckles all morning trying to track down a slight problem with a 9mm automatic. I wonder what this person found out."

Travis almost smiled. "I never hit anybody."

"No, but Larry says you held him against the wall with a fist at his throat when he told you he was too busy to talk."

"Those weren't exactly his words to me."

"You denying it?"

"No. Larry's a prick."

"No argument there. What did you find out?"

"Between the hours of eight A.M. and two P.M., someone took a zippered paperbag down off the shelf, opened it, wiped the prints clean and put the weapon back onto the shelf. No bag."

"No chance of it being an accident?"

"No. No way." Travis flipped the property tag onto the desk top.

A silence stretched between the two men, not abrasive, yet not companionable. At last Hammit dropped his hand, sat up, and looked at Travis. He reached for the file as though he suddenly needed something to do with his hands.

"Sorry about Adam Larkin this morning."

"Yeah. He's a real son of a bitch," Travis answered, tonelessly.

"Worse. I don't know why Burrell asked him to sit in. Especially now, with the department scaling down the open-door policy so much. He's, ah . . . he's a problem."

Something in Hammit's tone made Travis sit up and note his expression. It was pensive and slightly grim.

"I take it you have some bad news." Travis kept his voice cool—the only sign of his swiftly rising anger was the stillness of his body, the placid calm of his expression.

Hammit took a deep breath, exhaled. He met Travis's eyes for an instant, then quickly broke the contact and looked at the file he held.

"As you know"—Hammit's voice was at its impersonal best, the tone he recited unpopular regulations in, a tone Travis hated—"the private sector can cause an occasional problem with the way they view police, police procedure, and situations requiring and resulting in violence . . ."

"Hey, cut the crap." Travis's lips twitched downward. Hammit jumped at the flat tone and once again met Travis's eyes, then looked away.

"You want it straight?" He fiddled with the file.

"You know I do."

"All right, we'll do it your way." His voice hardened. "Larkin feels there may have been an element of conspiracy and revenge in the shooting in the alleyway. He feels

this revenge may have involved the way Soloman died."
Hammit paused. "He's talking death squad."

"Bullshit."

"He and Holstein feel that until a thorough and complete investigation can be made, you and Wilson need to be kept off the streets."

"Administrative duty," Travis spat.

"No. Not for you. Immediate and indefinite suspension."

"Susp..." Suddenly the effect of more than forty-eight hours of foul-ups and sheer stupidity broke over Travis. He found himself laughing, pounding the desk top, rolling back in his chair, holding his sides, threatening to fall, his voice echoing into the hallway. Then as quickly as it started, it was over. Travis's face was harder than Hammit had ever seen it, and when Travis came forward, hands shooting out to grab his shirt front, Hammit shrank back, his eyes wide. Travis lifted him to his feet and stood, towering over Hammit, his mouth saying the things he had held in all day long. "You know damned well there was no conspiracy. There wasn't time for one. Rojowski got hammered and Soloman turned on us. I had to shoot. Wilson was witness. I did what you, Burrell, or any of us would have done," he shouted, shaking Hammit.

"I admit I'm glad he's dead and I'm glad I was there to do it. But there wasn't any revenge. There wasn't time to even think about Marlow. You know that. And there wasn't time to plan a kill. Jarvis blew the stakeout and we lost three good men and three pieces of scum. Now some businessman wants to play cop and say what he would have done in the situation when we both know he would be dead right now if Soloman had drawn on him. Then somebody fucks up by wiping the fingerprints off the gun. You don't say that you're starting an investigation about that. You don't say anything, but just, 'Hey man, sorry.' Or that I'm crazy and dreaming the whole thing up.

"Hammit, you've got to be fucking kidding. Nobody makes all those mistakes."

Finally, through a haze of anger, Travis saw the throttled flush of Hammit's face, his bulging eyes and slack mouth. At the same time he realized where his hands were and released Hammit instantly. The smaller man slumped to his feet, rubbing his throat where Travis's fingers had knuckled his windpipe.

"Sorry, Hammit. I'm ... sorry."

"Well," Hammit said hoarsely, "at least you didn't treat me like the chair outside the review room. You rattled water glasses with that one."

"I'm on suspension?"

Hammit paused and looked at Travis uncertainly, gauging his reaction.

"You're on suspension. But I won't add to your troubles by reporting this latest little incident."

"What am I supposed to do while you guys have your fingers up your butts investigating a shooting that doesn't need investigating?" Travis's voice was tight.

"Go fishing."

"I don't fish."

"Well think of something. Do whatever you normally do when you're off duty."

"I can't. It's illegal."

Hammit grinned, carefully tucking his shirttail back into his pants. "Go home, Travis."

CHAPTER 4

Day Two—Midday

TRAVIS turned in his badge, then packed the few things he would need from his locker and desk—those personal things that would be an intrusion to the man who would be assigned his duties for however long the "immediate and indefinite suspension" would last. There wasn't much. It took all of five minutes, but those five minutes were enough for the haze of anger to fade and his mind to begin functioning normally again. The thoughts that occurred then came rapid fire, and Travis left the half-packed bag and headed for Records and Whizzer.

Whizzer was a pale-skinned, flame-haired kid with strange, almost orange eyes, and a way with computers that bordered on the mystical. When Whizzer sat down at the keyboard, slender freckled fingers flying, information came from sources most Computer Records people weren't even aware of. Less than a year ago, working after hours, Whizzer had single-handedly sent a major crime figure to prison on IRS tax-evasion charges by breaking the code on the man's new business computer. The papers had loved it, agreeing to keep the computer whiz's name secret for the sake of his safety. But the name had stuck. Whizzer.

And Whizzer loved a challenge. He was a graduate of a half-dozen universities with specialities in as many different fields, a genius who had finally found himself in the strange arid world of computers. Travis liked him, though half the time he didn't understand him.

When Travis pushed open the glass door marked RECORDS, Whizzer looked up and grinned. The look on his face was triumphant, as though he had just won a bet with himself. His words cemented the impression.

"Wondered how long it would be before you showed up." Travis pulled a chair up close to the console and raised his brows, questioning.

Whizzer's grin widened. "I entered a series of reports this morning. One dealt with the lack of fingerprints on a certain 9mm automatic. Yours, I believe. Knowing you, you couldn't let it lie. I knew you'd be around sooner or later." Whizzer's voice, a well-modulated alto, congratulated himself smugly.

Folding his long frame into the chair, Travis relaxed.

"Is there anything around here you don't know before the rest of the world?"

"Nope." Whizzer leaned back in his chair and reached for a Hires Root Beer, the contagious energy sparkling in his eyes. Condensation on the can rolled when he lifted it, and dripped onto his turquoise "I Love Shakespeare" T-shirt. He smacked his lips appreciatively. "So, Officer Travis, what can I do for you?"

"You can tell me who wiped those fingerprints clean," Travis said, feeling the slight burn of residual anger.

Whizzer laughed. "Contrary to popular opinion, I'm not God, Travis."

"I figured you could just break into God's computer records," Travis said wryly.

Whizzer grinned at the compliment. "I could if I knew where it was. But other than that, what else can I do for you?"

"How 'bout a list of recent parolees matching the description of the man at the stakeout yesterday."

"The one you chased?"

"The same."

"Which prisons? Federal?"

"Yeah, I guess so. Surprise me."

"Okay, it'll take about an hour. Care to wait?" Whizzer asked, his questions coming fast, almost on top of the answers.

"Got nothing but time, Whizzer."

"Yeah, I know," Whizzer said slyly. "Immediate and indefinite was the way it was phrased, I believe."

Travis sighed. "Like I said—is there anything you don't know?"

"How big your private parts are."

"That is privileged information. Besides, you wouldn't believe it!"

"Don't enter it into a computer," Whizzer said, only half joking.

"It hasn't entered into anything lately. I'll be back in an hour," Travis said, heading for the door.

"Yeah. Why don't you clean up the splinters outside of 102 while you're waiting. Somebody busted a chair against the wall."

Travis turned, surprised, but Whizzer was already engrossed in his keyboard.

Forty-five minutes later Whizzer buzzed him. Travis again entered Whizzer's private domain and pulled his chair back up.

"What do you have?" he asked.

"Nothing, nothing really. Four men over six feet, slim

and black. But none with green eyes and all were accounted for. Sorry."

Travis looked away, feeling the only avenue of investigation close up on him, and Brevard slip away. He sighed, "Guess it was a long shot anyway."

"Not really," Whizzer said. "A sensible move. But what now?"

"Now I guess I go fishing," Travis said, rising. "Two civilians gave me a paid vacation."

"Yeah, I wondered about that," Whizzer said, his eyes taking on a familiar gleam. "Administrative duty I could see, but suspension? Sounds to me as if somebody either likes you or wants you out of the way."

Whizzer's tone was odd, and Travis cocked his head, curious. He had a strong feeling Whizzer was about to open a door for him.

"What do you mean?"

"Oh, I don't know," Whizzer said, but his tone and the excitement in his eyes belied the words. His fingers rested for a moment on the keyboard before he continued as though what he would say was determined by the feel of the plastic keys.

"Except... those must have been pretty powerful civilians. And, too... I think it's rather odd—all the...coincidences...."

"Like what?" Travis asked, sitting back down and leaning forward intently. Whizzer had an idea, and Whizzer had one of the fastest minds Travis had ever known, a sweeping, inventive mind. Travis felt his blood begin to rush, and a strange heat passed over his skin.

Whizzer's voice was suddenly sure, his strange eyes piercing. "Like somebody went to an awful lot of trouble to clean that automatic. Like you were the only one to get a real good look at man number four. Like all the reports I've been filing on the results of the SRB and

IAD investigations play down the existence of the fourth man. Like nobody but you tried to run a trace on him, and now you're the only one to get put on suspension."

"Wilson?"

"Administrative duty."

Travis sat back. "Now that is interesting. Harshel?"

"Voluntary vacation. Four weeks accumulated." Whizzer's burnt-orange eyes gleamed in the reflected light of the display screen, calmer now that he had spoken. "Coincidence enough for you?"

"So." Travis spoke slowly, leaning back in his chair. "You think we're being set up."

"No, you're being kept off the streets and away from the action. Any action. You're being kept away from the other officers at the scene, away from comparing reports and discussing the 'Soloman incident.'"

Travis leaned forward again, laced his fingers, and smiled slowly.

"Why don't we run a trace on these powerful civilians and see if we come up with more...coincidences."

Whizzer grinned, his lips stretching across his face.

"Done."

He reached over and tore two pages off the computer printer and handed them to Travis.

Travis shook his head.

"No wonder they call you God down here."

"Professor Ronald Holstein checks out. He's a bit of a wimp but he's okay. Adam Larkin, however..." Whizzer let his voice trail off.

"Yeah, see what you mean. Not much info on a guy who's chief of a big company, and not much on the company either except profit and loss figures. What does Aztec Systems do, anyway?"

"I don't know," Whizzer said slowly, eyes glowing. "But it's interesting. I followed the usual procedures, identifiers, and so forth, and all I got back was that," he said, pointing to the last line on page two. "Very interesting indeed."

Travis read the lines.

INFORMATION UNATTAINABLE. NO CLEARANCE.
CODE 399024XB.

"I don't get it."

Whizzer leaned forward, the gleam in his orange eyes suddenly unleashed and growing.

"Seems like Aztec Systems is mighty powerful. It either has government contracts dealing with the intelligence community or national defense, or, quite simply...it is the government," he said, stressing the last three words.

"What...what makes you say that?" Travis said, trying to fit this latest information into the picture he had of the list of Whizzer's coincidences. And into his knowledge of Brevard, and Brevard's tactics.

"Two things. It's a very respectable address, the makeup of the security system, and the code number especially. It's only two digits off from another company I've been playing with."

Travis questioned with his eyes, thoroughly confused. Then: "That's three things," he said. Whizzer ignored him.

"In my spare time I've been compiling a master list and chain of responsibility of so-called private businesses dealing with the government. All this for a writer friend of mine. Aztec is new to me, but it reads very similarly to the information listed by a company called RHEASTARR." Whizzer let his voice drop dramatically. "And they create a surveillance equipment for the CIA."

The gleam in Whizzer's eyes had settled slightly with the pleasure of the telling. Now he was smiling the relaxed easy smile of the victor. Travis was glad Whizzer was so happy. For himself, he was no closer to understanding the puzzle. The pieces were growing stranger and seemingly less related to one another. He shook his head slowly.

"Whizzer, can you break the code? I mean break it so that it can't catch you?"

"I'm being paid big bucks to do just that. It's part of the research my friend is interested in," Whizzer said, fingering the logo on his T-shirt.

"Who is that mysterious writer friend you've been talking about?" Travis said.

"You ever heard of... Ludlum?" Whizzer asked seriously.

"Yeah. I'm impressed."

"Well, it's not him."

"None of my business I take it."

Whizzer just smiled. "I'll let you know when I have something."

"I'll have Dan Matthews check with you periodically, just in case you can't find me. Remember, I've got a vacation coming up."

"Fly casting," Whizzer said smiling, returning to the keyboard.

Day Two, P.M.

It was still daylight when Travis left the department. There was a lot of backslapping, name-calling, and best wishes from everyone as he left. Considering the events of the last few days, no one seemed to see anything odd in his suspension, several echoing Hammit's words about civilians playing cop. Travis was expected back in one or two days anyway. Everyone treated it as a lark—everyone except Whizzer, who had a bunch of mums delivered to Travis's desk along with a condolence card. Below the flowing Hallmark sympathy lines Whizzer had printed six lines from Shakespeare's *Hamlet*:

Hamlet: Indeed sirs but this troubles me. Hold you
        the watch tonight?
All: We do, My Lord.
Hamlet: Arm'd you say?
All: Arm'd, My Lord.
Hamlet: From top to toe?
All: My Lord, from head to foot.

The lines contained a warning, and Travis felt slightly chilled. For all his strangeness, if Whizzer had a premonition it was usually based on fact. Whizzer was a good source of information. But for Travis there was another.

When daylight dimmed, Travis hit the streets looking for answers. Though there were some places on the streets that a cop didn't go unless he took an army, there were others which were relatively safe. If he went well armed.

The streets were his domain and always had been. Only one other place had ever had a similar effect— Vietnam. There, with death on every side, where even the village washerwoman might be concealing a hand grenade, a man felt different; poised on the brink of death, a man felt most intensely alive. Travis had talked to others during and since the war, and most had felt the same. For some, like him, it was addictive. Every time he went onto the streets, he got the same rush.

Tonight, in the part of town the tourists seldom tour, there were uniformed servicemen, hookers, female impersonators, men in drag—or shims as they were known on the streets—johns, gay men in groups of two or more. The lights were garish, the odors sickly sweet, the clothing costumes, the people TV creations. There was a lot of neon and purple hair, four-and-one-half-inch spiked snakeskin shoes, fishnet stockings and garter belts, suede skirts slit hip high, coke spoons on silver chains, and, defying the cold, loud polyester shirts unbuttoned to show curly chest hair. Travis wondered if they had it professionally permed.

He drove for an hour while a deep fog came in off the Potomac and settled around the city, softening the harsh lights, hiding the worst of the filth littering the sidewalks, and promising at least some anonymity for a too-tall, out-of-uniform, possibly ex-cop. Finally, he parked the Trans Am, not bothering to lock it. Locks were generally a waste of time, guaranteeing a broken window in this part of town.

Travis checked an ankle-holstered .32, and his personal weapon, a .45. He slid it into his shoulder holster and headed for Amorous Gertie's. Gertie was a fifty-two-year-old ex-hooker who, by the name of her place—which flickered neon red—and by the advertisements pasted inside the doorway, proclaimed her willingness to cater to any and all tastes. Most of the ads had pictures showing who offered what. Some were tattered, depicting Gertie herself in her younger days, strutting her lavish figure and making eyes at the cameraman. Gertie had been the youngest, most successful madam D.C. had ever seen, catering to anyone in any government from lieutenants stationed at the base to visiting dignitaries. Some even murmured she had seen a president once or twice, but when asked, Gertie would just smile, flash her once-magnificent eyes, and walk away. Nobody could walk away from a man like Gertie could. Even today.

Travis slid through the doorway past the entrance lights with his head down and melted into the shadows. There was an air of celebration in Gertie's tonight—an electric feeling that said to the world, Gertie was in the mood to party. The silk bow ties sported by the bartenders and waitresses said she was going to do it in style. The habitués who recognized the signal were already stoned and waiting for the show.

Travis had learned to read Gertie's several years ago when he had been a new face to vice, and had entered a long series of illegal poker games where the house paid its losses with pretty boys or girls and then blackmailed the participants with films of their activities. Gertie had gotten a suspended sentence and left word at headquarters that Travis was welcomed at her place anytime. He had gotten a lot of ribbing about that one, but he dropped in from time to time to check on leads and pick up information. Gertie always sent him a drink on the house—the best bourbon, straight up. Tonight though, he wanted to be just another unrecognizable face in the crowd. Sometimes he cursed his height; it was hard to hide a face that stood five inches taller than average.

He got a table in the back and slapped a fiver down on the top to signal the waitress. She was new, lush, and very pretty, probably seventeen or so, but with a makeup job that had Gertie's signature all over it, and a sequined silk costume worth at least a grand. To her regulars, the fancy costume meant "Hands off, Gertie has special plans for this one." For those less accustomed to Gertie's subtle signals, a bouncer was assigned the job of keeping his eye pinned on her and anyone who got out of line. Some things, however, were expected, and when she brought his drink and change, Travis folded the one and slipped it inside the edge of her very low cut top. She smiled knowingly, raised his hand, and licked the palm, turning away instantly. The entire transaction took only a moment, her body shielding the encounter from the bouncer Travis spotted watching from the bar. Travis grinned. Gertie would make a fortune with this one. She was born to it. By starting out with Gertie, she would receive the training to turn talent to art. Gertie was a good teacher. Not only did her girls stay in the field longer than most, they did it with style.

Travis learned little in Gertie's. Everyone was celebrating the demise of Soloman, Irish-wake style, with two much liquor, lower prices on the girls, and even free food. Nobody was in the mood for words. Travis had to leave the bar sooner than planned. The hot little waitress had set her sights on him, and when she pulled his hand under her skirt, sliding it across her bare bottom, he knew it was time to look elsewhere. Seventeen—experienced and hot or not—was just too young for him.

Travis decided he needed safer ground. He left the window down on the Trans Am as he drove.

The rest of the evening was only slightly more profitable. The feeling he got on the streets was odd, out of place. His sources all knew about Soloman—and who had put him away. Everyone was willing and eager to talk to the man who had been there, the man who had done it. But not one admitted to knowing about the fourth man. Most were probably honest. At least three were lying. The moment he brought up the fourth man, they clammed up. Total silence and odd, half-frightened stares were the only replies, though once a working girl, who called herself Lily, laughed in his face and walked off, hips swinging hugely, laughing all the harder when he followed her asking more questions. Something just wasn't right here. Something... but he couldn't put his finger on it.

And then, at the airport, standing out like a beacon

light, he saw Nikki. She was picking up a john, a wealthy-looking businessman with a self-satisfied paunch and a briefcase. Travis could see the curve of her breasts beneath the sheer red fabric of her shirt. Nikki liked red, the more transparent the better. The businessman laughed at something she said, hailed a taxi, and helped Nikki inside, his hand lingering longer than necessary on her back and then sliding around front. Travis grinned.

He followed the taxi into town to one of the hotels Nikki worked whenever she had a good one and planned a long, very expensive session. Travis watched them walk along the breezeway, Nikki's long legs sliding against the thin fabric of her skirt. They paused outside the door of room 117.

Nikki turned from the man to work the key. The man dropped his briefcase and his arms went around her, his hands against her breasts. Travis could tell he was working the buttons of her blouse. Nikki stood completely still, a statue bent slightly forward, straining.

He could hear her moan. It wasn't just a practiced sound. Nikki enjoyed her work.

Travis, moving fast, slid out of the car and up to the couple.

"Nikki." The couple whirled, and the man's hands dropped suddenly to his side as he turned away to avoid being recognized. Travis could have laughed. Nikki, though, was amused rather than embarrassed. Her sheer nylon blouse was open to the waist, the full curve of her breasts visible. She smiled and drew her fingers across her cleavage, widening the space between the fabric.

"Hi, Travis," she purred, looking up through lashes black with mascara. Nikki was twenty-two going on thirty, but knew how to use her eyes and body to make money. Lots of money. And besides, she had once explained to Travis, "I like the business. I like the men. I like getting fucked." And she did. They had an understanding though—two more years and she would have enough money to get out, to go back to Boise and open her dance school. He had agreed not to bust her one night and had learned her life story, her dreams. Two years, he had promised her. She reminded him of his promise now with a sultry smile and a further widening of the red blouse until one nipple was almost exposed.

"I got business right now, Travis, from Boise. Come back later and we'll have a drink. Maybe you'll get lucky."

"I need to talk, Nikki. Tell your friend here to go wait in the lobby."

"You want to talk, go see a psychiatrist. You want a good fuck, you're at the right place." She smiled then and pulled the blouse together, letting the fabric drag across hard nipples.

"I said we need to talk. Now."

"And I said I'm busy. You'll have to wait." Turning to the red-faced man standing in the shadow, she said, "Come on in, sugar," and pushed open the door.

Quickly, Travis positioned himself before the doorway, smiling. He knew what the response to his next words would be, but Nikki had left him little choice. He had questions and wanted answers. "We talk or I bust you and your john. Now, Nikki. Not after he pays you."

At the word bust, a seventies cliché, the businessman gasped, grabbed his heart, stumbled backward a few steps, and took off running, his briefcase forgotten.

"Hey, wait," Nikki yelled. "Goddamn it, Travis. That was a two-hundred-dollar trick. Do you know how long it'll take me to make up that much? Angie got that one for me special. He's gonna be pissed as hell."

"Stop shouting. I couldn't care less about your pimp.

Or the john," Travis said, laughing. "You should have sent him to the lobby."

"We had a deal, you bastard."

"Yeah, well I just canceled it. We talk now or I take you in. Soliciting for the purpose of prostitution. Write home to your grandmother about that one."

"You fucker. You ain't shit. You can't arrest me. You ain't even a cop anymore."

The impact of Nikki's words slid over Travis like ice water. It had been less than ten hours since his being put on suspension. How the hell did she know about it already? Travis, his hand still holding Nikki's arm, shoved her inside the room and kicked the door shut. Some of what he was feeling must have shown in his eyes, for Nikki was suddenly subdued.

"Button your blouse." Then more softly, "I hope I didn't bruise your arm."

"I hope you did. Maybe Angie'll let me off the hook if I say his special john did it to me."

"Nikki, how did you know I'm not working now?"

Without bothering to button her blouse, she answered, "Beverly told me. Her roommate was down at the station today. But I heard it on the streets too, if that's what you're asking. Everybody knows Soloman's executioner is in deep hot water."

Travis sat slowly on the bed. Soloman's executioner. Who in the hell started that one?

"What else have you heard?"

Nikki opened and then closed the door, and laid the forgotten briefcase on the scarred bureau.

Nikki shrugged. "Way I heard it, you and some guy planned the whole thing and popped it to him in some alley. Back of the head stuff. Must admit though, Travis, it don't sound like your style. You're smart. You would have made it look like an accident or something. Not hard to do. Especially for a cop. Connections and all that."

"I shot Soloman in the line of duty, Nikki. It was legit."

Nikki shrugged again. "Whatever. What did you want, Travis? Make it snappy. I got two hundred bucks to make up."

Travis turned and looked at her reflection in the mirror over the low bureau. She was striking, with short dark hair, black eyes, the grace and stance of a dancer. She dressed the part too. Always in red. Sheer stuff that left little to the imagination. She tossed her head irritably, setting the feather earrings she always wore swinging, and opening the unbuttoned blouse a fraction. She returned his look in the mirror, and he smiled when he caught her fingering the gold and diamond crucifix she wore—whether out of sentiment or belief or a macabre sense of humor, he had never asked. It was one of her trademarks. It said "Nikki," as surely as the red blouse.

"I'm looking for a man, Nikki."

"Cute, Travis. I thought you liked girls. No wonder you never give me any." Her back still to him, she lifted both arms and adjusted her hair in the mirror. The blouse gapped hugely. Nikki smiled and licked her red lips, teasing.

"Wanna play games, Travis?"

Travis groaned. Nikki in a somber mood was trouble enough for any cop. Nikki feeling playful was downright dangerous. Quickly, he described the fourth man and his proximity to Soloman. The whole time he spoke, Nikki kept her back to him, adjusting her hair in the long mirror. After a few moments, it became difficult to keep his eyes on her face. "Anyone that close to the king has to have been seen somewhere, Nikki," he finally finished.

Nikki smiled and turned, facing him where he sat on

the edge of the bed. Quickly he stood. She laughed, and, not bothering to rearrange her blouse—which was now bunched under her armpits—she walked over, backing him against the bed. When his backward movement was effectively stopped, and her body was pressed full length against his, she smiled.

"Let's say I know about your pretty boy. Everything has a price, Travis."

"I don't have the two hundred to compensate for your customer."

"Not money. You. I always did have a thing for a man in uniform. Show me a good time and I'll talk. Maybe."

"Nikki. You just offered me payment in return for sex," Travis laughed. "Something's a little backward here. And besides," he said, pushing her gently away, "I'm not in the mood for games. Now talk, or I'll turn you over my knee and spank your pretty bottom."

"Sounds kinky. Let's do that first."

Her hands were pulling out his shirt, which had somehow become half unbuttoned.

"Nikki," he said, laughing harder, "I'm old enough to be your father."

"Even kinkier. Let's play."

"Nikki, stop it." He grabbed her, turned her around, and held her still, her back pressed against his chest, one arm pinned down. If her breasts hadn't pressed so snugly into his arms, it would have been a quite effective hold. As it was, his breathing was a little labored. He spoke softly into her ear.

"Now, little girl, talk to daddy. Who is the man, where can I find him, and what do you know about him?" He bit lightly on the ridge of her ear.

Minutes later he had what she knew and made for the door. Much more of her squirming and he'd have been in trouble. She had managed to get one hand free and had played havoc with whatever clothes and body parts she could reach.

"Oh, Travis."

He paused, the door open and his exit secured.

"Zip up your fly. And if you ever just want a good time... No charge." She let her words trail off and touched herself meaningfully.

The cold of his car helped his flushed face and steadied his hands as he drove. As soon as his breathing was easier, he thought over what Nikki had said. A man with an accent and previous business dealings with Soloman had made himself at home in D.C. in the last forty-eight hours. Nikki was scared—word was he was a mean bastard, and would slit your throat as soon as look at you. Nikki said something about being casket bait if anyone knew she had talked. He was the quintessential mystery man. He had no name, no ID, no history. But he'd somehow usurped the line of authority in Soloman's hierarchy and taken over. He had a lot of pull... even at police headquarters.

Travis was thoughtful, his mind whirling, as he drove to Chris's apartment for their date.

Day Three, A.M.

Chris sipped slowly on a cup of imported Dutch Chocolate coffee, enjoying the silence and peace of the hour. The noisy kids next door had left for school, and the man below her had finally turned off his blaring TV and gone to sleep for the day. The old building was calm except for the squeaks and groans of her apartment's ghost and the soft crunch of her cat at breakfast. It was the best part of the day, and Chris felt wonderful. Travis had not spent the night, and her back wasn't sore from the unaccustomed weight of another body in the bed, her shoulder had improved, and she had already been to the spa and ballet practice, soaked in the hot tub, showered, had a facial, and picked up groceries. It was 11:00 A.M. and she had the rest of the day to herself and her sketch pad.

Finishing the coffee, Chris buried herself in the pad for almost an hour, finishing up a sketch of Nino sleeping-in among her clean laundry. It was good and she was rather proud of it.

While she was washing up afterward, her buzzer rang, and Chris answered cheerfully.

"Yes?"

"Christine Lattimer?"

"Yes."

"We hate to bother you, Miss Lattimer, but we stopped by the design house and they said you were off. I'm Howard Long from Alvin Fabrics and wondered if perhaps we could talk a moment."

"Couldn't you come back later? I'm off today." She had never heard of Alvin and wasn't interested.

"I suppose we could come back next month, Miss Lattimer, but your boss said you were the buyer, and we can offer a special on our line, seventy percent on wholesale, if you buy this month. It's an introductory offer, and I'd really appreciate it if you would at least give me fifteen minutes to show you my product." He mispronounced four words and sounded nervous, as if it were his first day on the job.

Chris sighed. It was just like Charlie to fob a green, half-trained salesman off on her on her day off. He probably had gossiped with them an hour before sending them over with a complete set of directions. He'd done it before. Sometimes she hated Charlie.

"Okay. Fifteen minutes. But remember, this is my day off."

"Oh. Are you expecting company? I guess we could drop by after lunch if you like."

God, there were two of them. A training run. So much for her quiet morning.

"No. Come on up." Chris sighed again and pulled a sweater on over her sweatshirt.

A knock sounded on the door.

CHAPTER 5

Day Three, A.M.

THERE were no answers. Not without an ID on the green-eyed man—a green-eyed man no one had seen and who had no fingerprints. A man who, according to the SRB, *wasn't relevant*. Wearily, Travis released the seat belt and slid out, taking his basketball, his shorts, the box holding his personal weapon, and the groceries with him. His legs quivered on the stairs. After a four-hour game, he felt rubbery and sticky all over, and his exhausted body, steaming in the cold, felt sweaty and quiet. If only his mind were as calm, but it still boiled with questions. A shower might help. At least it would help the smell. He rounded the corner to his apartment head down, fumbling for his keys, and stopped. He could quit looking for the key.

The door hung open, cold air whistling in, the gouges of a crowbar pressed deeply into the wood. Travis breathed tightly and slid the groceries slowly to the ground. His fingers trembled from the cold as he opened the box and lifted out the .45. Without taking his eyes from the door, he checked the weapon, his thumb releasing the safety.

Travis pushed open the door with his foot and checked the room. It was empty. He advanced through the apartment, his breath white before him. They were gone—had been for a long time. But they had done a good job. Thorough. Holding the gun, he brought in the groceries and forced the door closed. Light showed through where the crowbar had dented the wood. The heater whirred softly overhead. *My electric bill is going to* . . . It was a stupid thought. But it was easier than thinking about the room.

Everything was bashed, ripped, or shattered. Everything. A ceramic lamp he had used as a child was cracked apart like a broken egg shell. The couch cushions were strewn, the couch itself overturned with the bookcase lying on top of it. Books were everywhere. Dishes and food had been pulled off the shelves onto the floor. The refrigerator hung open. His albums were scattered, pieces of several in the kitchen sink. His stereo had been pushed onto the floor, the equalizer dented . . . his stereo. Why hadn't they taken . . . he ran into the bedroom. The TV screen was smashed, and someone had urinated into the opening. Some of his clothes were slashed, and the bed was stripped, the sheets and blankets in a heap at the foot. Perfectly centered on the floral gold mattress was a folded bundle of red cloth. The only neat spot in the vandalized apartment.

It wasn't a robbery. It was something more.

The gun had warmed to the temperature of his hand. The apartment was already slightly warmer. His breath no longer blew white. Water dripped unevenly into the bathroom sink. Travis noticed all the extraneous stimuli, felt the passage of time, yet he could not make himself go to the bed. That neatly folded piece of cloth kept him at bay, and for the first time he wanted to run. Instead, he stepped over and with the tip of the gun pushed at the cloth, unfolding it slowly. It was unfamiliar—a woman's sheer nylon blouse, marred with dried blood stains. Chris would never wear anything like it, and then he remembered. It had been yesterday—last night. The blouse had been a calling card to every john for blocks. He had followed the color to the breezeway of the hotel she worked out of and into the hallway. She had still been wearing it when he forced her into the room for a little chat—a chat about a green-eyed man who didn't exist.

Nikki...

He didn't bother to look for the phone to call the station. He didn't have a burglary to report. He had a warning. She had told him she could end up in a box. The dried blood might mean she was right.

Travis pulled off his coat and strapped the shoulder holster into place, then strapped on his .32 in its ankle holster. In the closet, he pushed around in his Army footlocker until he found a box of shells, and, as an afterthought, he tossed some shirts and shorts into an overnight bag along with some tools he'd once borrowed from a B and E suspect. The vandals hadn't bothered to take a thing. They thought a lot of him. Travis smiled. It was a cold smile.

He stuck the shells into his pocket, sheathed the .45, and headed for the door. He was outside trying to make the dead bolt turn when he heard the muffled sound of the phone. "Shit." He stood for a moment, then with a violent shove reentered the apartment. Two rings. "Where's the Goddamned..."

Travis stood up the bookcase, shoved the couch upright. "Great place for a phone—under the couch, of course." On the fifth ring, he answered.

"Yeah." There was a moment of silence, and then he heard a deep, shuddering breath.

"T... Travis... Trav?"

"Yeah, who... Chris?"

"Help me... I'm hurt. They said... went too far... warning... for you..." Her voice stopped.

"Chris... Chris? Damn it, talk to me!" He could hear the sound of his own fear in the silence.

"Chris, where are you?... Chris?" he shouted.

Suddenly he was in the breezeway, flying down the stairs, and then at the wheel of the Trans Am. The steering wheel's leather covering was cold against his palm as the engine turned over and as he pulled into the street. It was ten minutes to Chris's apartment. He never slowed down. He didn't think. Couldn't think. It was enough that he could still breathe and that the gun was hot against his chest.

The manager was entering the building with a load of clothes when Travis got there. Travis's explanation was hardly coherent, yet something must have made sense, for the manager dropped the yellow basket and grabbed his ring of keys. Here too, though, keys were unnecessary. The door was unmarked, but open. Travis drew his weapon and entered slowly, the manager behind him. The room was a shambles, a replica of his own.

"Chris." No answer. "Chris?"

The apartment was silent. Too silent. Sidestepping, Travis pushed open the bedroom door. Like his own, the sheets were piled at the foot of the bed, but instead of a neat bundle of cloth in the center of the bed, this time it was a person. Curled around herself.

"Get an ambulance," he heard himself say as he replaced the weapon. The manager responded and was gone. Chris was bleeding about the mouth, and there was blood trickling from her scalp, but she was alive. The smell of semen was brittle in the air. A bloodied bat lay on the floor, Travis's bat, the one he used during the summer softball season.

"Christ, no... Oh, Chris. Chris...."

She couldn't hear. Carefully he picked up a blanket and tucked it around her, noting half against his will the bruised places on her shoulders, the red welts down her thighs. There was blood puddling into the mattress from between her legs. He sat beside her and smoothed the hair from her face. It was slick with sweat and tears.

He heard himself talking, his voice alternately soothing and angry, incoherent as something in his mind— under strain for too long—snapped. That something had quivered before, singing like the coiled and twisted steel cables of a long suspension bridge battered by winds. Now one of the strands had given way, and he felt his mind tilt dangerously. Another snap followed as Chris moaned hoarsely, and Travis's mind fell away into a fierce burn. For all of the years before Nam he had believed in an innocent world, a world where right was right and wrong was wrong and the law was God. It was the only way to live. There was no choice.

Yet in Nam there had been no law.

Until he took control and created one.

Until he meted out justice to the guilty.

With his own hands.

For all the years since, the two parts of himself had balanced out. Suspended tautly between opposite shores, the Nam warrior and the civilized, educated police officer had faced one another in limbo. Not even Marlow and his guilt had changed it.

Stalemate.

Till now.

Travis thought he had forgotten how to cry, and so the tear that fell onto Chris's face surprised him. He watched as it was joined by a second, and they trickled down her cheek and neck. Her eyelids fluttered.

"Chris?"

She swallowed, swollen lips moving slowly.

"Chris?"

She opened her eyes.

"Chris . . ." he breathed, touching her cheek.

Her voice rasped, broken and mewling.

"Don't touch me," she said, turning her face into the crook of her arm.

The ambulance arrived, wailing, and so did the police. One of them was a woman, tight-lipped and wide-hipped. She rode in the ambulance with Chris, holding her hand. The other officer took down Travis's statement and let him go. Travis didn't even remember what he'd said. Nothing mattered but Chris's words. "Don't touch me."

From the hospital, during the hours while he waited, he called his mother, concerned about the rest of his family. She was all right, but agreed to get out of the house for a few days. She would be going to Tony's in Silver Springs. He called Tony and warned him, too. His brother's last words hung in the air between them after he'd hung up, and finally entwined themselves with Chris's.

"Sounds like you're way over your head, kid, way over."

"Don't touch me."

The doctors x-rayed Chris, and blood was drawn. Travis saw the rape kit in a nurse's hands. The tight-lipped patrol woman—her name was Abney—never left Chris's side for three hours. Later—for Travis it was a lifetime—she came out and handed the other officer a preliminary report. Then she turned to him.

"You Travis?" she asked crisply.

He nodded.

"I think you need to hear this, too."

He walked over, lead weights on each leg. He really didn't want to hear.

"She said it was four men. Two black. We got descriptions. They asked a lot of questions about you. Two did all the talking. Talked about a guy named Soloman and another one. I couldn't spell it. Here, I spelled phonetically."

She handed him a piece of paper. His eyes traced the letters. Sayaad.

"They got in as some kind of art salesmen. She a decorator or something?" Travis nodded. "She opened the door for them. They started asking questions. When she wouldn't talk, the two in business suits left. Then the other two got nasty. Real nasty. The doctor can tell you how bad." She paused, obviously puzzled by whatever emotion she saw on his face. "They used a bat on her. In ways bats weren't designed for. It'll all be in the report. I'll leave a copy on your desk. You okay?"

Travis met her eyes. They were softer than her mouth. Compassionate.

"Yeah, I'm okay."

"Oh, one other thing. Something they forgot to tell you guys in the rape-seminar classes. When a woman's been through what she has, it changes her. They get harder or softer, meaner or more dependent. Angry. But all that comes later. First they feel ashamed and dirty. And being touched by a man, any man, but especially one they care for, is unbearable. She told me what she said to you. Be patient with her. She needs you. It'll take a long time before sex is good to her again." She cocked her head. "Your Chris is a strong lady, though. I think she'll be all right. Oh, one other thing. She needs to know how you are feeling. Your answer to that question will be the most important thing in her life. Think about it carefully."

Travis nodded and watched the officers leave. The nurse's explanation left him sick and weak. Chris's attackers had done everything imaginable to her. She was already in surgery to repair and/or remove what was left of her vagina and uterus. She had lost at least two pints of blood. Maybe three. The only thing that made the explanation bearable to Travis's cold mind was the nurse saying, "She passed out when they used the bat on her. She won't remember a lot of what they did to her."

With the two hours or more that Chris would still be in surgery heavy on his mind, Travis left the hospital and drove to the station to leave a further statement and read the report filed by the officers at the scene.

Sitting at a desk in the corner, he read slowly, methodically, the details there feeding the slow burn.

The two men who had worked over Chris were probably unknowns, temporarily unidentifiable—one white with acne, one black with yellowed eyes. The black was uncircumcised. They had left a message with Chris. The officers had included it in their report.

"Tell him Sayaad says to back off. He's in way over his little boy's head. And this other," the white man had said, unzipping his pants, "this is for Soloman. For his executioner. And we'll burn him too. You tell the ex-cop. He's next."

Travis tasted blood where he'd chewed the inside of his cheek. Blinking back the fresh tears that threatened to fall, he flipped to the section of the report headed "Descriptions" and he froze.

Perhaps the officers at the scene didn't know who was being described, but Travis did. The two in business suits were Tallitt and Carver, Soloman's lieutenants. As sure as there was a Satan in Hell.

Suddenly his mind, weighed under by the trauma Chris had undergone, began to function again. Slowly, then fully, it came to life with a heat that left him breathless as the anger took on purpose. He hadn't felt exactly like this since Da Nang and Saigon, when Alain Brevard had slipped away. And since the day he had found Marlow. The personality Nam had shaped and nourished flexed and began to find control. A man he hadn't seen in over a decade reached out and planned grimly. If Brevard was indeed the power behind Soloman's organization... if Sayaad had been the liaison... then that made Brevard ultimately responsible for what had happened to Chris. Tallitt and Carver would lead him to Sayaad—and to the men who had raped Chris.

Tallitt and Carver. Travis had just finished a three-week investigation into everything they did. He knew every move they made, everything they owned, and every thought they attempted.

"The little boy" was going to find them. From them he'd ask only one thing. Two names. It might take some persuasion. Maybe a lot. Two names. He swallowed when he envisioned his plans for the two who had raped Chris.

But first there were a few details to attend to. And he needed help. He pulled the phone to him and held it while he worked out his first move.

Dietrick was home, and the conversation between them was short and pointed. Travis had no time for amenities.

"I need a favor," he said, not bothering to identify himself.

"You got it."

Travis could almost see the quiet eyes and the quiver of the too-long mustache. He began to relax. "I've got a sick friend who needs to be looked after."

"Yeah, I heard."

Travis paused, surprised. "News travels fast, doesn't it?"

"Anything about you does these days. You know who did it?"

"No. But it was sanctioned by Tallitt and Carver. They were there. At least for the first part."

"Why? They had no reason to cross the line. They'd be next up for Soloman's job. But involvement with something like this'd spoil any hope they had. They'd be in jail instead of in charge."

"My guess is they think *I* went over the line. Let it get personal. Also, word's out I didn't get suspension. I got canned."

"Because of Soloman?"

"Bingo. Is it gonna be a problem? Say for two, three days?"

"No, not at all. I could use a break from the bullshit for a while. What room is she in?"

"Don't know. She's still in surgery. You'll have to check."

"No problem," Dietrick said.

"Thanks." Travis was glad Dietrick had asked no questions.

"Hey. Remember. Peace. Love. Dove."

It was an old joke between them always delivered with a sixties peace sign. Travis laughed mirthlessly and broke the connection. "No way. Not tonight," he whispered.

The next call was for Nikki—to the city morgue, considering the blood-stained blouse. It was the first place to start looking. And it was busy.

"Damn." He slammed the phone down and called Records, asking Whizzer to run *Sayaad* on the computer. "Give the results to Matthews." Whizzer laughed. "You think I own this frigging machine, don't you, Travis?" Travis grinned and rang off, reaching for the directory, his hands hard in the fluorescent light. He needed to be moving. The energy of rage was making even his skin tingle. Flipping through, he missed his page twice, but finally found and dialed the number of the hotel Nikki worked out of. The desk clerk had a nasal voice that reminded him unpleasantly of Jarvis.

"The Piedmont."

Travis winced. "I'm looking for a girl," he started.

"So who isn't," the clerk laughed.

"I'm looking for a girl named Nikki."

"Don't know any Nikki."

Suddenly Travis was cold with pent-up anger. His fist clenched. His voice, softer than a breeze, carried a menace that communicated itself even over the phone. "Listen, asshole. She works out of the Piedmont. Five six, short dark hair, walks like a dancer and likes to wear red. Sheer stuff—and feathered earrings. A crucifix. She might be hurt and I'm going to find her." He paused. "And you're going to cooperate or an asshole is all you'll have left to remember yourself by. Now—do you remember a Nikki?"

There was a long pause.

"You say she might be hurt?" The voice was mildly curious. Unconcerned by the threat.

"Could be."

"In that case I might know your girl." Suddenly the man laughed a short bark. "Don't know anything about a crucifix, but they pulled one out of the alley across the street this morning. Call the morgue. Your Nikki could be on ice." He laughed again. Travis cut him off, heading for the door. Perhaps he'd been right the first time.

The morgue parking lot was almost empty. The coroner's and technicians' cars and the ambulance were lined up in a short row. Inside it was quiet. The night crew was sitting around a ceramic slab eating tuna sandwiches and potato chips. Connelly, the ME, looked up and grinned.

"Hey, Travis! Hungry? How 'bout a gut-and-meatball sandwich?"

"Nah. Just had one," Travis said coolly, his face immobile. "Can we talk?"

The strain must have shown, for the grin slid off Connelly's face to be replaced with the noncommittal professional expression they teach all doctors in medical school. He picked up his Coke and left the others.

"Sure. What do you need?"

"Hear you brought in a Jane Doe from the Piedmont Hotel area," Travis said expressionlessly.

"Yeah. About ten o'clock."

"Got an ID on her?"

"Come on, Travis. You've been in vice long enough to know how these things work. The average hooker doesn't carry around a birth certificate. We might never ID her."

"Yeah. Well, I may know this one. Can I take a look?"

"Sure," Connelly said, his expression still distant, considering. "Come on."

The room, lined floor to ceiling with spotless stainless-steel refrigerator doors, was icy. Connelly checked several ID plates, then pulled the handle of a door lying chest high. The tray slid out, neatly pedicured toes first, then leg and thigh, wounds dry and gaping. Travis's lips pulled tight against his teeth at the sight. He had seen many bodies, the results of ice-cool professionals and passion-driven murderers alike. But it had been years since he'd seen anything like this. Carefully he schooled his face to calm, fought down the reaction that claimed his body.

This was Brevard's work—vintage Brevard, although admittedly far more brutal than his Vietnam murders.

The man had obviously evolved a whole new category of death. Travis wondered if he'd trained his Nam psycho to these heights or if he had found a new crazy to kill on cue. Because Brevard didn't actually wield the scapel that killed. He only choereographed the action and took pleasure in the death.

Travis wasn't sure why Connelly had let him see the "Doe." This had to be one of the bodies the Feds were keeping so mum about, one of the murders the white shirts were trying to keep out of the media—the murders which matched the ones in D.C. ten years ago. And those in Viet Nam.

He had been nineteen and scared shitless the first time he saw Brevard's dirty work. Two victims had been piled in a garbage heap—both Vietnamese, of course. One had been strangled, bloated tongue and eyes protruding. The other had been like this—slashed.

Connelly, reading the statistics, was a dimly heard haze of sound in the background.

"White (or possibly Asian), female. Five six, one hundred ten pounds, brown and brown, early twenties. Discovered approximately eight A.M., Riggs Place and Fourteenth Street in an alleyway. Nude. Preliminary report indicates body was dumped after the fact. Death occurred approximately ten to twelve hours prior. About ten P.M. to midnight. Cause of death, multiple stabbing and lacerations." Connelly looked up, the carefully schooled expression slipping a little. "Whoever did this worked her over real bad. Over two hundred slash marks, no pattern, average one-half to three inches deep, some two feet long. No murder weapon at the scene." He looked at the face, crisscrossed with dry wounds. "Not much left for a visual ID. You know her?"

Travis's mind was cold, blank, but for Brevard. Where

was he? "I don't think so. I don't know. What do you make of it?"

"Professional medical opinion or gut feeling?"

"Whatever."

"You got some crazed son of a bitch who gets his rocks off by slashing women."

"Any sign of intercourse?"

"Chemistries on vaginal washings aren't back yet. Don't know. Might never know if he used a condom."

Travis dragged his eyes off the body. "Any personal effects?"

"Not much. This way."

The refrigerator door slid shut with a rattle and clang. At the desk Connelly pulled out a tray of manila envelopes, chose one, and dumped the contents onto the desk top. With his forefinger, Travis pushed the few things around.

"No crucifix. No feather earrings. And I never saw Nikki without them. They were her trademarks."

"Well?"

"You said possibly Asian. Why?"

"Teeth. Skin tone. Could be tan I guess, but . . . your girl Asian?"

"No. Could be her if she's Caucasian. The question is, did somebody know her well enough to remove her things from her and replace them with this stuff? If so, why? And another thing. Her blouse wasn't torn or slashed. Just a little bloody."

Connelly looked up. "What?"

"Nothing. Just thinking. Call me when you finish the report." He ignored the curiosity on Connelly's face.

Outside, the cold hit him like a physical blow—the temperature was dropping fast. Travis zipped up his jacket, checked his watch, and slid into the seat of his car. It could have been Nikki. The physical characteristics were right. But the time element was wrong. He had seen Nikki at 10:00 P.M., and he had scared off her john. Tallitt and Carver or their thugs could have been tailing him and taken her right then. But Tallitt and Carver weren't Brevard. And the kind of death he had just seen took time. Tallitt and Carver would have raped her, beaten her, and put a bullet in her head. Not slashed her to death. Only Brevard would have done that. Somehow, Travis knew the body he had just seen wasn't Nikki. There were too many things that didn't fit. In the hour left to him before Chris came out of surgery, he cruised the bars Nikki worked out of and drove through the Piedmont looking for a hooker in a red blouse. It filled the time, kept him busy, helped keep his mind off Chris and the anger he kept in check by clenching his jaw. . . . Chris and the strange puzzle pieces, none of which quite fit.

The recovery room nurses badgered her, making her cough, drying her tears, insisting she couldn't go to the toilet. She was catheterized, they said, but the urge was still there, a painful pressure in her groin. Her groin. . . . She closed her eyes and slept.

When she woke again, she was in a room, softly lit, and she was disoriented. Her mouth was dry. Tubes lay along the bed beside her and ended taped to the backs of her hands. One carried blood.

"I'm thirsty." It wasn't her voice. It cracked hoarsely. She tried to lick her lips, but her tongue was dry and her lips burned.

"Here."

She turned, accepted the straw, and sucked, swishing the last bit of water around in her mouth. It stung. Looking up, she met Travis's eyes.

And she remembered. Closing her eyes to shut out the scenes his face forced on her, she turned away.

"Don't turn away from me. Please."

His voice was hoarse, rough, and softer than she had ever heard it. The softness, so unusual for him, brought back another memory—faint—of tears...of his tears hitting her face to the soft accompaniment of his voice, telling her he was sorry—so sorry.

"You came for me," she whispered. "How did you know?"

"You called me," he said.

She felt the movement of his fingers through the hair at the nape of her neck. "I don't remember."

"Look at me." His voice was insistent. Gentle.

"No. I don't want to look at you. I don't want to see you. Not now. Go...Go away, Travis. Please, just go away."

"No. Look at me."

She could feel the tears in the corners of her eyes as she squeezed them tighter. "How...How can you stand to look at me, Travis?" she whispered past the tightness in her throat. "How can you stand to see me after...after what they did?" There was a silence. He suddenly turned her head and held it in his hands gently. Time passed, and still she refused to open her eyes.

"That's just it, Chris," Travis finally whispered. "They did all that *to* you. Forced it on you. You had no choice." His voice was tender. She could feel his lips move against the side of her face, his breath warm. "There's no guilt or shame in what happened. Not for you." He paused, remembering the officer's words: *She'll want to know how you feel. Your answer will be the most important thing in her life.* "I wish...God, Chris...I should have been there. I should have...when I saw you, curled around yourself...I thought..." He breathed heavily. "Ah, shit, woman, I care about you. Please don't close me out... Please."

Tears slid down her face, tingling against her bruised skin. She could hear a clock somewhere close. His words hung between them, leaving her a choice she wasn't ready to make. She felt a surge of anger followed by a helpless emptiness. Even now, her mind clouded and her body still under the effects of the sodium pentothal they had used to put her to sleep, he forced her to think... to feel... to react to him. Chris, clinging mentally to the touch of his hands on her skin, took a deep breath.

"You wouldn't lie to an old friend, would you?" she whispered.

"Never." His voice was sure, strong, certain.

Slowly she raised her hand and placed it against the back of his neck, slid her fingers into his hair. He breathed out in one long pained breath against her cheek. She never was quite certain what he said.

Later, after he left, she looked at Dietrick sitting slouched in the chair by the bed, his eyes dark in the shadowed room.

"You're really here to act as bodyguard, aren't you, not just to keep me company? In case... in case they come back."

Dietrick tilted his head, smiling slowly under the long mustache, and relaxed under her scrutiny. "I always told Travis you were the smartest thing he ever did. If you ever get to the place where you can't stand him anymore, give me a call. I like a beautiful woman with brains."

She snorted. "I don't fit either description, Dietrick. Especially after today," she whispered. He didn't answer and she was glad. Dietrick, too, was smart.

"Is Travis going to do something stupid?"

He raised his eyes. "Travis? Do something stupid?"

He thought for a moment. "Probably. And if I wasn't here with you, little lady, I'd be helping him."

Day Four, A.M.

The dream was murky, tied together with all sorts of loose ends. Or did they all connect? David, wearing a fireman's hat, unzipped his fly and sprayed at a burning hut in a backwater village. From within came screams. A woman, her clothes in flames, rushed from the doorway. She moved in slow motion, her sluggish hands beating at the flames. A burst of fire cut her down, blood spurting in normal time. Smiling, Alain Brevard stepped over her and slung back his weapon. Like some sort of priest, he nodded to David and held out his hands. David, without resistance, lifted his head from his shoulders and placed it in Brevard's hands; his body wavered and vanished. Brevard sighed sadly and tossed the head at Travis. Slowly, it rolled through the air. Travis caught it. It was Jack's, drool sliding from its lips. Travis screamed. The woman, hearing the scream, rose and came toward him, her arms outstretched, her body bloated and stinking. It was Marlow. Dan was holding him down as Marlow came closer. Then, like David, she vanished, taking with her the stench. Dan turned him away from the burned hut, and Randy held out his hands, guiding the two men to the back of Catcher Joe's. The green-eyed man, Sayaad, served up mugs of beer. Travis's mug was brass. Reverently he drank.

Travis woke with a start. An aching back proclaimed reality. His hands shaking and sweaty, he rolled off the sofa. Moving slowly, he laced up his Pumas and stretched, hearing glass crunch beneath his weight. It was a tiny pink hand, the fingers ground into fragments in the carpet. The body, once a delicate ballerina, lay in sections nearby. It was like his dreams—all broken pieces. Shaking off the last effects of the dream, he looked around. Whoever had worked Chris over and trashed her apartment had given special attention to her collection of glass figurines. Only one piece, a small crystal mouse, was undamaged. Rescuing it, he added it to the bag he had packed for Chris, placing it so it would be the first thing seen when the bag was opened.

While coffee perked, he showered, shaved, and put on fresh clothes. The T-shirt wasn't his and hung a little loosely. The owner must have been a monster—maybe the man she had alluded to as keeping her in practice. If so, he was short one shirt and one girl.

The coffee and the last two croissants made a quick breakfast, and Travis remembered to stop in at the manager's and arrange for a cleanup service for the apartment on the way out. The manager was sympathetic, helpful, and plied Travis with a dozen questions, none of which were answered. Travis was in a foul mood.

In his own apartment, Travis repacked a bag for himself to store in the trunk—just in case—and took the time to clean and load his .45 and a Smith and Wesson Model 64. The .45 was soon shoulder-holstered again, and his snub-nosed .38 in its snug ankle holster replaced the smaller .32. It was his own version of police backup.

On the way out he spoke to the apartment manager, who had a few choice words to say about the condition of Travis's apartment and a certain tenant's irresponsible behavior regarding a variety of subjects. Travis gave him the number of his insurance company, the number of the cleanup service he had called for Chris's apartment, the number of the local law enforcement agency, and politely told the manager to shove it. Outside, it had started to sleet. Yes, he decided, he was very definitely in a foul mood.

Across town in the hospital his mood abruptly worsened. Dietrick, tired-eyed and grim-voiced, softly explained that Chris was in recovery again. She had started hemorrhaging just after midnight, her pressure dropping dangerously low. Just after 6:00 A.M. two surgeons had wheeled her back into surgery, two bags of blood dangling.

"Why didn't you call me?"

"I tried. You didn't answer your phone."

"I slept at Chris's." His voice sounded so calm, so matter of fact, but his eyes blazed. He dropped Chris's overnight bag beside the bed. "My apartment was in worse shape than hers. It got trashed yesterday, too."

Dietrick eyed him curiously, drawing his own conclusions. "You report it?"

"The apartment manager will, but there's really no need to. I find the guys who got to Chris, I'll have the ones who trashed my apartment."

Dietrick sat down slowly and reached for his Coke can. After a moment he grinned, but rather than explain he asked, "Leads?"

"Two. Tallitt and Carver. They were there. With any luck and a little persuasion they'll give me the other two. On a platter." He didn't mention Sayaad. Or Brevard. He never had before. Why start explaining the past now?

"Sounds like you got enemies in high places, my boy," Dietrick drawled, "or low places, as the case may be."

"Or both."

"Could be. You armed?"

"Well enough. But I may need your key."

DEATH WARRANT

Dietrick raised his brows. "You planning to start a war, Travis?"

"Walk softly and carry a big gun. Reagan, circa 1980."

Dietrick grinned and stretched out a leg as he fished in his pocket.

"I take it you can't find your own."

"You take it right. Besides taking a leak into my smashed TV screen, the aforementioned vandals aka rapists broke lamps, records, my stereo, and rearranged my furniture. Postmodern scheme of decoration. That's my apartment now."

"Postmodern? You mean punk?"

"In all its trashy glory."

Dietrick passed him the key and replaced his key chain. "Don't use it all in one place. Remember. Peace. Love. Dove."

"I'll remember it to them personally."

Travis added the plain key to his own chain. It was a nondescript, heavy-duty, aluminum-alloy key that opened unit number 174 BB of Springfield's largest U-Store-It complex. Inside was an assortment of snow skis, a bicycle, a console TV, a set of olive-brown luggage, and a low trunk filled with goodies—enough to start Dietrick's war should Travis need to.

"Ah, Travis?"

Travis looked up. Dietrick was looking at his Coke can.

"You know, don't you, that . . . ah . . . well, Chris can't have children . . . not after what they did to her."

"So they tell me. So we'll have a dog or adopt. Or both."

Dietrick grinned crookedly and finished the Coke, popping it into the garbage. "Contemplating the state of matrimony, are we?"

"Yes, we are. How long before she's out?"

"Since when?"

"Since she rearranged the coffee cups and I didn't know about it. How long before she's out?"

"Might be her now."

It wasn't, and they talked another ten minutes before Chris was wheeled into the room, pale, asleep, and with only one IV, of clear fluid—D5W. Somehow that relieved Travis.

When the nurse woke her, she was groggy and complained of pain, ignoring Travis and falling asleep again almost immediately. The nurse injected something through the IV line and left.

Travis smoothed her hair, massaged her free hand, and talked nonsense to her. When he left, it was without a word to Dietrick. His throat wasn't working properly.

Day Four, P.M.

Chris realized she was awake, her eyes already adjusted to the darkness. She swallowed, painfully, and tried to clear her voice to speak. Instantly someone was beside her. She started.

"It's okay, darlin'. Just me. Here, let me turn on a light."

"Dietrick?"

"The one and only."

"I'm thirsty. My throat hurts."

"They intubated you. Tends to have that effect. Here, sip." He held a straw to her mouth. "Especially since you've been to surgery twice now."

"What all did they take out this time?"

"Nothing. They just closed a little bleeder."

She sighed and lowered her head. "Has Travis been here?"

"This morning. You were asleep."

"I look pretty bad, don't I?"

"I'm sure to a woman there's some logic to that transition of subject matter, but somehow I just can't follow it."

"You're talking like Travis. Answer the question."

Dietrick flipped on another light and rested his arms on the bed rail. His eyes were a soft liquid brown, like a large spaniel's, and almost as sad. "Yes, m'am. You do." He paused. "I suppose now you want a rundown."

Chris managed a half smile and winced with the effort. "Yes, if you don't mind. My mouth hurts. Start there."

"Top to toe?"

"Just the salient points."

"Salient? Now who's talking like Travis?"

"Sorry. It's catching."

"Okay. Well, let's see. Your mouth is swollen and you have a cracked tooth, both of which will heal all by themselves. You got two black eyes, a broken nose—but it looks fine to me—multiple bruises and contusions, scrapes, and six units of other people's blood in you."

After a moment she spoke, her face still in the dim room, her eyes staring at the ceiling.

"Did I hear someone say I can't have children?"

"Shit. I mean I... Ah," Dietrick sighed, "I'm sorry, Chris. I'm real sorry." His voice, a slow Texas drawl, dropped lower. "Sorrier than you can imagine."

When she didn't respond, he added softly, "Travis said he'll just adopt. A kid and a dog. One of each."

Chris turned, stared at him steadily, and finally spoke. "How soon can I have a bath?"

"How soon do you want one?"

"Right now. And my hair washed. And my own

nightgown. And my teeth brushed," she ended emphatically. She heard him chuckle.

"Demanding lady. Good thing Travis brought a bag for you this morning. I'll call a nurse."

"And Dietrick? A shot, too, if it's time. I hurt like hell."

It was after dark, and Travis's mood had turned from foul to frustrated before he finally located Tallitt. His car, a brand-new Jag with a strawberry-red customized paint job and a customized license plate that read SCANDAL, was parked in front of Rendezvous, a restaurant-bar Tallitt owned.

Travis remembered from the reports that it was a real rough place—not to be entered without backup. It would be hard getting in and harder getting out. But Travis was tired of waiting. The building was situated in the center of a well-laid-out and well-packed parking lot; its exterior was of nondescript, windowless brick, with two rear fire exits and a double-door entrance guarded by two mountainous and very ugly black men. As Travis watched, an '83 LTD parked near the street, and four lean, young black men went in, pausing to dap with the Bobbsey-Twin Gibraltars, their palms sliding across one another in the street version of sport's low five. Their greetings were lost on the winter air.

"Shit. I could wait here till morning and I'd still be the only white boy in the joint." Travis frowned. Why couldn't something today be easy? A private, unwitnessed tête-à-tête with Tallitt was out of the question tonight. And Travis had particularly wanted it unwitnessed—and off the record. He'd have to change tactics. He sat until his anger had calmed somewhat, and he had himself under control.

Travis unzipped his jacket, checked his .45, and slid

out of the car, not bothering to lock it. He might want back in real fast. He grinned. Already he had the Bobbsey Twins' attention. They stood solidly in front of the doors.

Low-browed, round-jawed, flat-nosed, and with poor-fitting off-the-rack suits—not Tallitt's best talent. Travis's grin widened. He might get his butt kicked, but at least he was doing something. Finally.

One of the Bobbseys spoke.

"Where you be goin'?"

Travis kept moving. "I be goin' inside." The two men looked at each other and grinned.

"De place's got a dress code."

Travis slowed and looked down at his jeans and Pumas and back at the Bobbseys, his lips pursed, musing.

"It got a color code too?"

"Matter of fact it do," the other Twin said.

"Well good. You won't mind I be meeting my lady then."

Instantly the Bobbseys relaxed, one shaking his head.

"Amanda's latest white boy," he said scathingly.

"She usually likes the three-piecers."

"Must be the body."

"It sure ain't de clothes."

Travis grinned and walked on in. "Thank you, Amanda," he whispered as he entered. "Whoever you are." With the first obstacle cleared, he breathed a little easier.

Travis stepped into the shadowed entrance alcove, behind a healthy green plant which turned out to be some kind of stiff cloth. "Never needs water or sunlight," he said to himself, and scanned the room. It wasn't exactly the hole in the wall he had expected.

Rendezvous was decorated in shades of cream and green, from the pale, curving bar and the oval tables to the latticework between the booths, and to the textured, upholstered walls. The carpet and seating were forest green, and brass accents gleamed softly in the recessed lighting. Waitresses in low-cut cream dresses and green aprons carried plates of broiled steaks and seafood between the tables. And a live band played less than earsplitting music for the packed, centrally placed dance floor.

The clientele was posh too—white-collar workers, clerks, and black yuppies. Not the crowd he'd have expected of a joint with Tallitt's name attached.

And Tallitt. Travis felt a spurt of anger, quickly cooled.

In a large, circular corner booth facing the entrance sat the owner, a glass of scotch and a bowl of peanuts on the table in front of him. He sat like a benevolent Buddha, legs crossed and left arm draped across the booth's back.

Travis almost whistled. "Not bad, Tallitt. Not bad at all." Yes, he'd very definitely have to change tactics.

Clint Eastwood would not work here.

"Do you have a reservation, sir, or are you just out slumming for the evening?"

Travis turned at the sharp voice and smiled. She was pretty, with high cheekbones and black eyes, her hair close-cropped, and the blackest skin Travis had ever seen—and a knockout black dress that left nothing to the imagination. She was full-breasted and had a challenging stance, and Travis didn't know what to look at first. Travis would have bet his next month's pay that this was Amanda. Then he remembered there might not be a next month's pay.

"Slumming for now. Reservations for later." Suddenly it was easy to change tactics, and Travis smiled.

"Well, if you're slumming, get out of my bush," she said, returning his smile. By the look in her eyes, this was very definitely Amanda.

Travis started to step away, grinned, and reached back.

He slid his hand along the smooth stem to the leaves and shook it slightly.

"Nice bush, Amanda."

Surprise flickered and was gone. She tilted back her head and met his eyes straight on. Suddenly she laughed.

"Nice of you to notice. But if you're going slumming, you should have dressed the part."

"I'm passed slumming. Now I have a reservation." He checked his watch. "At eight-thirty. And besides, these are my best sneakers."

"Reservation?" She eyed him slowly up and down. "Uh-huh."

"Yeah, really. With Tallitt. I'm a little early."

Presenting him with a mouth-watering side view, she checked the reservation book. "Mr. Tallitt," she said, stressing the first word, "doesn't have an eight-thirty appointment."

"I know. It's a surprise."

"You a friend?"

"You could say that. Tallitt and I go back a long way. To 1984. Three years for peddling dope."

The light went out of her eyes.

"Cell mate," she said flatly, slamming the reservation book. "I don't think . . ."

"Not quite," he interrupted softly. "I put him there."

Suddenly the smolder was back. "A slumming cop. I always did have a thing for a man in uniform."

"Oh, yeah? What thing is that?"

She grinned. "You think that badge is going to get you in?"

"No," Travis said, pulling out his wallet. "I've got clout." He handed her a card. "The American Express Gold Card."

She laughed, plucked the card from his fingers, and

slipped quickly across the dance floor. Second obstacle cleared. And Travis suddenly realized he felt just fine.

Travis scanned the room again. Tallitt was drinking his scotch. Two bodyguards were sitting at the bar, one pointedly staring at the entrance, the other watching Amanda. The band ended a soft version of an old Billie Holiday song and after a moment broke into an energetic version of "Play That Funky Music White Boy." The band leader saluted Travis.

Travis sighed. So much for an anonymous entrance and an unwitnessed interview. Across the room, Tallitt stared at the card, looked up at Travis standing framed in the entrance alcove, checked his watch, and nodded.

Four or five people laughed and waved at Travis. Travis realized there wouldn't be any trouble. It was too easy. Part of him was disappointed. Very. Whoever had written the police report either owed Tallitt a favor or had never made it past the Bobbsey Twins. Now the most Travis could hope for was that Tallitt would invite him to his office for a chat—where maybe Travis could convince Tallitt to part with a name or two. Fat chance.

Amanda left Tallitt and went to the bar, then carried a glass filled with white frothy liquid to Travis. Smiling, she handed him the drink.

"White Russian?"

"Milk. With Mr. Tallitt's compliments."

Travis grinned, and took the glass and his card. There was something taped on the back. Amanda's personal card—name, address, and phone number. Great. And some things tonight were too easy.

"Don't leave home without it," she said archly.

Yes, Miss Amanda certainly did have a thing for white boys. Even ones in jeans and sneakers. He smiled as warmly as he could and slid both cards into his back pocket. He started across the floor. Midway he remembered to salute the band. He lifted the glass of milk and drank. The leader made a quip about chocolate syrup and vanilla ice cream. Everyone in the bar laughed—everyone except the table for five to the left. They were slit-eyed and muttering. One of the bodyguards-cum-bouncers moved closer to the table.

Travis watched Tallitt. He was cool and calm, perfectly serene. Travis really would have preferred being Clint Eastwood. Just this once. A man leaned over the booth, shook Tallitt's hand. They laughed, and Tallitt pointed to a waitress. The man left. Just ten feet from the table, two women passed in front of Travis, heading to the ladies' room in back.

For only that instant, Travis lost sight of Tallitt. When he saw him again, Tallitt's legs were unnaturally splayed, his kinked head cradled against his arm. From a small hole high in his forehead, a single trickle of blood flowed steadily into glazed eyes. Something sticky and red clung to Tallitt's swelling tongue. It was peanuts.

Travis swallowed the urge to run, and turned and surveyed the room, his hand on the weapon at his left shoulder. "Play That Funky Music White Boy" taunted. People danced...ate...talked. There were no quiet looks, no hurried movements. No one moved toward the exits. Whoever had just shot Tallitt was cool and professional, blending into the crowd. Quite unlike himself.

Suddenly Travis felt terribly white. Whether by chance or design, he was undoubtedly the prime suspect in a murder. They had his name from his gold card, his prints from the milk glass, and his own bad timing to incriminate him. It took little effort to imagine the weapon would be found on the premises. No prints. He had three alternatives. Run. Or find the killer. Or sit and make it easy on them.

"Shit."

Slowly he nodded to Tallitt's body, managed a smile, and moved in the direction of the bullet's most likely trajectory.

Nothing.

He circled the room, checking the fire exits. Both had alarms. That left the front door.

Carefully, nonchalantly, Travis turned and headed for the front of Rendezvous. In the darkened entrance alcove was movement. A sleek head turned slightly as the outside lights caught its sheen, and then the doors swung shut. Just a glimpse, the merest hint of movement, and Travis was sure—the green-eyed man. Sayaad—the illusive fourth man who wielded so much power and yet didn't seem to exist. His ticket to Brevard.

Travis grinned tightly and moved fast.

"Hey, white boy. Don't I get a tip?" Amanda, softly mocking, stepped in front of him, blocking the entrance alcove.

Travis dropped the milk glass into her hands, grabbed her shoulders, and whirled her into the darkened entry, still moving. "Amanda, Tallitt's dead. I didn't do it. In two seconds the cops will be here. Don't mention my name. I'll explain it to you later." Releasing her he exploded through the front doors, sending one of the Bobbsey's sprawling. Would Amanda talk? If she did, he was ass-deep and sinking fast.

Behind him, the alarm had been given, and a mass exodus took place. Rendezvous emptied of every person carrying a gram of coke or an ounce of pot, or owing a supper bill. Fifty wide-eyed blacks burst through the door as Travis reached his car. Ahead of him, a silver BMW pulled smoothly onto the street.

Travis's Trans Am roared to life, spun in a tight circle, and followed. A dark Chrysler pulled in front of him. Travis gunned his engine and passed, losing sight of the

BMW as it made a left. The Trans Am's back wheels spinning on the slick asphalt, Travis spun into a wide turn just as the BMW made a quick right a block ahead.

Two more turns and Travis was gaining. The space between the Trans Am and the BMW's taillights was lessening. The traffic, the lights, the pedestrians ceased to exist for Travis as he took a hard right and gained another ten feet. Instantly, high beams glared into the rear window of his car. The Trans Am shuddered. A pattern of shots shattered the windows and battered into the body of the car. Travis, splintered by glass, hit the brakes, pulled hard to the right, and fell into the seat as the Trans Am came to a hard, jolting stop against the curb. One hand holding his weapon, Travis turned off the ignition.

Silence.

Freezing rain pattered against the car and onto his face.

Nothing moved. No car doors, no footsteps. Nothing. After several moments Travis slowly raised himself up in the seat. The street was empty.

He had lost him again.

CHAPTER 6

Day Four, P.M.

"I GUESS it wasn't sensible to ask for washed hair this time of night and so soon after surgery." She paused. "I guess I still look grungy, even after the bath, huh?"

Dietrick moved around the room opening drawers and finally turned on the light. "One head of clean hair coming up."

Chris jerked her face away from the sudden illumination and Dietrick's dark penetrating eyes. "No. I didn't mean ... you can't ..." She felt herself flushing as she stared at the far wall, her fingers clutching the bed clothes. There was a short silence interrupted by the sound of water scudding against plastic and collecting. Chris glanced over to see Dietrick add a squirt of shampoo to a plastic washtub, then more water until bubbles frothed to the edge. His back was to her. He lifted the plastic tub, and, turning, he walked gingerly to the bed and the adjustable hospital tray beside it. Dark and gentle, his eyes spoke before his lips moved.

"You want clean hair? I got time." He paused, smiled. "Scoot over here. Move slow so you don't pull stitches."

An answering smile tugged at the corner of her lips.

Dietrick leaned over to the wall speaker, buzzed the nurse's call bell, and demanded towels. He soaped a rag, eyes still smiling.

"I said scoot over here."

"You . . . can't," she whispered, more of a question than a denial.

"I can." And reaching out a large, rough, calloused hand, he cradled her blood-crusted head and pulled it over the side of the bed.

Half an hour and three sudsings later, her scalp tingled cleanly, free of the oil and blood that had accumulated and dried there. The last rinse was clear, and the towels arrived after only two reminders, a splattered, smiling Dietrick taking them from the tight-lipped nurse.

Chris smiled broadly, wriggling her shoulders as he dried her hair. "You should have waited a while for your shower. You're all wet."

"No problem, little lady. That smile makes it all worthwhile. Here." He handed her the bag Travis had packed. "Find a comb. I'm going after a cup of coffee. Want one?"

"No thanks. Dietrick?" The gentle eyes turned on her for an instant. "Thanks."

"My pleasure," he said, pulling the door to after him, change rattling in his pocket.

On top in her bag was a small crystal mouse—Herman, a long ago gift from her mother. Travis must have placed him there. Chris smiled and set Herman by the phone. She combed out her damp hair and while Dietrick was gone risked a look at herself in the small makeup mirror Travis had packed. She touched her broken nose through the taping, traced the purple bruises beneath her eyes, and put chapstick on her dry lips.

"Bedtime for Bonzo," she whispered to her reflection. "All I need now is Ronald Reagan." She didn't remember being hit so much, but she remembered enough. Wrenching from the memories she slammed down the mirror, then, on second thought, threw it across the room and against the ugly blue wallpaper. It shattered, the splinters falling noisily, glinting in the dim light.

A last arrhythmic slurp, and Travis swallowed the final chocolate taste of a shake. A last bite of a Whopper with extra onions followed.

Travis glanced at his hands. They had started to shake at about the same time his mind had begun to function again. That had been in the yellow cab that had taken him from the hotel parking deck where he'd ditched his car to Dulles where he'd rented another—an interminable ride in which he'd alternated between moments of extreme nausea and icy calm. The questions and answers had bounded around in his head, the ludicrous with the sensible, and he'd been unable to determine which was which. So he'd gone for a Whopper.

Travis popped a straw into the large Coke and opened the apple pie. As he did, glittering, rounded shards of safety glass fell out of his sleeve. His insurance company was going to love this one. Turning the ignition, Travis headed home.

The apartment looked better but was still unlivable. As he cleaned up and picked through the mess for something clean to wear, he remembered Nikki. That was one more to chalk up against Sayaad. Because, no matter how he put the pieces together, the puzzle still said the same thing. Sayaad. And behind Sayaad was Brevard. Somewhere. He was the key ingredient for everything that had happened.

"Okay. So who's Sayaad? What does he want from me? Why does he want it?" Travis stood in his BVDs, his wet hair plastered to his head, a pair of mismatched blue socks on his feet, and three fingers extended. Finally he uncurled the last two. "Is he tied in with Aztec Systems, and if so, then how far will they go to get whatever it is they want?" The sixth question, left unasked, was, "What tied in to Brevard?"

Travis still wasn't sure how to go about finding out, but Whizzer would be a good start. Feeling better about having decided something, Travis dressed, found the phone and the directory, and made his calls. The one to Chris was strained, stilted. Dietrick was more blunt. Travis had "better drag his slack ass in and quit playing cowboy."

What happened to "peace, love, dove?..."

Whizzer was out. And Amanda definitely was not feeling sweet.

The Rendezvous was "crawling with uniformed vermin all because some eighteen-year-old white basketball-sized piece of shit decided to crash the joint. I got company I'm expecting at eleven P.M. sharp."

Travis took the hint and hung up, hoping she had misphrased the part about basketball-sized. But he'd be there at 11:00. He just hoped he could explain. Setting the alarm, he curled up and slept an hour.

At 10:55, Travis, in his rented, copper-colored Nissan, puttered up to the classiest six-story in Wheaton proper—and puttered on by. Positioned half a block down from the Wheaton Arms was a dark Chrysler with two men in it. As his headlights glanced into the car, Travis got a distinct impression of Latin American features. The Chrysler was the same make and model he'd passed just before his car got blasted. Somehow the coincidence wasn't comforting.

Travis found a pay phone and dialed Amanda.

"Hello."

"You sound sweet again."

"It's 11:02."

Travis winced at her tone.

"So much for sweetness. You got two Latins in a Chrysler sitting half a block from the Arms. Tenants?"

"Not likely, white boy. *I'm* the only darkie in Uncle Tom's neighborhood. Of any nationality. Are you bringing trouble?"

"Where's the fire escape or the service entrance?"

"White boy, I got to be crazy."

"You wanted an explanation."

Ten minutes later, cold, damp, and frustrated, Travis rang the bell of 402. And found himself staring down the barrel of a chrome-plated .32. Holding the gun and the door was Amanda, wearing white silk pajamas. And nothing else. From the fire in her eyes, it was obvious she hadn't decided whether to seduce him or shoot him. Or both.

Perversely, Travis decided to make her decision more difficult.

"Ah, jeez, not you too. Everybody's got a gun. And I'm getting real sick of all of them pointing at me."

"You make a good target."

"I make a better highball." Stepping into the apartment, Travis slammed the door shut and headed for the kitchen at the far end of the great room. "Where's the bar?"

Deliberately ignoring the gun, the provocative outfit, and the way she sputtered when he passed her, Travis banged cabinets and rattled dishes until he found two glasses and the ice cubes.

"What the hell do you think you're doing?"

"Found your voice, huh? Where's the bar? And will you put that stupid thing away." At the look on her face Travis was torn between irritation and laughter, and decided irritation gave him the best odds on not getting shot.

"Tell Tallitt it's stupid. A little firepopper like this was the last thing on his mind tonight."

"What? A .32?" He turned back to the cabinets. "You gonna tell me where the bar is?"

"Under the cabinet."

Travis pulled out a bottle of Jack Daniels and a bottle of Classic Coke. Suddenly sweet, he looked up at her, his eyes all innocent. "Oh. Would you like something?"

Amanda sighed and the .32 wavered slightly. "Brandy. No ice."

Travis felt he had made great headway. Carrying his drink he led the way back to the living room. It was a stark room, black and white, with strong pink accents that Chris would have called fuchsia or something. Travis sprawled onto the sofa and drank deeply.

Amanda sipped her brandy from the far wall, the .32 still pointing in his general direction.

"I thought I told you to put that thing away."

"Not until I get some explanations." She smiled sweetly. "Sorry, white boy." But she didn't sound sweet. She sounded as though she were enjoying herself. Immensely.

"You can start with who's watching my apartment."

"I don't know."

"You're doing real good so far," she shot back.

Travis ignored her. "They're not cops. Could be the same two that jazzed up my car a couple hours ago."

"I don't talk cracker slang. Say it in plain English."

Travis ignored her again, but his frustration was growing more acute. He had a strong feeling she wanted him to take away the gun. Forcefully. Mentally, he shrugged. Maybe she liked rough stuff.

"Just after Tallitt got shot, I saw a man I've been after

for a while. Could be Middle Eastern or Colombian. Like your two bird-watchers downstairs. Anyway, he took off. And just as I'm about to catch up with him, someone starts spraying my car full of bullets. Now," Travis leaned forward, his eyes catching Amanda's, "two Latins show up here, sitting in a dark Chrysler like the one at the scene. Seems a bit peculiar." His eyes settled on the gun, his voice deepened. "Maybe I should be the one holding a gun on you. Who did you tell I'd be here tonight?"

"Listen, sweetheart," she said, still sarcastic but not as belligerent, "I covered your ass tonight. If I'd wanted to give it away, I could have given it to the police and not even be messin' with you.

"I lied about you to the cops and took their shit for two hours. Then I came straight home. I talked to nobody but you when you called at the club."

"So who was listen' in?"

"Nobody. The number on my card is Tallitt's private line and Tallitt was in no condition for eavesdropping."

"What about a bug?"

"The man was careful. He liked his privacy."

"Terrific," Travis breathed, and finished off his drink. Then, more loudly: "That means they've got me pegged."

"I told you about that honky slang."

But this time she was smiling, and the .32 was canted at a definite angle. Travis stood slowly, his face strained and wry.

"What I meant was, I called you from my apartment. My phone must be wired. He's got more... Want another?"

"No. He who?"

"The guy I was chasin' tonight. Sayaad."

"What's he got?"

"I'm not sure." Ice clinked. "Couple of days ago we iced a guy named Soloman."

"Yeah, I read about it. A real fuck-up."

Travis ignored her, stirring his drink.

"I don't know what their connection is, but Sayaad was with Soloman. I chased him. He got away."

"Strike two."

It was getting harder to ignore the little barbs.

"Next thing I know, after the usual red tape, everybody involved gets cleared—put on active administrative. Me... Good old Trav gets suspended. And nobody knows nothing. It came down from God himself."

"And you think this Sayaad arranged it?"

"Oh, there's more."

"More, yet more."

Amanda was definitely not on the same wavelength, he concluded. She seemed to be getting happier by the minute. This girl had a strange way of reacting to bad news.

"Right after that, somebody snatches a friend of mine, chews up my apartment, and then goes to my girl's. Ditto there, but beats and rapes her and leaves her nearly dead. She's still in the hospital."

"Those two guys downstairs?" Amanda had suddenly sobered.

"Don't know. Actually I thought it was Tallitt's idea and Tallitt's hired help."

"What are they after?"

"Don't know. At first I thought it was a warning. Now I'm not sure."

After a moment, she grinned. "Like I said! A real fuck-up."

Amanda bounced back fast.

"Anyway, two of the four involved fit the descriptions of Tallitt and Carver, dropped the names of Soloman and Sayaad with Chris, and took off. Tonight I find Tallitt." Travis drained his second drink. "You know the rest."

"Not quite," she sighed. "But I do know you didn't do Tallitt. I never took my eyes off you. Not once."

"I'm not that stupid. I watch TV. If I'd wanted Tallitt, I'd have done it in a way that no one would ever know."

"Well," Amanda drawled in her best Deep-South Gullah, "be's you ain't feedin' me a line, then I'd say somebody's puddin' the Mo Jo on you, Home Boy."

"Yeah. And I think it's this Sayaad. But why me? And what does the government have to do with it?"

"The gov'ment? Now you sayin' the gov'ment's in on this too, white boy?"

Finally Amanda sounded sad. But not disbelieving.

Travis spread his hands. "Popular guy."

She grinned, her eyes tracing a slow path up his length. "I can see why. So what do you want from me?"

"I want you to put that stupid gun away. And amnesia. I don't want you involved. I don't want you getting hurt. Forget a certain white boy named Travis was at the Rendezvous."

Travis walked from the bar slowly across the room to her and replenished her brandy. Her eyes measured his, an appraisal different from the coy sexual tease of the past moments. Finally, she leaned past him, sat the .32 on the table, and lifted her glass.

"For a while, white boy. For a while."

Their glasses clinked.

Chris jumped, the sound of screaming loud in the room. Hands held her and she struggled, fighting. She couldn't breathe.

"No. No. Please . . . No." The words penetrated. They were her own. On their heels, like a litany, were other words, gentle.

"It's okay. It's only a dream. It's okay. Come on, Chris. It's okay."

Dietrick. She stopped fighting. The room was silent, punctuated with heavy breathing and sobs. Dietrick's arms held her, her face in the soft folds of cloth at his shoulders. He smelled fresh, like pine and leather. She shuddered. *Thank God he doesn't smell like sweat*. The men in her dreams had smelled of sweat. The door opened, silhouetting a nurse's head.

"Is everything all right?"

Dietrick turned, shielding Chris. "Fine, thank you ma'am. Bad dream. But... would you get her a Coke or something? It might help her calm down."

"Sure. Be right back."

Dietrick's hands soothed her, and Chris slumped against him, her rigid body relaxing. His rough hands kneaded her flesh through the split in her hospital gown. It was calming, tranquilizing, asexual, like a mother's hands. As the nurse reentered, she pushed him away. Later, after the Coke, after Chris's vitals were taken and her dressing was changed, and she had received a shot for the pain that came in waves, and the room had fallen silent, he spoke.

"The dreams *will* fade. Soon you'll be able to sleep a whole night without them and wake up not being afraid when the alarm goes off.... Eventually you'll stop looking at every man as a threat, even when they want to go to bed with you.... Someday you'll even open your door to a stranger again, not thinking, or just wanting to be helpful. Not right away. But someday."

She heard him move in the quiet room and wasn't surprised when a tissue touched the corners of her eyes.

"When?" she whispered.

"It took my mother two years. But then she didn't have the benefit of counseling, therapy. All she had was me and the love of a good man. You have all four."

"So where is my good man?" she whispered, smiling up at Dietrick.

"Out doing something stupid."

They both grinned. Chris sobered first. "I think my good man is right here."

Their eyes met and held. In that moment something changed. Silently, Dietrick returned to his chair.

Before midnight, Travis had decided on a plan which would tell him several things. The first was how far Sayaad had penetrated into the department, how fast he could utilize department information, and whether or not his informer was one of Travis's personal friends. Like Hammit. The possibility made Travis slightly ill, but it was a possibility he couldn't overlook. Second, was whether Sayaad wanted Travis personally or just wanted to keep an eye on him. And third, if he got lucky, was what Aztec Systems had to do with rape, vandalism, and kidnap. Who was using whom?

First, making sure the bug was still in his phone, Travis called the department.

"Officer Matthews."

"Dan. Can you talk?"

"Ah, Wendy. Yeah, I been trying to get hold of you."

Travis paused, surprised, an amused grin tugging at his lips. "Wendy?" he laughed. "Last I heard the only Wendy in your life was an ugly, sixty-pound bulldog. You must have company."

"Right," Matthews drawled, his voice suddenly seductive. "Listen, Wendy, when can I see you? I've been missing you, babe."

"I don't know," Travis said, trying to control his laughter. "What have you got?"

"A hard-on, and the night is yours. Give me time to go

home and change and we could catch a late flick. You still wear that Tabu perfume I like so much?"

Travis laughed. "Tabu, shit. On a bulldog? Okay. I'll call you at your place in half an hour."

"That sounds good. Ah, Wendy. Wear something sexy."

"Right," Travis hung up grinning and checked his weapons.

The phone rang only once. "Yo."

"Dan, Travis."

"Travis, Dan, " Matthews said jokingly, undisguised pleasure in his voice. "Rats, I was hoping for Wendy."

"You always did have a preference for dog-faced women," Travis said, relaxing instantly. Dan always had that effect on him. Sometimes he thought Dan would even be calm at Armageddon. He would cock a brow and, with his unique ability for rational understatement, say, "What a mess."

"Yeah," Dan said. "But you're the one who liked the real bitches. Forgive me if I remind you of one high-strung mongrel called Candy..." Dan let his voice trail off suggestively.

Travis groaned, laughed, and agreed, remembering a woman who had liked scenes, the louder the better.

"Speaking of dogs," he said finally, "do you remember when we were on patrol and worked the ten-eleven cases?"

"Yeah," Matthews said slowly, his voice changing as he recognized the old code. "It's been a long time since we worked those. What do you have in mind?"

Ten-eleven was a code they had used years ago when they had worked patrol on the B shift. Then, within the department, there had been some back-stabbers reporting on officers who met for conversation while on duty. To protect themselves, the men on Travis's shift—one of whom had been Hammit—had inverted burglar-alarm codes, to schedule times and locations for meetings, using the seldom-used ten-eleven dog-case code as a clue to the officer being contacted for a meeting. The ten-eleven was a code to invert the burglar alarm location that followed. It had been Dan's idea. Travis just hoped Dan would invert the code properly and understand the time change he was asking for.

"Well, Adam five, minus one, two," Travis said distinctly. If there was a tap on Matthews's phone, and the person responsible had ready access to police procedure, they could find him now. They would show up at burglar alarm Adam four at two A.M. But Matthews, if he understood the old ten-eleven the way Travis hoped, would show up at Zebra five at one A.M. And he would be careful. The use of the code in itself was a calculated warning.

Dan's voice was slower than normal, the tone registering confusion, then acceptance, and finally understanding of the warning. All in three words. "Yeah. Okay . . . Okay."

Suddenly Travis grinned. "Oh, wait a minute, Dan. You don't have to wear anything sexy tonight."

Travis could almost see Dan smiling over the phone. "Your loss, Wendy."

Thirty minutes later Travis drove by Zebra five and spotted Dan leaning against a doorway, as inconspicuous as it was possible for him to be. At almost six five, and lanky as a bean pole, it was hard for him to blend into the woodwork. Dan's angular, spare face was lit by his perpetual smile—until he saw the car. Shaking his head, Dan bent low and crawled into the Nissan. His knees hit the dashboard and his crown rested against the roof. Laughing, Travis pulled away from the curb. No tail at

Zebra five. Hammit knew to invert the code. So it wasn't Hammit.

"Almost didn't recognize you in this tiny thing," Dan said softly. "How come?"

"Well, my usual mode of transportation is now permanently air-conditioned."

"Oh?" Matthews looked up, interested.

"Yeah. Like a sieve. I stepped in somebody's shadow."

"Shadow, hell. You stepped in somebody's shit if you got to be using that ten code. We usually save that for the real big pricks. Who you expecting to show up and why?"

"Last question first. Somebody's listening in on my phone."

"Oh, yeah?"

"Yeah. I think it's Juan Valdez."

"Who?"

"You know. The coffee-bean farmers. The llama jockeys."

"Oh, you mean de Co-lom-beans?"

"As in white powder by the kilo from south of the border."

"I guess that explains the code."

"Yeah. A certain need for anonymity."

"Anonymity, shit," Dan laughed. "Did Tallitt have a desperate need for anonymity tonight?"

Travis felt himself cool. "Yeah. A need unfulfilled. That's why he checked out with such a big fanfare."

Travis drove for some minutes, finally breaking the silence. Dan wouldn't.

"I was in Rendezvous, waiting to talk to Tallitt—waiting in public, the only white face for two blocks. Every eye in the house was on me. I made quite a stir. Someone else used the opportunity to get to Tallitt."

From the corner of his eye he could see Matthews

nodding. "One James 'Good Boy' Johnson recognized you from when you busted him couple or three years back. Gave name, rank, and serial number on you. Only reason there isn't a warrant out right now is he maybe had a grudge. And one feisty little black lady said the kid who did it was eighteen and had jet-black hair and eyes. Maybe a PR out to make a name for himself."

"Whose version gets accepted?"

"My bet's on the Good Boy. You'll be implicated by morning."

"Terrific."

Dan reached over and turned on the radio to the slow country station he worked for part-time. Crystal Gayle's low voice filled the car as he settled back against the seat, readjusting his knees. At the end of the song, Travis felt Dan's eyes on him and questioned with his own. Dan spoke slowly, drawing Travis's own conclusion.

"Sounds like some of the big boys are out to nail you."

"Yeah. But why? Which big boys? Ours or theirs?" Travis stared out into the gray mush sliding against the windshield.

A few moments later they arrived at Adam four and Matthews looked around. "What time do you expect them to show?" The previous conversation was set aside.

"Two," Travis said, grinning, knowing what was coming next.

"Great. We got time for a beer."

"You read my mind. I picked this spot for just that reason. We can watch Adam four from Jackson's."

"Jackson's?" Matthews said, surprised.

"I told you not to wear anything sexy," Travis laughed.

"You wasn't just joking."

Jackson's was a dirty corner bar across from the mid-block location of Anderson's Jewelers, burglar-alarm code number Adam four. In front of Anderson's was a bus stop with a short, rickety bench and plenty of empty parking spaces. The ones that were occupied contained empty cars. No one was waiting for them.

Travis parked the Nissan on the side street beside Jackson's, and he and Matthews unfolded themselves from the car advertised as big enough for football players. The manufacturer must have meant Pop Warner, because the lack of space had left the two men's legs cramped. Walking stiffly, they pushed open the side door of Jackson's and paused just inside.

"If I remember correctly, it's your turn to buy," Travis said. "I'll get us a table with a view, and speak to one of the ... uh ... ladies."

"Don't breathe too deep. You might catch something."

With that advice, Travis found Delores and cashed in on an old favor. No charge.

When Matthews came back, wearing his usual straight-lipped, head-wobbling, Gomer Pyle grin, he was carrying a pitcher and two mugs, a basket of nacho chips, and some cheese sauce with jalapeños. He set it all down carefully, the heavy glass mugs thumping softly.

"I thought you didn't like hot peppers," Travis said.

"I don't, but I had to do something to combat the odor of onions on your breath."

Travis grinned. "Sorry." Now he knew why Amanda had let him leave.

Dan filled both mugs and pushed one to Travis, taking a long pull from his own. "I like your type of surveillance. It has definite benefits. Yes. Yes," he said, W. C. Fields-style. "But, uh, Travis, what if the people we're waiting for are in here waiting for us?"

Travis grinned. "Then they buy the next round."

They talked sporadically between mugs in the easy camaraderie of a long friendship. The conversation paused often, whenever a car pulled by slowly as if it might be watching for someone. Finally, at 1:45, with a fine snow covering the streets, a clean, shiny, oddly snow-free Olds pulled by slowly, smoked windows obscuring the occupants. It wasn't a Chrysler, but it was compatible with other expectations. In this weather, only a car just recently removed from covered storage would be free of snow. Not a common thing this time of night, not this side of town.

"Looks interesting," Travis said, glancing at his watch. But the car pulled on by and out of sight. Exactly two minutes and forty-five seconds later, the same car reappeared from the opposite direction, cut its lights, and glided into an empty parking slot two doors down from Anderson's.

Travis grinned and looked at Matthews, who was watching him over the rim of his mug. He swallowed the last drop and set it on the table, his lips moving.

"Bingo," they said in unison, their grins widening.

Travis shrugged and snapped his fingers for a waitress. "Look and learn," he said to his friend.

Matthews's brows came together, puzzled.

Travis turned, nodded to Delores, and then looked back at the car.

Matthews groaned. "What you gone and done now, Travis boy?"

"All a part of the plan."

Matthews pulled an alfalfa-green-and-white baseball cap with a prominent Silo Feed Pro logo out of his back pocket, snapped it open, and shoved it on his head. At Travis's look of inquiry, he pulled a doleful face.

"Disguise. I'll never be able to show my face at Jackson's again if you're doing what I think you're doing."

Travis smothered a comment and turned to watch Delores.

A half-Mexican, half-black, half-drunk woman, full-bodied and well-rounded, Delores was just past her prime. But she hadn't caught on to the fact yet. The best thing about Delores was that she liked to play.

Exposing one round shoulder, Delores grabbed Evelyn, a washed-out, dropsical blonde and, chattering an explanation, headed into the street. Dropping a bill on the table, Travis and Matthews followed.

Delores put on quite a show. Slithering around the car windows, exposing first one and then another part of her buxom body, she offered a variety of treats to the occupants of the darkened interior, her broken Spang-lish a litany of prices and suggestions. Evelyn pulled a parched, slow invitation after her.

Travis looked at Dan, who was half hiding behind his Silo Feed Pro while the other half was being thoroughly entertained. Her back to the watching cops, Delores opened her blouse and rubbed herself over the passenger window. Dan nearly choked.

It was the final ticket; down came the window with a smooth automatic slide. A head and arm came out, shouting Delores away from the car.

Stunned, Travis stepped brokenly into the street—and stared straight into the startled eyes of Adam Larkin.

CHAPTER 7

Day Five, P.M.

It nagged at him like a familiar pain, a sore tooth, a rough place on the tongue, twitching at the corners of his memory, dusty and half-formed like an unfinished puzzle long forgotten. It reminded him somehow of the smell in the condemned building the morning Soloman was killed. The smell. . . . Unbidden, his mind made an intuitive leap. Suddenly the pieces slid together with an audible click in his mind.

Nam. It was just like Nam.

Stymied at every turn, information withheld and discovered piecemeal, constant bureaucratic fuck-ups, disinformation, confusion like a game with half the pieces missing, and him running around like a horse with blinders on. It was like being pitted against Alain Brevard, where both sides played against the middle, with him and those he loved caught in the cross fire.

In Nam, the intelligence community had been in bed with the enemy. More intimate than lovers, Alain Brevard's drug runners and the CIA's jungle-fighting intelligence gatherers had moved together in a torrid, tainted, mutually dependent relationship that polluted everything it touched. But Brevard had never really known who Travis was.

And he certainly was not aware that the "Ace of Spades" was still on the trail after all these years, like a toothless old hound with his nose still to the ground. Travis laughed mirthlessly at the comparison. So Brevard wasn't staging this. Someone else was.

Sayaad.

Angry at his own blindness, confused at the parallel, Travis downshifted into second and passed a stalled car, touched his left blinker, and turned. A girl in red caught his attention. Too short and too demure. Not Nikki. She nagged at him too. Another piece of unfinished business, warped and left hanging, like Jack and David and Alain Brevard and the last move on the board—the final checkmate Travis had been cheated of. The war had just ended too soon, and Alain Brevard had vanished in the chaos, leaving two too many evils hanging in the balance.

Travis pushed the Volvo into third and then fourth, hearing the smooth transition of the gears. He'd traded in the Nissan on something a little larger, a little more powerful. He liked the way it moved, like a tank, but quick.

It was late afternoon and the skies were clearing. A weak sun peered at the bedraggled earth and slid behind another cloud.

"Coward," he snarled. Nam.

Talking to Matthews had helped, but the appearance of Adam Larkin the night before had thrown him. Larkin was intelligence—most likely CIA, according to Whizzer. But who was Sayaad to call in such powerful backup? Somehow the government was tied in, yet the connection was missing. There were too many people and too many loose ends. It was like trying to tie together a half-remembered dream.

Once he had played their game. After all, they'd taught him the rules: how to play around with taps and tails, how to work around panicky bureaucrats and defend himself against good street agents—how to live on the edge. But that had been a long time ago. He'd been alone there. There'd been no one left to be hurt but him. Now he was out of practice, his reflexes slower, his intuition dulled by living in safety too long. This time the picture wasn't clear, and Travis didn't know which way to go. Not yet. Not when Chris was still in danger.

Travis's hand tightened on the stick shift. He'd gotten to the hospital at ten and met Dietrick, tired, grim, and not his most pleasant self, in the hall.

Dietrick's balled hands had pinned him against the wall outside Chris's room and, though he stood a head shorter and fifty pounds lighter, the strength in his wiry body warned Travis not to resist.

"I don't give a good Goddamn what kind of day you had. You could have found time for Chris. She..." Dietrick's tired eyes watered. "She..."

"Randy." Gently, Travis pushed against Dietrick's unyielding hands. "I was coming. But I couldn't be sure I wasn't followed. Not after somebody sprayed my car with bullets."

Not slackening his grip, Dietrick searched his eyes. "Ever hear of Ma Bell?"

"She's got big ears. And she's nosey as hell. Tapped. I had to find out who. And what they wanted."

"And?"

"Trouble's coming at me from both sides. I still don't know what's going on. I didn't want to lead anyone to Chris."

"You're here now."

Travis grinned wryly. "I took precautions."

Dietrick released Travis's crumpled shirt and rolled against the wall, the early morning light harsh on his face.

"I wish I had."

"Say again?"

Dietrick sighed and rubbed his eyes. "I caught some nurse giving out information on Chris over the phone. Said it was Chris's brother."

"Chris doesn't have a brother." Travis's voice was carefully expressionless.

"I know. And she's already contacted anyone who'd be interested."

"Could be nothing, though," Travis said, knowing instinctively there was more.

"Does the following description sound familiar?" Dietrick closed his eyes, resting his head against the wall. "Six four, curly, short, black hair, dark skin, green eyes. Accent."

Travis sucked in a slow breath. "So?"

"He paid Chris's hospital bill yesterday. Crisp new hundred dollar bills. Forty of them."

The two men shared a long look.

"You'll stay with her?"

"What the hell have you gotten into?"

"Yes or no?"

"Don't be an ass, Trav."

Travis relaxed slightly and tried a grin. "I'm not sure. I'll tell you when I am. And thanks. I owe you one."

"You owe me several, but this ain't one of 'em. This one's on me."

Travis slowed the Volvo and waited at the light, his eyes watching his rearview mirror. The view was still clear. No tail. The light changed and Travis moved ahead.

After they spoke in the hall, Dietrick had left and gone home for a shower and clean clothes, allowing Travis to enter the room alone.

Travis had taken in the room instantly—the wallpaper,

decorated with tiny blue patterns, the utilitarian lights over the bed, the rough sheets and chrome bed rails. The smell. It had all screamed of hospitals and pain.

Even then, even this morning, the smells and his subconscious had been trying to force on him the memory of Nam—the parallels between then and now.

He had shut his eyes to block out the sight of another hospital room in another part of the world, in another time. Caught off guard by the force of the unexpected memory, Travis had sucked in his breath and turned to the bed, blinking rapidly. The memory faded. But not before he saw that ravaged, drooling face. Jack. Brevard's last victim before Travis had gone after him alone.

Downshifting, Travis passed another car.

"We had a bet on whether you would come today." Chris's voice was soft in his memory, soothing the edges of his pain. Travis had blinked, focusing.

"Oh?"

"I owe Randy a pizza after we get out of here."

"Thanks. Such faith." His words had been short, but his tone gentle.

She had been sitting up in the bed, her head raised almost perpendicularly, her fragile body lost in the sea of white sheets and white nightgown and white skin two shades too pale. Purple bruises and pale lipstick provided the only color. She was beautiful. He had told her so.

"Thank you for the balloons."

Tied to the head of the bed had been a pink bouquet of helium-filled balloons, bright curly streamers acting as stems. Walking to the bed, he had read the card.

All my love, Travis. P.S. How about a bulldog?

He owed Dietrick another one. He hadn't thought to send flowers. He had tried to tell himself it was all right, but a heavy weight settled in his chest.

"Chris." He had startled himself by saying her name.

His voice had been full of tears or anger, he couldn't tell which. Blindly he crossed the short space and took her in his arms. She resisted only a moment before melting into him.

Silently they rocked and, later, neither one mentioned the tears. She felt so right, so delicate and gentle against him. And so abused. He could feel her bones and the tight bandage that held her broken ribs stationary. But her hair was shining, lightly braided in one long braid to the middle of her back. Her scent was sweet, blocking out for a while the antiseptic smell that had sickened him.

Even now, the remembered feel of Chris in his arms was sweet, clean, and fresh. Travis pulled into the parking lot, and rested his head on the wheel. Exhaustion overwhelmed him, and sadness. Before he had left he'd pressed something into her hand—a small smoke-crystal tennis shoe he'd picked up at a specialty store. Dietrick had returned about then—he'd said it was the first time she had really smiled.

It took him six hours to break the code. Now exhaustion battled excitement in his mind as he looked at the flashing green screen. He was "in" Aztec. Fingers trembling, he hit the keys that opened the company like a flower to his eyes. The printer clicked on and reams of information began piling onto the floor. One page caught his attention.

AZTEC OPERATION IDENTIFIER:
TO INVESTIGATE, IDENTIFY, NEUTRALIZE INFORMATION DEFICIENCIES
RE TROOP INVOLVEMENT LEBANON 1983–4
RE TROOP INVOLVEMENT CLANDESTINE ACTIVITIES
RE CONTRAS: NIC
RE L. T. FACTION: IRAN

Re Ripcord: Madrid, Spain
Re Gato: Colombian Drug Routes to U.S.

The list went on and on, two pages full. Whizzer breathed out slowly.

"As Travis would say, Bingo."

A chill wind has sucked the heat out of the car and still Travis sat, eyes closed, his head resting on his hands, dusk falling, the parking lot security lights a dull gleam. Nobody would steal the stiffs from Connelly's funhouse and morgue tonight, Travis thought. No sir'ee.

A lilting, fluid conversation echoed in the empty lot—Spanish, half-remembered from college but too quick to translate before it faded from memory. Travis smiled into the darkness and waited for the speakers to leave.

Measured footfalls passed the car, paused, then continued on. The cadence was smooth, athletic, and graceful, striking a cord in Travis's memory. A car door opened and closed. Suddenly breathing deeper, Travis turned his head just in time to see a silver BMW and a dark Chrysler pull out of the parking lot into the street.

Sayaad.

Travis's first instinct to follow was swiftly checked by a memory of spraying bullets and flying glass. The nonexistent green-eyed man apparently always traveled with nonexistent backup. And every time he showed up in the same locale as Travis, people died.

Travis felt himself grow cold. Connelly. There must be a half-dozen people inside. Dead. Travis got out of the car.

Memories of Nam, half-settled confusion, impulse, and fear battled inside his head. Questions bucked away the answers. Just how good *was* the opposition? What would Sayaad want with Connelly? How did Sayaad know to come here? Had the Trans Am been bugged? What if it hadn't been Sayaad? Coincidence? Fat chance.

Puffs of breath whipped into the wind as Travis neared the entrance. There wasn't time to jimmy the locks on the service door. Travis looked around, then slipped inside. It was quiet. Quiet as a morgue. In other circumstances he'd have laughed.

The offices were empty. Slipping into the darkened hallway, Travis went quickly down the stretch of newly waxed floor. His skids squeaked with each step. If he was going to play this game again, he would need new crepe-soled shoes.

Glancing into each room he passed, Travis stopped at the second one to the left, stunned. The space was small and jumbled, dimly lit by a long view box for slides, and the sharp white light of a microscope. Grouped around the room on shelves were dozens of large glass jars, all nearly filled with slightly cloudy fluid and a denser, submerged mass.

Tiny faces stared as if startled at his intrusion or as if slumbering peacefully on. It reminded him simultaneously of Chris, curled fetally on her bed, the mattress soaked a bright scarlet, and the broiled monkey served in Da Nang on ornate lacquer trays, impaled by long gleaming spits.

The odd paranoia that had gripped Travis in the parking lot was suddenly overpowering. Behind him a door opened, and Travis whirled. Connelly stopped, both hands raised, staring at the barrel of the .45. His eyes bulged.

The relief was so strong, Travis felt almost sick.

"Ah, Jesus. You're *okay*," he yelled.

"Son of a bitch, Travis. And I ain't Jesus. Put that damned fuckin' thing away. Didn't your mother tell you those things were dangerous? And stop yelling. There's dead people in here." Connelly habitually ran unconnected subject matter together. He could have sold used cars.

Laughing, Travis sheathed the .45. "You're right. No one should ever fuck with a gun. It could cause tissue damage."

Connelly snorted. "Scared the piss outta me, boy. I don't know what I was doing when I came out here, but right now I got to find the head. You can talk while I tinkle and explain why you were holding a gun on my fetus collection. You're not one of those bleeding-heart antiabortionist fools, are you?"

"Were those aborted?"

"No. In here." Connelly pushed open a door, led Travis into a brightly lit, stainless-steel restroom, and proved his point.

"I can see now why your wife left you."

"Cute, Travis. But remember, you followed me into the john, not vice versa. What kind of company are you looking for anyway? I don't pay for my fun and games."

"Who was your visitor?"

"Why? Were you listening? Sounds like a cop's question."

"Old habits are hard to break."

Connelly turned from the urinal, retying the rumpled strings holding his surgical greens beneath his stomach. Bending around his flab, Connelly washed his hands and rinsed, using the sterile techniques of the medical profession.

"Got a question myself."

"Oh?"

"I did the PM on one Edgar Ralph Tallitt with a nosey D.A. breathing up my ass."

"Sounds uncomfortable."

"He asked a lot of questions about you, made several inferences about your, ah, colorful and violent past. All in reference to the aforementioned stiff."

"Shit."

"It's okay. I knew the style, and I think ballistics will

bear me out on this one. If I guess right, it's out-of-town talent brought in to clean up what's left of Soloman's crew, so that one of the survivors can step into the king's shoes—or crown, or whatever the appropriate analogy. But the point is, while I was trying to convince this prick you were innocent and he was getting sick at the stomach, he got a phone call. Came back looking queerer than when he left and said he guessed I was right. Hell, I hadn't even gotten the skull open yet."

"Mighty powerful phone call."

"Back to that cop's question," Connelly reminded him.

"Right. So who was your buddy?"

"You mean the guy in the twelve-hundred-dollar pinstripe?" Connelly pulled out a half-dozen paper towels and patted his arms. "You tell me. Guy comes waltzing in here, claims he's from UPI working on a story. Makes sense. The Feds declassified these Does this afternoon. You'd know the media would jump on it."

"You get his name?"

"Yeah. Grier. Jack Grier. Come on. I'll buy you a Coke."

"You want fun and games. It'll take at least a chocolate bar and silk stockings."

"In the hall, Romeo," Connelly said, holding the door. "I got my reputation to think of. I can't be seen in the men's room with just anybody."

"Gee whiz. I thought I'd be quite a catch."

"That's why we're getting out of here."

Travis laughed, the tile walls throwing back an echo. "You think he's for real?"

"Is your mother a virgin?"

"So what did you tell him?"

"Nothing about you. He's not your type."

Connelly put some coins in the Coke machine and

tossed Travis a can. "Just because I'm buying, don't think that means I'm easy."

"I never kiss on a first date."

Connelly laughed, popped the Coke top, and drank deeply.

"More to the point was what he told me." Connelly burped. "That's the real reason my wife left me. No class."

"Such as?"

"Such as burping."

"No," Travis said patiently. "Such as what Grier told you." Sometimes it was impossible to get Connelly to give a straight answer.

"Are you still talking about that guy? I told you. Not your type.

"For one thing," Connelly continued, without a break, "he was interested in the same Jane Doe I showed you the other day. Very specifically interested. He asked about the lacerations. Asked about sliced cartilage. This girl had slashed cartilage across her nose, ribs, and one ear. Only an unusually sharp instrument would cut cartilage that neatly; her nose was sliced clean through. Not your common butcher-knife kind of wound. And then this Grier suggested it might have been done by a scalpel."

"Oh?" Travis kept his face carefully neutral. Travis knew full well what instrument had made the slashes in the victim's body—and who had wielded the instrument. A muscular youth, fifteen or so when Travis was in Nam—a real psycho who'd do anything Brevard asked. Anything. He followed orders like a well-trained attack dog. He'd had no name in Nam—needed none. Travis was certain that Brevard had not left his dancing bear behind.

Connelly drank again. "You know, Travis, when I

worked this girl up, I thought about a scalpel as a murder weapon, but I didn't put it into the report. This Grier knew too much. Too many details and specifics. In-depth medical information. Even the jargon. Threw a couple words at me I haven't heard since residency."

The two men had left the drink machine and walked up the hall. Connelly commented on Travis's squeaky shoes and Travis shrugged.

"Anything else?"

"Amyl nitrite."

"Amy who?"

"Amyl nitrite. It's a vasodilator. That was another odd thing. He asked me if she had it in her system, and when I said no, only cocaine, *he* informed *me* our tox screens don't even test for it. *He* told *me*. Said I'd have to run a gas chromatography or mass spectrophotometry on her urine sample to detect it.

"That kind of information is pretty specialized. And then I looked up the information on the other Jane Does, and they all had amyl nitrite in their systems. Every one. This guy knew more—"

"Wait a minute, wait a minute. This is the second time you've used the plural. What other Jane Does? You got more of these?" Travis finally realized he was being offered a bonanza of information.

"Yeah. Twelve in all, over the past two years. More, if you count the ones in other areas of the East Coast. And that's just the ones we've found. FBI's in charge of the investigation, but it's been real hush-hush. Not telling the locals diddly. Probably because it ain't going anywhere. They all but gave up on it about six months ago."

"Gave up? When there's still . . . Shit." This part was news to Travis.

Connelly shrugged.

Silently Travis added it all up. Six months ago Sayaad

had first come to town. Six months ago the FBI had dropped an ongoing investigation. Six months ago he, Travis, had been put on Soloman's trail again. Why? So someone could keep an eye on him?

"Anyway, he must have studied the previous PMs and the FBI reports. In detail, because he mentioned animal blood. Reports, by the way, so classified that not even you could get a copy of them."

"Cops don't classify information. That's military talk," Travis said absently.

Connelly grunted.

The two men entered the carpeted reception area and sat in Connelly's office.

"Animal blood?"

"Yeah. In some of the previous cases, animal blood was dripped onto them after death. It was detected because of the odd patterns of splatters.

"Animal blood. Like in fanatical religious sacrifices, witchcraft? That kind of thing?" If so, it was a new twist. Something Brevard had added only recently.

Connelly tipped his chair back on two legs, crossed his hands over his middle, and considered. "Possibly. But I'd still say it was sexually motivated."

"Why?"

"Four reasons. One—most were hookers, not virgins. Two, our acid phos' and semen testing on vaginal washings showed positive. All had engaged in sexual relations. Three, the amyl nitrite. If it's there. It's sometimes used as a sexual stimulant. Four, the blood was watered down. Like butcher-shop blood. Not fresh."

"You going to run the other tests?"

"Tonight. But I told Grier it'd take a week at least."

Travis smiled at the beatific expression on Connelly's face.

"Thanks. One last question."

Connelly rolled his eyes.

"This guy. Was he tall, six three or four, slim, long-distant-runner kind of physique, light-brown skin?"

Connelly nodded.

"Eyes?"

"Two. Green, my friend. Like fine old jade, well-polished and priceless."

"Terrific." Somehow hearing it confirmed made Travis's head swim. Slowly he rose and headed for the door, then stopped. "Any chance I could get a copy of these PM reports?"

"Not a chance."

"Figured."

"Oh, Travis."

"Yeah...."

"Something I neglected to tell our friend. Most of these girls had similar stomach contents. Grier didn't bring it up so he may not know. Your favorite."

"What's that? Cold pizza?"

"No. Close. Seafood. Japanese style. Probably raw, though it had been affected by stomach fluids. Squid. Oysters. Seaweed. Fish. And all the girls had eaten less than four hours prior to death."

Travis looked down at the plump pathologist and smiled. "Thanks. Sit on it for a while?"

"Sure. I'll give you till the gas chrom comes back. You know. A week."

Travis grinned. "Thanks."

Later, sitting in his car, Travis remembered to breathe and tried to force the tension out of his body. Before he'd left the morgue, he had looked once more at the Jane Doe in the cold, stainless-steel room. Travis had seen his share of bodies both in Nam and since. The Jane Doe wasn't the worst, but she twisted something deep inside

Travis. She was a savage reminder of Nam. Like everything else lately, she triggered something that pointed into his past. In Nam it had been the two MPs who'd gone under with him—gone under and not come back.

David had had a wife and kid, a wallet full of photos, and a line of jive that would have put Eddie Murphy to shame. David had gone out to score six kilos of pure unrefined opium one night and somehow gotten separated from his backup. The next morning his head had floated up against a barge with a soft thud. Travis had been the one to find it, the soft, low tapping sound on the hull as bait. They had run a rope through the severed neck and out the mouth in a loop, then tied the loose end to the boat—the boat Travis and Jack passed several times a day. They never recovered the rest of him.

Jack had been the big brother, the father confessor to the two younger men. The next day, heavily armed and angrier than Dante's seventh circle of Hell, he'd gone after the guy David had bought from last—the man who must have made him to Alain Brevard. Jack simply vanished. Nothing for three months. And then he'd been dropped off at headquarters, a drooling, incontinent figure marred all over with half-healed torture scars and track marks—a pitted shell, dependent on others for feeding and cleaning and for providing the chemicals his ravaged body craved. All because of Alain Brevard.

Travis, Davis Moss, and their commanding officer, Jack Delane, had been assigned to find out where the drugs were coming from. Understaffed, underfinanced, and overwhelmed, they had found themselves fighting a battle against both sides—a battle that had claimed Jack and David. It was a battle that would never have begun if the man in charge of the docks had been in contact with the CIA.

Communication between the services in Nam had been shitty. Jack and David had paid the price.

These had been the first two. Since then there'd been more.

And now there was Chris.

An overwhelming guilt settled painfully on his shoulders as Travis started the Volvo and headed home.

It was a dark, cloudy night, and the snow from the night before was a slick slush freezing beneath his feet. His clothes were damp, his hair was damp, and all he could think of was sinking into a hot tub with a cold Bloody Mary and a good book. Feeling more weary than he cared to admit, Travis climbed the stairs to his apartment.

The new key fit the new lock snugly; the crowbar marks had somehow been obliterated; the new-paint smell was faint in his nostrils. The door opened without a squeak and Travis stood transfixed. Two new couches faced one another across a gleaming walnut coffee table. Wooden bookshelves neatly stacked with books and knickknacks replaced the horrid metal shelves last piled in a heap against the wall. Two lamps, one brass and one a pottery jar, cast soft circles of light in the cream and taupe room, while Huey Lewis played softly on a new stereo in one corner.

"Like it?" Her voice was soft.

Travis stared and shook his head slowly.

Simply clothed in a clinging, pale-pink, wool-knit dress, smiling uncertainly, Nikki stood framed in the doorway to his bedroom.

"I don't believe it."

"Close your mouth and shut the door. Hungry?" Travis's eyes widened and traveled her body, searching for the signs of injury he'd expected to find.

"I'm okay, Travis. Really." She smiled, her full lips moving slowly. "Like it?"

"Yeah. It's quite a change from all that red." Travis closed the door and crossed the room.

"No. I mean the apartment."

"And no feather earrings. Gold. Nice." Travis pushed aside the loose folds of pink wool at her neck. "Still wearing the crucifix though. You want to tell me what's happened here?" Travis's fingers lifted her face, his hands gentle on her skin. Relief smoothed his features.

"You look beautiful, lady."

Suddenly Travis grinned. "I don't believe it. You blushed. You really blushed."

"You're dead on your feet," Nikki said crossly, pushing him away. "I'll fix you an omelet. I could hear your stomach growl from across the room. Go get a shower."

"Yes ma'am. But I'd rather have a hot bath and Bloody Mary."

"So go draw the water," she said, shooing with her hands. "I'll bring the drink when I bring the omelet."

Too tired to argue, Travis headed for the bath, then paused and looked back. Nikki, ignoring him, was busying herself in the kitchen, lips slightly pursed. She looked almost domestic. Travis shook his head again slowly and headed into the bathroom.

Pushing aside the bubbles, Travis slid into the tub, sighed, and relaxed. The bathroom was dim, lit only from the next room, which made the pine-scented bubbles glow greenly. Travis rested his eyes as heat seeped into his bones. Only when he sensed movement did he grin and rearrange himself in the tub.

"One queen of drinks with celery stick, one—as you call it—garbage omelet, and toast on the side."

"Mmm. You remembered."

"I remember a lot of things, Travis. Where do you want it?"

Travis grinned and ran his eyes slowly down her body.

"The food, Travis. Remember the food?"

"In my stomach. Drink first." He stretched and pulled a one-by-twelve across the tub, making a tray.

"Hedonist."

"You should know. Didn't you once suggest champagne and hot oil in a hot tub?"

She ignored him. "Bubbles? Somehow I took you for the cold-shower type." She settled the tray, then pulled in a chair from the next room.

"Had my share of those, too. Um. This is good. Extra Tabasco.

"So what's the story?" he asked, around a mouthful of omelet. "Last trace I had of you was a red blouse on my bed."

While he ate, Nikki filled him in. The night he spoke with her in the Piedmont he'd been followed. They had picked her up not fifteen seconds after Travis left. Mean, vicious, and flying on something that made them even meaner.

They'd roughed her up pretty bad, played games for a while, then thrown her in the trunk of their car. The next day was worse. They were out of whatever they'd been on the night before, and it left them shaking, frenzied— two punks with orders they weren't following.

"They kept talking about some guy named Tallitt and . . . I still haven't got it all straight yet. But they made a mistake. They took me to where this Tallitt guy was supposed to be and instead s . . . someone else was there.

"For modesty's sake you better run more water, Travis. Your bubbles are almost gone."

Travis grinned and passed her the tray. "I think not. I'm already shriveled."

"Shriveled? Sounds like a personal problem."

Travis laughed. "Out, woman. Fix me another drink."

"You don't have time. I'll lay out your suit."

"Suit? I'm wearing the only suit I got." Travis flicked the drain with his toe.

"You have a more appropriate one for your appointment. I bought it this afternoon." The water level dropped slightly as Nikki rose and headed for the bedroom.

"What appointment? Don't you think it's a little late to go calling? Nikki? . . . Nikki!"

Nikki stuck her head back through the doorway and grinned when Travis, standing in the tub, didn't bother to hide himself.

"Sayaad."

Standing in a copper-toned private elevator, his stomach still one floor below, Travis reviewed the last hour with astonishment, not untouched with anger. Almost effortlessly Nikki had coerced him into a series of foolish and probably dangerous actions. Irritable, out-maneuvered, and increasingly curious, he had let her force him into a new, ill-fitting suit—one probably cut for a eunuch—then push him out into the cold and lead him across the city to parts unknown in a car that wasn't his. All without a single explanation, with no phone call for backup, and without his .45. Those she had vetoed. That covered the dangerous parts. The foolish part was, he had let her.

All because of the name Sayaad. And a 9mm round she had delivered with the man's compliments.

It was an unusual invitation. Travis had no doubt where the round had been obtained—from a rooftop, eight stories up. A nice touch. And it worked.

However, all things considered, no one but Nikki could have made him agree to this meeting and its strange conditions. Travis had a cold, itchy feeling Sayaad had known that, too.

The only detail that gave him a measure of comfort was the .32 strapped to his ankle. Nikki didn't know about that one.

The elevator doors opened and Nikki moved out ahead of him, through an alcove and to the only door. It wasn't locked. Travis resisted the urge to dive into the room, pull his .32, and lay down a pattern of cover fire, Crockett and Tubbs style.

Sayaad might consider it impolite. Travis grinned hugely and suddenly relaxed.

The penthouse apartment was gun-metal gray and shades of teal, with recessed lighting and leather furniture that contrasted pleasantly with oriental antiques, objets d'art, and an old, black, baby grand piano, a Steinway. It wasn't exactly what Travis had expected. The city, brilliantly lit, was spread out just beyond the room, a glittering backdrop arrayed in a twenty-foot-long window.

Sayaad stood, his back to the room, watching the lights below.

Somehow, until that very moment, Travis hadn't expected to find the elusive green-eyed man. His grin faded to a half smile, which Nikki returned before leaving, exiting down a dimly lit hallway to the right. Travis scarcely noted her departure.

Slightly reassured by Sayaad's deliberately vulnerable position, the lack of bodyguards, and the proximity of Nikki, Travis moved into the room. It was all special effects calculated to lull him into a feeling of confidence and compliance. Travis allowed himself to accept the gestures without becoming less alert. The thought of the too-tight tweed as funeral dress kept him wary. Consideringly, Travis fingered the brass casing of his invitation in his left pocket.

Slowly Sayaad turned. Attired in charcoal gray, he seemed a part of the airy, sophisticated room, or it a part of him. His expression was open, pleased, that of the gracious host. His eyes matched his smile. Welcoming.

"I shall have to compliment Nikki on the choice of your attire."

"Yeah. Well it has to go back." Travis realized he sounded churlish, and almost grinned at Sayaad's reaction.

"You don't consider it suitable?"

"For my funeral maybe, but if I'm expected to wear it and live, I need an extra inch in the crotch."

Sayaad smiled and walked into the light, moving with the easy grace Travis remembered from the day of the stakeout. The analogy of a cat leaped to his mind again, and Travis felt a slight prickling on the back of his neck.

The round in his pocket had warmed to body temperature. Somehow that bothered Travis. He released it quickly.

"Would you care for wine?" Sayaad gestured toward the bar.

"I've already started on Bloody Marys tonight. If you don't mind," Travis said, his voice deliberately discourteous. He didn't necessarily like being rude, but other than the .32, it was the only weapon he had. He hoped it was effective.

Sayaad shrugged. "Sounds barbaric. But please, help yourself."

Again swallowing a grin, Travis crossed to the bar and mixed his drink. Without seeming to, he was watching Sayaad as he worked. Beneath the pleasant expression of the café au lait face and the jade-green eyes was tension, but so vague Travis couldn't identify the cause of it. It ebbed and flowed, seeming at one moment indecision, then curiosity, and finally something cold and harsh. And unpleasant. Travis wasn't sure he wanted to find out what was causing the vacillation. Obdurately, for the drink's final stir, Travis used his finger, then licked it clean. The expression that crossed Sayaad's face was a classic, and Travis filed it away.

When Sayaad spoke, his tone was amused, and Travis realized Sayaad had been aware of his observations. "Americans."

"Yeah. Individualists. Pioneers." He paused. "Harvard?"

Sayaad's brows twitched with amusement. "Eighty-two," he said. "But actually I finished at Oxford," he added, his accent becoming very proper upper-class British as he spoke. "History, language, and finances."

"Platteville. Eighty," Travis responded. "Women, bars, and criminal justice. In that order."

"3.0 average. Too many bars and women and not enough criminal justice," Sayaad said.

"You sound like one of my professors."

"Direct quote, Dr. A. E. Randolph, criminal procedure. November, seventy-nine."

Sayaad was showing off. Travis found himself enjoying the game now that he knew the role he was expected to play—barbarian to Sayaad's sophistication.

"I see you do your homework," Travis said.

"A man in my position must."

"And what exactly is your position?"

"I, unfortunately, am currently the East Coast distributor of pretty boys, lavish women, hashish, heroin, cocaine, marijuana, and various other illicit drugs. Thanks to you. And now I need your help."

Travis nearly choked on the Bloody Mary as he digested the implication of the useless confession. He decided to ignore it—for the moment—while concentrating instead on the request for help.

"Help? Seems to me you got all the help any man could want. Speaking of which, where's Ugh and Boner?

I halfway expected them to be here to finish the job they started on my car."

"Oh, yes," Sayaad said with a half smile. "I expected you to be more the Corvair type." His eyes sparkled with amusement like sunlight on a green lake. "It's been replaced. The car you drove here is registered in your name."

"Kind of you. Just like my apartment and Chris's hospital bills. You do remember Chris and the method you employed to get my attention?"

A hint of something nameless crossed Sayaad's face and darkened his eyes. His voice, however, remained cool and polite.

"I deeply regret the misfortune suffered by Miss Lattimer."

Anger surfaced on Travis's face. "Misfortune... Isn't that sugar-coating it a bit?" His own voice made no pretense at manners. Sayaad's eyes darkened perceptibly.

"Perhaps. But all reparations within my power have been made."

Travis set down his drink. "There's no *reparation* possible for what she went through. Just give me the two guys who did it, and a judge, and I'll make the correct reparations."

"However much I understand your sentiments, that is not possible. They have already been dealt with in a manner far more thorough than the United States' apathetic system of justice could have provided."

Travis's eyes formed the question.

Sayaad explained. "In my heritage we practice an eye for an eye... a tooth for a tooth...."

"What'd you do? Castrate them?"

"The details of their punishment are none of your concern," Sayaad said sharply.

Inwardly, Travis flinched, less at the reprimand than at

the cold look in the odd eyes. They'd gone a shade pale. On first seeing Sayaad, Travis had thought them the most expressive eyes he'd ever seen. Considering the dead look in them now, he'd have to reevaluate that perception. Sayaad had continued, his voice still cold.

"Their orders were initiated by me while I was in competition for my current position. They overstepped those orders. It was necessary to, shall we say, clear the board completely when I assumed control." He paused.

Travis remained silent, remembering Tallitt and the small hole in his temple. One pawn eliminated.

"Tallitt. Carver. The two lowlifes who hurt Nikki. And others." Sayaad spoke more softly, his voice seeming to slither. "I administered justice"—he paused—"in a manner both you and I would recognize as fitting. Extreme prejudice—wasn't that the term... Sergeant Travis? We could call it common ground. Despite our ethnic and ideological differences...."

Those green eyes were suddenly intense, telling far more than his words, and Travis felt an instant warning that prickled down his spine.

Memories stirred like smoky images in his mind.

Nam.

Travis went cold. Sayaad knew. It was impossible. But it answered so many questions....

"What do you want from me?" He might have wished his voice a little more forceful.

"Simple. Just do your job. Accept whatever routine assignment you'll be given tomorrow. And stop chasing after Soloman's supplier." Travis carefully did not respond.

Sayaad rose and replenished his drink, moving with the lithe grace of a jungle cat. Again Travis's mind recognized the parallel. And the threat.

"Does that assignment include the new East Coast

distributor of boys, women, cocaine, hashish, marijuana, and heroin? And other illicit drugs?"

Sayaad laughed, his face instantly transformed, shaving away years. His eyes focused deeply on Travis. Travis resisted the impulse to smile back.

"Perhaps. Eventually."

Travis suddenly felt cold, detached. He was tired of playing Sayaad's game, whatever it was. It was time to play his own game. His eyes narrowed, the corners crinkling.

"You didn't call me up here to tell me to do my job. What's in it for you?"

"Again simple. You turn the other way so I can do my job."

"Job . . . ?"

Sayaad nodded, his eyes watchful as if he sensed the change in Travis.

Slowly, steadily, Travis slipped his left hand into his pocket and pulled out the 9mm round. It had cooled. Carefully, Travis leaned down and balanced the bullet on the coffee table, its rounded end pointing at the ceiling.

Then, straightening, he said softly, "No deal."

Sayaad's expression altered visibly, as if Travis had passed some final test to which he'd been put. He smiled.

"It's been a pleasant evening, Officer Travis. Perhaps we'll meet again. Nikki is in the car downstairs; you have the keys." His smile spread. "Good evening. And good . . . hunting."

Travis, aware he'd been dismissed, went to the door. The alcove was cool; Ugh and Boner stood at the elevator, its door yawning. Tensing, Travis stepped into the confined space. But the expected attack never came.

When he got to the Mazda—his Mazda, and Hammit would croak over the paperwork explaining this one away—Travis was sweating. Nikki was sitting inside, a natural fox coat turned up against the chill. She smiled.

Sitting beside her, he asked, "Where to?"

"Your place." Her smile warmed. "And this time I'm my own agent. All questions receive an answer. By the way—you look great in the buff."

For the first time in hours, Travis laughed.

The interview had been short and strained, the undercurrents strong and twisting. And though Travis had refused the request put to him, Sayaad had seemed pleased. It was almost as though he'd hoped Travis would refuse. The whole conversation was confusing. In fact, the only thing Travis had gained from the interview was the Harvard '82 comment and an allusion to Oxford. Both had already been turned over to Whizzer.

And the man knew too much. Travis remembered the allusion to "extreme prejudice," undoubtedly referring to Nam—a different time and a different world... and a different Travis.

The man was intelligence. Or had ties to the intelligence community. But not the CIA. They wouldn't have called in a street cop.

And not MI-5 or MI-6. They'd not be acting on American soil without the complicity of the CIA.

Not KGB, GRU, or Department 13. The man had too much money and the style was all wrong.

Instinctively, Travis knew it wasn't Mossad.

The possibility that Sayaad was acting on his own occurred to Travis and was discarded. The money and power angles weren't right. Sayaad's expenses were phenomenal.

Except for the drug angle, it could be a cartel—financial magnates hiring and financing Sayaad for some legislative intent... trade agreements by blackmail. But, unless the backers included some freelancing CIA or Pentagon officials out to make a buck with the help of their security clearances, this operation was run by the government, for the government. Somehow Travis couldn't picture the current administration agreeing to the scenario that was unfolding. Second terms and political considerations would have made any government official shy away from the borderline illegalities. Yet, only the Pentagon or CIA could have gotten to his service record. It was still classified due to the sensitive nature of the accusations that surrounded his honorable discharge.

That left the possibility of a splinter group acting on its own—a deeply buried splinter group, perhaps financed by outside help. A coalition? A splinter group *and* a cartel? The ramifications were enormous.

When Brevard had vanished at the end of the war, Travis had returned to the U.S. sector just in time to be airlifted out. Exhausted, malnourished, he had recuperated at an Army prison hospital stateside; charges against him were held pending his recovery and a thorough investigation. The charges were never filed.

In the aftermath of the U.S. pullout, a great many things were dropped or ignored. Strangely, the charges against Travis were included. But, while in prison, he'd learned a few things from another inmate imprisoned for being AWOL and for drug use. Alain Brevard had gotten away—on a U.S. Army helicopter. And Travis had never given up the hunt.

Travis turned over; the crisp freshly laundered sheets whispered beneath him. Sleepily, Nikki murmured and curved her body into his. Her skin was cool and Travis pulled her closer to warm her.

What Nikki had told him added confirmation to his speculations, mostly from the money angle. Sayaad had given her twenty thousand dollars to bring Travis. And a new car. And the coat. It was all a part of Sayaad's *reparations*. She had been abused by the same men who had attacked Chris. The man was generous to a fault. In all, Travis calculated Sayaad had spent in excess of forty thousand dollars. All of which sounded like drug money. He had also redecorated and refurnished Chris's apartment. Nikki had seen to it. Travis grinned in the dark. For a hooker, Nikki had great taste. Tasted good too.

Still smiling, Travis woke her.

Day Six A.M.

Fumbling, Travis reached for the phone, more to stop the noise than out of any real curiosity. It was 8:10. Nikki still slumbered beside him, teeth marks visible on her shoulder in the dim light. By the time the phone reached his ear, Travis was smiling.

"Hello." Nothing came out. Clearing his voice, he tried again.

"Hello, your ass," the caller responded. "Your fishing holiday is over and you're late to work. Get it in here."

Instantly Travis was awake, his face impassive. Sayaad moved fast.

"What do you mean, I'm late to work?"

"Back on duty. Special assignment. Have your ass in here in thirty minutes." The phone clicked loudly in his ear.

Hammit was in a good mood, Travis thought sourly, replacing the phone.

"Like hell, thirty minutes. I'll spend that long in the shower."

"What?" Nikki asked sleepily, rolling up against him.

Travis grinned. As it turned out, he was very late to work.

CHAPTER 8

Day Six, A.M.

PROMPTLY at 10:00 A.M., Travis, unshaven, pleasantly tired, and thoughtful, dropped into a chair outside of Hammit's office. Without missing a beat in the report she was typing, Jessie looked up and flashed a smile.

"Enjoy your fishing trip?"

Everybody was a comic. "It had its moments. Is he in?"

"Little boy's room," she said, indicating the hallway with her head. "He's a bear today. Watch out."

"So what else is new?"

She took him literally.

"They put up green flowered wallpaper in the women's john. We had to use the men's room for two days."

Travis laughed, feeling suddenly at home, aware at that moment of his initial discomfort. "Sorry I missed it. Sounds like fun."

"It was. Angela Cordy walked in and caught Lieutenant Jarvis with his pants down. Literally."

"Oh, yeah?"

"Yeah. Said it was no big thing."

Travis grimaced. "I walked right into that one, didn't I?"

"Like a lamb to slaughter. By the way, you've been cleared."

A small electric shock pulsed through Travis. Instantly he was alert. Wary.

"Of what?"

"Tallitt's murder."

"I see. I didn't know I was implicated."

"You were. You aren't." Jessie shrugged.

Travis decided not to mention he already knew about his change in status.

"Just like that?"

"Um." She stuck a pencil between her teeth and rolled a fresh sheet into the Smith-Corona.

"A little unusual, isn't it?" he prompted.

"Everything about you is these days," she mumbled past the number-two.

"So. What is this special assignment I'm to be given?"

"Beats me. Paperwork went straight to Hammit's desk. Sealed."

"No grist for the rumor mill?"

"Not a grain."

Footsteps sounded behind him. Hammit paused, grunted by way of greeting, and passed into his office.

Travis and Jessie exchanged grins. "Same old shit." Travis wasn't sure who had spoken first, but they were both still laughing when Travis shut the door from inside the captain's office.

Travis slouched into the least uncomfortable of the two office chairs. "Thought I was supposed to be fishing."

"Things change."

"Wrong time of year anyway."

Hammit grunted. Apparently he wasn't in the mood for small talk.

"You're cleared. You're back on active duty. Don't ask me no questions; I got no answers." Hammit spoke without making eye contact, his gaze locked onto the desk top, his voice gruff and staccato.

"You're a captain. You're supposed to have answers," Travis said. But the captain hadn't been in an elegant penthouse last night bandying words with Sayaad. Travis could have offered enlightenment, but didn't.

"Being captain don't make me omniscient. Orders came down from God himself. Again. Along with this shit." Hammit tossed a manila case into Travis's lap. It was still sealed. "I'm instructed to provide you with any and all assistance and two detectives of your choice as support. All with no questions asked. So I got no questions. Not officially." Finally Hammit looked into Travis's eyes and held them with his own. "But privately I'm curious as hell."

"I'll share. Who can I have?"

"Matthews and Dietrick, if you'll call him back from playing nanny."

"Done on the way in. It's why I'm late." Travis was only half-truthful. His visit with Dietrick and Chris had been short. Not that they'd noticed. Their eyes kept straying from him to one another. Somehow that stung, though it eased his guilt about Nikki's presence in his bed all night. And all morning. "Thanks," he concluded.

Hammit grunted again. "So I'm a nice boy and you're the Three Stooges. Don't fuck it up, whatever it is."

"Do we get cars?"

"No."

"Come on, Cap'n."

"Life's a bitch and then you die."

"One car," Travis said, lowering his bid.

"You twisted my arm. Now get out of here."

Grinning, Travis rose and left. Waiting at Jessie's desk

for the necessary voucher for the car, Travis heard Hammit bellow, "Don't forget you promised to share."

"Yeah. Yeah. In the morning," Travis yelled back.

Jessie paused in her typing. "You boys playing games? Sharing toys?"

"Something like that."

She looked disappointed—no grist for the rumor mill at all. Conspiratorially, Travis leaned closer and she brightened.

"Did you know that life's a bitch and then you die?" he whispered.

Lifting a brow, miffed, she returned to her typewriter. "If you're lucky and someone doesn't fuck up your paperwork."

Travis grinned. "Warning taken."

At his desk, Travis found a bowl of stems, wilted. The flowers had been snipped off hours previously. Attached was a card and, making a bet with himself as to the sender, he opened it and read.

While you here do snoring lie,
open-ey'd conspiracy
   His time doth take.
If of life you keep a care,
Shake off slumber and beware.
   Awake, awake!
      The Tempest. Act two.

Travis frowned. He'd won the bet. Whizzer. He'd call him as soon as he finished scanning the file. An hour later Travis was forced to close the door to his cubical office, shutting out the well wishers. Apparently he'd been missed. It was gratifying, but, like Hammit, he was curious, too.

Sipping his coffee he broke the seal and slouched back to read.

The paper was thick and slick, sliding easily in his hands. The pages rustled slightly, cool to the touch. Travis felt himself grow cool. Sayaad *had* worked fast.

This was no vice-offense report, it was about homicides—dozens of them. Most were over ten years old. One, six months old, was from the Rockville Police Department, followed up by the investigative unit of Montgomery County. The second was a Jane Doe of more recent vintage—this week. Initial and follow-up reports had both been compiled by D.C. city police. The cause of death in both cases was blood loss and multiple lacerations.

Travis had a vivid memory of the slashed body in Connelly's morgue—the same Jane Doe that Sayaad had paid an interest in, the same method of death favored by Brevard in Vietnam. Prickles raised on Travis's neck. He resisted the urge to inspect the blank wall at his back. Ignoring the homicide reports—he could come back to those—Travis flipped to the sealed folder.

In ten pages of neat, single-spaced paragraphs was a history of the suspect: an itinerary of the last six years of his life; a paragraph about several videos that tied him to the murders; a list of known associates both living and deceased; a paragraph summarizing some white shirt's concerns that drugs were somehow involved in the man's financial picture; a financial statement that put him into the seven-digit category; a list of aliases.

A picture.

Travis found himself staring into the eyes of Alain Brevard.

His first reaction was elation, a wild howling, dancing excitement. Scenes flashed through his mind, so real they made him ache. Alain Brevard, his body jolted by repeated rounds. Alain Brevard, jerking as thousands of volts ripped through his tightly strapped body. Alain Brevard, floating face-up, blue, in an oily, sluggish tide. Alain Brevard, an ace of spades tucked beneath his bleeding, dying body.

Somewhere in the back of his rejoicing mind a calmer voice spoke, half-ignored, yet insistent.

After more than ten years, to find Brevard. No. To be handed Brevard on a silver platter. By an unknown called Sayaad. Coincidence. Too much of a coincidence. The prickles on the back of his neck sharpened into a warning sensation not unlike that experienced in Nam. Then, it had been almost a sixth sense as he stalked the darkened docks. Now it was clear forboding. A premonition. *Travis had to unravel Sayaad.*

But the voice went unheeded as something primeval twisted and leaped deep inside Travis's mind.

Whizzer was tacking up a new Shakespeare poster when Travis entered. His sharp face breaking into a grin, he came forward.

"You sure took your own good time to..." Bright orange eyes flame-lit, he paused and stared. "You looked in a mirror lately?"

"No. Why? I look funny or something?"

"Or something. You got a look..." Whizzer hesitated and tilted his head, studying.

"Yeah?"

"Closest I can come to describing it is unholy glee. You plotting a murder?"

"Yes." Travis's tone was meant to be lighthearted, but Whizzer's eyes glowed and narrowed.

"Anyone I know?" His voice held a warning Travis disregarded.

Travis grinned lopsidedly and tapped the file he held. "Alain Brevard." His voice almost hissed.

Whizzer's eyes never left his face, and when he spoke his voice was measured, cautious. "You mean Amory Beauvier. I scarfed a copy and scanned it earlier. Unsavory character with a lot of holes in his background, a lot of money in the bank, and a massive waste of man-hours and the taxpayers' money." He paused, his eyes boring into Travis's.

Travis blinked, Whizzer's words beginning to penetrate. "Wh-what?"

"Amory Beauvier. The case you've been given rightfully belongs to the FBI or DEA, if I'm any kind of judge. Travis, come back from whatever never-never land you landed in. Mr. Beauvier will never see the inside of a jail. Even asking this department to investigate is a waste of time."

The joyful, whirling maniac that coexisted inside Travis reacted to the words, whipping his mind and reflexes with instant anger, a coiling fury. Barely, some part of him that still clung to sanity heard the warning in his whispered name.

"Travis . . . Stop it. . . ."

With an effort that rivaled any he'd ever exerted, he calmed himself. Blinked into a haze. Breathed. And found a shred of reason.

"Waste . . . What do you . . . ?" Travis steadied himself against a CRT and eased down into a chair, his drowning consciousness struggling to the surface. Some part of his mind registered Whizzer's reaction as if in slow motion. The wiry body relaxed from the tightly coiled spring it had become. Distantly, Travis recognized the stance and felt surprised. When had Whizzer learned advanced, unarmed self-defense? And why would he move into the position of one who faced an armed enemy . . . ? Following Whizzer's eyes, he looked at his hands. Slowly, shocked, Travis replaced his weapon.

A bubbling pop and the sound of escaping gas brought Travis around as he accepted a cold Coke. Whizzer had been down the hall to the machine and back. Travis hadn't noticed and wondered if he was losing it all. As he sipped, his mind began to function again. Stunned, he reviewed his mental state since he had seen the picture of Alain Brevard. And he recognized within himself the existence of a second mind, a second purpose, a second Travis. He knew this other self. Intimately. It was the self of Nam. Wild. Rabid. Uncontrolled. It had been with him for days now. Ever since he had seen Chris curled around herself on her bed. Bleeding.

Out of long habit, but with limited success, he calmed this second self—tucked it away, bound but growling. Minutes later, the uncontrolled turmoil was deeply buried.

"What do you mean, waste of money and man-hours?" He was pleased. His voice was almost normal.

Whizzer continued to watch him steadily, but answered easily enough. "The financial section explains it all, Trav. If you did get evidence enough to make an arrest, the trial would be held up for a year in legal maneuvers, continuances, and plea bargains. *If* you managed a conviction, which I highly doubt, he'd flit from court to court on appeal for five, ten, twelve years—and eventually get thrown out on a technicality. Finally, if God held back the sun and it looked like he might do time, he'd just vanish. The man does business in over two dozen countries, several of which do not honor extradition.

"He'll never see the inside of a jail, Travis. Never. And that's what makes it a waste." Whizzer's eyes were compassionate, gentle, as he watched the conflicting emotions on Travis's unguarded face.

"By any vision . . . of logic . . ." Travis paused. "This

"... this disease ought to be wiped out," he finally concluded. Whizzer nodded encouragingly. "But you're telling me he'll never be punished."

"True. You've said it to me a thousand times. Any system of logic would dictate removing a threat to human existence. Place the verified threat against a wall"—Whizzer cocked a finger and fired—"and eliminate it. Logical. Any computer in the world would tell you that. Unfortunately for you boys in blue, as you are euphemistically called, the law is not logical."

"You're not making sense. Law as a system is logical. Only its interpretation isn't."

Whizzer smiled tightly, sipped from a Dr Pepper, and sat back in his chair. His body was still tense, ready, but the readiness was subliminal. On the surface he was relaxed and casual. Travis was grateful.

"Allow me to elucidate."

"Elucidate. Is that like computer dating?" The pun fell on deaf ears.

"Neither our system of law, nor its application is logical. It was not intended to be. Logic is as the Muslims and the Orientals see it. Cut off the hand of a thief, castrate a rapist, blind a peeping tom. Equal justice for all, regardless of station. That's logic." Whizzer's voice had become clipped, hard, his eyes unyielding, and Travis felt he was in the presence of a stranger—a stranger who sounded remarkably like Sayaad, and remarkably like himself. "Any threat to society and its commonly accepted mores is wiped away. In public, so that justice has the threefold purpose of punishing the guilty, warning the innocent, and working as a stopgap for those whose need for violence can be temporarily sated.

"Our system is more humane and more... human. And that's where the loopholes appear."

"What did you mean by unfortunately? For us? For cops?"

"Because you are trained to see the law as a logical process. Crime. Evidence. Suspects. Separate the innocent from the guilty." Whizzer ticked each item off on his fingers, his voice ungentle. "Arrest the guilty. Trial. Jail. Simple. Logical. But not the way the system works. And you boys are caught in the middle."

"Go on."

"It's what makes you cynical. It's why you call it a game. It's the major cause of police burnout. All because you persist in viewing what you do as logical, when in reality you have the least logical job in the world. You stand between the blind, unknowing, mostly innocent public and the twisted, depraved, vicious criminal element. And your ultimate weapon is illogic. The law."

Suddenly Travis was far from Whizzer's quietly taut body and relentless voice, in a smoky, black void of slapping waves and diving bats. In a place fouled by the smells of rotting fish, greasy cooking, open sewers. In a place most easily identified by the sucking, moaning sounds of death and the quick dull echo of a distant shot.

Nam.

The illogic there. The situation of peril from all sides and not knowing who was the enemy. Who among the allied forces was connected to Brevard, held close with the bondage of drugs, women, murder? Who was free of this taint? Who could—maybe—be trusted? The reasons why Travis snapped, went rogue. And why, eventually, he came back. In a convoluted flash he saw it all. And somehow for the first time, it began to make sense.

He focused on Whizzer's eyes, glowing softly in the green light of the display screen, a Garfield poster behind his left shoulder.

"All right. So I'll never get Alain Brevard into a jail."

His voice grew hard. "What do I do? Ambush him in an alley? Track him down and use a throwaway to eliminate the 'threat to the populace'?" He didn't mention the fact that he was perfectly capable of such tactics.

"That's one way."

Travis felt his face work in surprise. "What's the other?"

"Arrange so he draws on you."

"Legal murder. Seems I've heard of that before. It's the same accusation that sent me fishing a few days ago."

"With witnesses if possible. With you wounded if not."

"How am I supposed to arrange this... this..."

"Logical response to a threat," Whizzer finished for him. "Simple. You keep him tied up on the street. I work on the computer angle. Somehow we'll box him in. I don't know how. But somehow. If you want it bad enough."

"I want it bad enough," Travis said, his mind grasping the one sane element in this conversation.

"I figured. Here. This might help." Whizzer grinned his old familiar grin and tossed a folder onto Travis's lap. "Makes interesting reading and even better speculation. Mr. Sayaad is quite a character. It's not complete, of course, but still, it is very good work if I do say so myself. My friend Dubchek in Records contributed to the research. You owe him one.

"Now. Just two things."

Travis looked up, meeting Whizzer's eyes.

"One. Obviously you know this Amory Beauvier" —he stressed the name—"from somewhere."

"Nam."

"So does he know you?"

"I did business with him twice," Travis reflected, "in

a GI uniform over fifteen years ago. I've added twenty-five pounds, an inch, a lot of years, and longer hair. I don't think he'd recognize me. Besides, I was one of hundreds, and I was never alone with him. Always one of a crowd." *And once I became the Ace of Spades, he never saw me.*

"Okay. Number two. It doesn't take a crystal ball to see this is personal for you. If Hammit knew, he'd block this. No matter what it took. He'd give it to someone else."

"You trying to tell me I ought to back out?" Travis leaned forward, his whole posture one of menace. Whizzer stayed relaxed.

"Yeah, you ought to. But you won't."

"No. I won't."

"Tell me why?"

"Once upon a time I let two friends go in after him alone. One came back in little pieces. The other is . . . recuperating. He's just learned to wipe his ass after using the toilet. It took him twelve years. David Moss died. The imbecil was my commanding officer, Jack Delane."

Whizzer was silent.

"Nobody knows Alain Brevard better than I do. Nobody wants him as bad as I do. And nobody else is going in after him. Not without me." Travis's voice was a sibilant whisper. "And nobody is going to Hammit about our past . . . relationship. Right?"

Whizzer grinned his old grin, shrugged, and said, "What relationship?"

It was dark as pitch when Travis finished studying all the folders. A legal pad full of notes tied all the tenuous pieces together, with supposition and Whizzer's research as cement. It was conditional, provisional. But he knew he was right. And Sayaad was the key.

Travis pulled the sheet of computer paper and photostats to him again. Sayaad. A man with a past as shady as a deep-cover agent. A man whose name was no name. A man who, to all intents and purposes, did not exist. Sayaad. A man whose life was more questions than answers.

Whizzer's history of the man began in the Middle East. A fuzzy newspaper photograph of Bashir Gemayel's 1982 funeral showed a distraught, angry young man standing on the fringes of the family in front of some government building. He was not identified in the caption, but it was Sayaad. Travis had no idea how Whizzer had found the photo. Dubchek, likely. An earlier photograph showed the same man dressed in a quasi-military uniform, stiff, at attention in a group of similarly dressed young men. The caption was foreign and not translated, but Travis had seen enough of war to recognize the special aura of an elite corps. That was in 1980. Three years later Amal Leahr was decorated with Oman's highest military honors and promoted. His new rank was equivalent to lieutenant colonel. After that he vanished. Completely.

Whizzer had confirmed that "Sayaad" was not a name but rather the Arabic word for hunter spelled phonetically. If it hadn't been for Travis's tip about Harvard '82, that bit would have been the entire file on the stranger who had caused so much trouble in Travis's life.

Fortunately, Whizzer had found an '82 Harvard yearbook and a picture of Sayaad—a young man named Amal Leahr. He had been an exchange student, an unexceptional history major with few interests: no club memberships, few talents, no sporting interests. It all seemed to fit. Until, while thumbing through the yearbook, Travis came across the section dedicated to memorials and his eye was caught by a name.

There was no picture of Michael Leahr—no picture of the exceptional young man anywhere in the yearbook. But he had been a brilliant chemist . . . a poet . . . a classical musician. He had died at the end of the year in a freak explosion in a chemistry lab.

Travis remembered the gleaming Steinway in Sayaad's apartment. Thoughtfully he made a few notes, called Whizzer, and continued reading.

The rest of the file was a composition of facts and hearsay about an underground quasi-political organization referred to as the Huntsmen. The organization's members were shadowy figures with connections to dozens of countries—France, Taiwan, Italy, Great Britain, Saudi Arabia, and the United States among them. Also included in the list were Iran, Colombia, Panama, Peru, El Salvador, Nicaragua, Cuba, and the Vietnams. Travis didn't like the way that read. Not one bit.

The governments had an informal agreement permitting any agent free access to work within their borders at will. Which was peculiar in itself, as many of the countries on the list were at war with one another, or at least not speaking. Half were Western democracies. The rest were Third World dictatorships and drug-growing capitals. The list read like a drug trafficker's wet dream. Free access from prime coca-growing capitals to rich, decadent Western heartlands. Travis flipped to the back and had his suspicions confirmed.

DEA, Interpol, and FBI summaries all mentioned the Huntsmen as probably worldwide drug traffickers. But getting any of the Western governments within the Huntsmen's field of influence to act against them was another matter. Part of the problem was that the Huntsmen provided certain services to any of these governments on a pay-as-you-go basis—services they called *hunts*.

And they hunted for anything: security leaks, elusive world criminals, terrorist groups, corrupt officials. And because they had the tacit approval of the governments and because they did not have to adhere to legal procedures, they were successful. Very. They had an estimated 98 percent success rate on cases previously considered hopeless and abandoned. Sayaad was a recognized field agent of the Huntsmen....

The governments, of course, did more than simply turn a blind eye to the agents' methods of investigation. They assisted within the framework of semiprivate businesses, with almost unlimited funds, and with liaisons in the public and government sectors—like the D.C. police...and Aztec Systems.

In his summary, Whizzer had made a definite connection between Aztec and the Huntsmen—and a definite connection between the Huntsmen and South American drug trafficking. Worldwide. Travis liked it less and less.

The Huntsmen had had their conception in the sixties in Southeast Asia—Cambodia, Laos. They owed their existence in part to CIA patronage, a CIA which knowingly set up drug growers and traffickers as guerrilla fighters, working against the Vietcong.

Intuitively, Travis made the connection. Alain Brevard had been working with these Huntsmen in South Vietnam. But if that was so, why had Sayaad just given him Brevard? It didn't make sense. Unless....

There were two possibilities. Either one presented major problems.

The pieces clicked into place. Sayaad had been working through Soloman to get to Beauvier/Brevard. That much fit either scenario. A monumental foul-up removed Soloman, and, like collapsing dominoes, everything afterward fell into chaos. Whatever Sayaad needed from Brevard, he couldn't get from the front door.

Travis, whose past with Brevard had been documented, had been kept nearby but on hold. Now, probably because Sayaad had reached a stalemate, he was being activated. He was Sayaad's "wild card." And Sayaad had known Travis would not refuse. With Brevard as bait, Travis was hooked. Which Sayaad had ascertained last night. Easily.

Sayaad would use the homicide investigation and its results as a smoke screen to get to Brevard and accomplish the Huntsmen's goals, whatever they were.

But the homicides were only a small part of a much larger picture, according to Whizzer's information—a picture already being investigated by a half-dozen agencies in the United States and abroad. Prostitution in its more vile forms had always been part of Brevard's stock-in-trade. These days, as in Vietnam, he was into snuff films—films where, after a suitably pornographic interlude, a woman was killed on-screen. According to Whizzer, the films were somehow being used to keep the drug lines open. Blackmail? Or willing assistance? Travis knew that Brevard's combination of drugs and sex was highly addictive. He had seen enough men ruined by it in Nam. Now, more than a decade after the war that had spawned and trained Brevard, were U.S. officials still being controlled and manipulated? Were they perhaps assisting Brevard in his aims? Who were they?

Travis knew it went a step further. Brevard's stock-in-trade was drugs and girls, just like any street pimp. But his love was secrets. Power. Travis would bet his soul that espionage was involved also.

"Trav?"

It was Hammit, looking weary but unrumpled for once. He didn't ask, but the question was evident. Would

Travis share the sealed assignment? Travis glanced at his notes to where Hammit's name was circled three times in red. He knew the captain was Sayaad's liaison with the department. Had to be. He was the only man with enough power and position to pull it off. But Hammit didn't look happy about it. And the business with Larkin did cast a question on the possibility. With one foot he pushed a chair in the captain's direction.

"Have a seat."

Hammit produced two Pepsis, popped both tops, and relaxed into the squeaky, vinyl-upholstered chair. Half an hour later, Travis stopped talking. When he finished, Hammit did the one thing Travis didn't expect. He laughed.

Rubbing his hand through his thinning hair, he shook his head. "Holy shit."

"I beg your pardon, Captain?"

"You heard what I said. And I know what's coming next. You think I'm this liaison this Sayaad character is working through. Right? Wrong. But I can help you figure out who it is. In fact, I know who it is." He laughed again. "Who deliberately left the alleyway beside Soloman's den unwatched even though there was a window leading out onto it? Who ignored requests for sharpshooters to take out the two bodyguards? And who gave the official go-ahead too early the day Soloman was killed? Jarvis didn't call off the operation when the two street punks failed to come out of the den. He didn't call off the operation when shots sounded from the den and Abdullah came out with a wound. He didn't . . . Shit."

Hammit rubbed harder at his scalp. "And all this time I thought Jarvis was only a monumental fuck-up. My guess is, your Sayaad was early that morning, and Jarvis went ahead with the operation because he didn't know what else to do. Your Sayaad was expecting nine or so actives and an arrest for trespassing. Instead, because his timing was off, he got twelve. And because of the two punks in the den he got screwed."

"Shift change," Travis said softly, putting it all together. "And Rojo..."

"Rojowski was off shift. He covered the alley because he privately thought it was a loose end. And the two street punks who went into the den weren't making a buy, they were making a rip-off. Soloman never climbs out of bed till noon. So the best time to hit a den and set up a rip-off is dawn, when the night's proceeds are still on the premises, and the big man is home in bed. The two punks were in the middle of cleaning out the place when Soloman showed up unexpectedly. Abdullah and Cooch took the two out, and with Abdullah wounded returned to the Caddy in the street. Jarvis should have called off the op at the first sign of trouble."

"Jarvis is a communications major. What can you expect?" Travis said. "Cops these days need combat experience, not a lit. degree."

There was silence then. A disturbance from further down the hall echoed hollowly. Finally Travis noticed his warm Pepsi and drained half of it in the suddenly hot room.

"Jarvis.... And Wilson and I left position."

"And you shot Soloman. Ending this Sayaad character's big plans with the king and setting him up in business as Soloman's replacement. With Jarvis as inside man here in the department."

Travis's grin was sickly. "Life's a bitch."

"And then you die. So what now?"

"You going to Internal Affairs about Jarvis?"

"Based on what? The speculations of two tired cops? We got no proof. Yet."

"In that case I waste department man-hours and go

after Bre-Beauvier, while you keep an eye on Jarvis. Do I get three cars?''

Hammit belched. "Bastard."

Twenty minutes later, a stack of folders eighteen inches high under his arm, Travis flicked off the light. Instantly the phone rang.

"Christ." Travis put down the stack and reached through the dark for his phone. "Travis."

"I presume you will accept the assignment." It was Sayaad's voice, his upper-class American accent predominant.

Slowly Travis sat down on the desk top, the files cradled on his lap. "You sound very confident of yourself."

"Do I take that as a yes?"

"I need a copy of the films. All you have."

"That can be arranged."

"And a meeting."

"I sincerely doubt you have anything to say that I would find interesting."

"Maybe not you. But some people around here would be very interested in hearing about the Huntsmen." Travis held his breath in the silence that followed his statement.

Soft mocking laughter floated across the phone lines and Travis allowed his lungs the luxury of air. "Very good, Travis. I'm truly impressed."

"Thank you." Travis wasn't sure who the laughter was mocking, but at least it was laughter.

"In that case, allow me to invite you to dinner. Eight-thirty, tomorrow night. My apartment. Bring your friend Nikki. Perhaps it *is* time for a meeting... between the Huntsman and the bearer of the ace of spades." The phone went dead.

His heart racing, his breathing too rapid, Travis leaned across the dark desk and slowly replaced the receiver.

Day Seven, A.M.

At 10:00 A.M. Whizzer received a dozen rare orchids and a job offer, salary unspecified. Whizzer framed it and hung it over his desk, centered on Garfield's stomach.

It seemed Sayaad had no doubts where Travis had obtained the name of the Huntsmen.

Travis slipped the new blue-black loafers on and wriggled his toes. "You get what you pay for," he muttered, unconsciously repeating the words of the shoe salesman. They fit wonderfully. Travis had never paid one hundred fifty dollars for shoes before. On a cop's salary, it wasn't extravagant. It was impossible. But Nikki had insisted. And they did complement the new dark-blue pinstripe, double-breasted suit he wore tonight. He had traded in the too-tight tweed on a new suit, crisp white shirt, and silk tie. For a little extra, of course. And a little extra on the "same-day alterations." And a little extra on the shoes. In all, he'd "a little extra'd" a good three hundred dollars in plastic today.

Splaying his legs, he "limbo'ed" down to where he could see his tie in the new mirror that hung over the back of the couch. Long fingers worked meticulously till the oxblood silk lay flat. Nikki said the gold flecks in the tie made his eyes look more green. But then Nikki was good at flattering a man's ego. "It was part of the job," she told him, grinning evilly as she reminded him about her not-too-distant-past occupation. Satisfied with the lay of his collar, Travis stood. Dressing would have been a lot easier if Nikki had not locked him out of his bedroom and bath. He'd never shaved at the kitchen sink before. But Nikki insisted she needed absolute privacy to work a transformation on herself.

Travis glanced at his watch as the door to his bedroom opened. Two hours. As women's magic went, not bad. Nikki glided into the room, a pleated silk designer dress flowing past her dancer's legs. Travis knew by the look on her face, he must be gawking like a school boy. But Nikki really looked spectacular. She grinned impishly at his low whistle.

"Thank you, kind sir. Sayaad had it delivered this morning before we went shopping. Nice, huh? Yves St. Laurent."

"Think he'd adopt me, too?" Travis said with a wry grin. He figured Sayaad had spent maybe a couple of grand on the dress. *Drug money*, his mind whispered. Travis's eyes narrowed at the thought. "On second thought, I don't think I need to be adopted."

Nikki laughed and crossed the room to him, her arms outstretched. She slid easily into him, soft perfume and tendrils of hair against his nose. And then she stiffened. Slowly she dropped her arms and stepped back. Eyes narrowed, her voice low and angry, she said, "Why do you have that thing on?" A beautifully manicured index finger tapped the slight bulge of the 9mm under his left arm so that he would not misunderstand her question. "This is a social occasion. Not cops and robbers."

Some things simply were not open to discussion. Travis smiled. "Come on. We'll be late. We don't want to spoil your entrance." He held open the door.

Nikki's eyes had lost all their sparkle. But she didn't argue. Lips tight, she led the way from the apartment, her new fox coat swinging from her hand. The sway of her hips let him know the depth of her disapproval and disappointment. Travis sighed. He figured he'd have to spend several hours coaxing her out of her funk.

Chris had never been so difficult. . . . But then Chris preferred Randy to him. Travis still felt a little sting at the obvious relationship growing between the two. And Randy couldn't quite meet his eyes.

In front of him and two steps down, Nikki suddenly flipped up the hem of her dress, exposing silk stockings, a black lace garter belt, and a bare bottom. Travis felt his body react, and laughed aloud when she cast a demure glance back at him. He caught up with her and helped her on with her coat, his hands lingering on her neck.

"What if some guy had been behind me?" he whispered into her hair.

"Lucky guy," she answered.

Laughing again, he unlocked the door of his Mazda and helped her in. "Lucky guy indeed."

Travis leaned his back against the copper-toned elevator and ignored a case of déjà vu. The last time he rode up to Sayaad's apartment, he'd been unprepared mentally for the experience. Tonight was a different matter. Quickly he reviewed in his mind the details of Whizzer's latest information and conclusions. Whizzer had been skeptical of his own work. Travis had been somehow unsurprised at the path the investigation was taking, for crime, reduced to its basics, is all the same. Whether a murder is committed by a poorly educated member of a low socioeconomic class or a well-educated white-collar worker, murder is still murder. Sayaad was indeed a great deal more—or less—than he appeared. Tonight was Travis's opportunity to discover if Whizzer's skeptical instincts and his own instructive ones about the man were indeed correct.

A cop who works undercover has to play many roles. But in his case they usually involved risky, tense relationships with dirt bags who ended up in jail—not cat and mouse with a sophisticated adversary in a penthouse apartment. Travis hoped he remembered the manners his mother had taught him. The ones the street had taught him wouldn't do tonight. Travis grinned at the thought of Baby May, Michael "the Blade" Bucknell, and Jimmy C in Sayaad's living room.

The door to the place Sayaad called home opened. The tall, dark-haired man smiled, greeting them himself. Sayaad moved like a black cat, his green eyes missing nothing, including Travis's inspection. Amusement in his eyes, he gestured them into the room. Before them, D.C. glittered like a thousand Christmas trees on display. Candles glittered around the gray and teal room. Sayaad's severely cut black coat and matching trousers gave the impression of a dinner jacket without quite the same formality. Travis glanced at the gleaming black piano— his reason for being here, if he could pull it off. It turned out to be easier than he expected.

Sayaad and Nikki engaged in banal chatter while Travis organized his thoughts. Their host passed out drinks. When Sayaad placed a long-necked Coors Light in his hand, Travis knew he'd found his opening.

Travis held up the Coors Light, his lips slightly pursed. Sayaad glanced at the bottle, then at Travis, his eyes questioning.

"I thought this was supposed to be much more formal."

Sayaad quirked a brow. "Would you care for a glass of wine?"

"Nah. Just a glass."

Sayaad grinned, plucked the beer from Travis's fingers, and walked to the wet bar. A heavy crystal glass materialized from its depths.

"Ah..." Travis halted him. "Would you mind tilting the glass? Americans don't like a lot of head on their beer."

Sayaad lifted both brows and tilted the glass, his eyes

questioning the angle. At Travis's grin, he poured gently and handed over the glass.

Nikki, having decided to ignore Travis, complemented the apartment, the smell of the food, and led Sayaad away. Travis stepped over to the piano. It was a beautiful old Steinway, aged, ivory keys a soft white in the candlelight. Travis wiped his glass and set the crystal on the piano top, seated himself on the stool, and ran his fingers over the keys. He was immediately aware of Sayaad's interest. The man crossed the room.

"Mr. Travis. Do you play?"

"Just the radio," Travis said, unfeigned regret in his voice. "I've always admired people who could sit down at one of these things and play. I could sit and listen for hours."

"I'm pleasantly surprised. You strike me as a Top Forty, jazz and blues person."

"No. Not at all. Turn down the lights, put on some soft classical music. . . ."

"And a beautiful woman?"

"Always. Do you play?"

"A little. Perhaps before the evening is over I'll entertain you with my meager talents."

Travis got up, took his glass, and gestured to the piano. "How about now? Do we have time before we eat?" He was gratified to see real surprise on Sayaad's face.

"I'm honored, Mr. Travis." Sayaad took the vacated seat. "Do you have a favorite composer?"

"Oh, you take requests? I'm partial to Rachmaninoff." Sayaad paused, impressed. Travis continued, "Actually there's a Concerto No. 5 by Rachmaninoff that's very quick moving. Staccato. A lot of runs. Bold. Demanding. I like it a lot."

"Very good. I can see why you would choose it. It fits you. I hope I do it justice." And he proceeded to play.

Travis grinned. Nikki caught his eye. He knew his grin was one of victory rather than pleasure. Travis had not expected to gain so much so quickly by his detached, relatively sophisticated demeanor. He'd just proved Whizzer's skeptical conclusions.

As the music played, Travis sat on the facing couch and moved his head with the movements. He glanced up after a moment and saw Nikki watching him. He realized she knew something was up—Nikki was very perceptive. Travis grinned, shrugged, and closed his eyes, his beer beside him on a table, his arms crossed in a characteristic pose as he lost himself in the music.

The piece came to its strong close. Travis sat straight in his seat, opened his eyes, and smiled at Sayaad. He applauded softly. "Excellent. I'm very impressed."

"Well, I made a few mistakes. It's been a while since I played that piece."

"It was still beautiful."

Sayaad smiled, pleased. "Come. Dinner should be ready."

"Great. Pizza Hut's delivered already." He couldn't help it. Sayaad made him perverse.

Sayaad sighed and shook his head. "Americans. No, actually I took the liberty of conferring with Nikki. And I had my cook prepare London broil, medium rare, topped with melted Swiss cheese and diced green onions."

"Oh, this sounds better than sex."

Sayaad grinned. "Thanks," said Nikki. Sayaad laughed.

A half-Cajun, half-black chef, Ramon, served up the broils with side dishes of sautéed mushrooms and double-baked potatoes. Short, smooth-skinned, mustachioed, Ramon moved like a bird and was always ready with fresh wine, beer, and other drinks. Genial conversation accompanied the meal. The food was delicious. Afterward, brandy was served. Travis relaxed, his attention again on the piano across the room. It was time to begin his little plot. He spoke thoughtfully.

"You know, I have a friend in South Carolina. His sister is a classical pianist. She teaches at one of the colleges now. It took her years of study to get where she is. I used to go over and she would be at that piano. For hours she'd sit and practice. I guess that's why I find it so impressive when someone can just sit down, play like that, and make it look so effortless. How long have you played?"

"Mr. Travis, I must admit there is more to you than your DD Form 214 and your personnel jacket suggest. For instance, your interest in classical music."

Travis just nodded, though Sayaad's casual mention of his Defense Department file had rocked him.

"In answer to your question. . . . My family was very musically inclined. My earliest memories are of the piano and a gray-haired music teacher who would probably have been a dragon had I not been so eager a student."

"So you've played all your life?"

"A good part of it."

"You're really an exceptional pianist. Why didn't you pursue it?"

Sayaad started to respond, then paused. A strange emotion passed over his face. "Perhaps there came a moment in my life when I realized there was more to life than music."

"Yeah. Well, it's almost a shame, as beautifully as you play. Once upon a time I wanted to make music my career, but I didn't have your talent." Travis spoke slowly, his eyes on the Steinway.

Travis and Sayaad met glances, and something passed

between them. Perhaps that strange emotion Travis had not been able to name.

"Everyone has a God-given talent, Travis. It is up to each person to find and tap into that talent." Sayaad seemed to mentally switch gears. "Which brings us to the whole purpose of this meeting tonight between the bearer of the ace of spades and the Huntsman." Their eyes were still locked on each other. Travis admired the way Sayaad moved, from genial host to systematic, blunt opponent.

Nikki sighed, wiped her lips with her napkin, and lifted her brandy. "Well, if you gentlemen will excuse me, I think if you're going to talk business I'll retire to the parlor." Both men stood as Sayaad helped slide her chair back, and she exited.

Sayaad lifted the crystal decanter. "More brandy?"

"No, thanks. But I'll take another beer if you have one."

Sayaad walked over to the wet bar, followed slowly by Travis. They stood on opposite sides of the wet bar, as they stood on opposite sides of most things, Sayaad facing the long window. Sayaad twisted the top off the long-necked bottle and set it before Travis, his face pensive, his eyes on the city beyond the room.

"I have a dozen films for you to take with you when you leave. I'll warn you in advance—they're not very pleasant viewing. Although I understand the Ace of Spades was fully informed of the nature of these films when he was in Vietnam."

"Perhaps *he* was. But what can you tell *me* about them?" Travis was giving nothing away either, tonight.

Sayaad appeared to think a moment, and he chose his words carefully. "We are talking about an entrepreneur with a strange background and a fetish for mixing sex and murder with drugs, who tapes live shows and distributes the films to a select group of clients. But then you know all that."

"Yeah, I know a lot of things. But what I don't know is why you would give him to me. You're supposed to be one of the bad guys." Travis lightly accented *supposed*. "Why would you turn another bad guy—your upline manager, Soloman's upline supplier—over to me?"

"I see your dilemma. Honor among thieves and all that." Sayaad smiled wryly. "But what would you do if you found a dirty cop? Send other cops in after him? Correct me if I misquote you, but haven't you said there's nothing worse than a dirty cop?"

"I have. But don't even try to make a comparison." Travis sipped his beer, his eyes on Sayaad's face.

"I wouldn't dream, Mr. Travis, of trying to place cops and thieves on the same level."

"I would certainly hope not. But most thieves generally take care of their own problems. They don't involve the authorities. Or even attempt to. So if some group of thieves had a problem internally, they would quietly and efficiently eliminate the problem themselves."

Sayaad started to respond.

"Please. Just humor me for a moment."

"All right, Mr. Travis. The floor is yours." Sayaad took his brandy and walked away. His back to the room, he stared out over D.C.

"Hypothetically speaking, of course..." Travis began.

He could hear humor in Sayaad's voice when he responded. "... Of course."

"Say this entrepreneur we were speaking of is a member of some illicit organization, for instance, the Huntsmen, and this entrepreneur suddenly turns renegade. These Huntsmen, acting much like a self-sealing gas tank, would remove the renegade and have another member simply absorb the renegade's interests. But before the Huntsmen could create that vacancy, they would have to have someone in position, ready to take over. Someone who would leave no loose ends.

"Unfortunately, the entrepreneur in this case had something over on the Huntsmen. Records or information or something that prevented the Huntsmen from going in the front door, even though the entrepreneur was on their payroll. So they sent in you—by the back door, undercover, so to speak—to retrieve the records or information or whatever loose ends there might be, and then eliminate the entrepreneur.

"How am I doing?"

"Far better than I would have expected, Mr. Travis." There was a strange sound in Sayaad's voice.

"Oh, I got more," Travis continued.

"Somehow, I'm not surprised."

"So you have it all planned out. But I get in the way."

"By shooting Soloman."

"Now you're getting the picture. And you try to keep me off the case. Until you hit a snag. You find out that somehow you can't accomplish whatever goals you were assigned. So you give the entrepreneur to me, hoping that through me you can accomplish these goals and not blow your cover to the entrepreneur. So far so good?"

Sayaad nodded, his posture tense, his back still to the room.

"There's only one problem."

"Oh?"

"Yeah. And that's you yourself." Travis took a deep breath. "I don't think even Amal Leahr could have gotten to my war records."

Sayaad became suddenly very, very still. Travis instinctively knew he was on very shaky ground—in danger perhaps for his life. There was something about the complete immobility of Sayaad, his posture, the tilt of his head. . . . Travis switched his beer from his right hand to his left and carefully reached under his jacket for his weapon. Softly, he continued.

"However, Michael Leahr, posing as Amal Leahr, would find it easy to get my records. How'm I doing now?"

Sayaad slowly turned, and smiled when he saw Travis's hand in his jacket. "You won't be needing that, Officer Travis."

"I'm not so sure."

"Michael Leahr," said Sayaad, "was killed in a chemistry accident at Harvard in eighty-two. Michael was my half brother."

"Ah, but it's a little-known fact that Michael Leahr was a stage-quality classical pianist, while Amal was barely proficient. I'd say your earlier playing was considerably more than proficient."

Sayaad stared at Travis. No emotion crossed his face, but his brandy was forgotten in his hand. He scarcely appeared to be breathing.

"And then there are the questions raised in Michael Leahr's postmortem about the questionable time of death. A problem with lividity, as I recall.

"And lastly, there's the computer enhancement of the features of Amal and Michael Leahr. A friend of mine says it's more than probable that with a little surgery and a lot of background research, Michael Leahr could have become Amal Leahr. Amal had strong ties to a terrorist organization originating in the Middle East—an organization known to be affiliated with the Huntsmen. Michael, who for reasons I haven't been able to uncover yet, may have wanted Amal dead and the Huntsmen infiltrated. Michael, as a holder of dual U.S. and Omani citizenship, and a linguist of no small repute, would have been a perfect subject for CIA recruitment—and Huntsmen infiltration."

Suddenly Sayaad laughed, his voice soft and calm and very amused.

"My playing must really have impressed you, Mr. Travis. And stimulated your imagination. Sounds like a movie script."

"Perhaps someday it will be."

"Really, Mr. Travis, you can take your hand off the weapon under your coat."

Slowly Travis removed his hand.

Sayaad, still grinning, said, "And who in this movie will play the Ace of Spades?"

Travis grinned, swigged at his beer, smacked his lips, and said, "Ahhh. Probably my twin, Mel Gibson. Unless you have something else in mind."

"I do."

"Well, I guess it's my turn to listen then."

"We have a mutual friend."

Travis tilted his head and raised his brows in question, in obvious imitation of Sayaad.

"Joshua. David Moss. Senior."

Travis felt the wind rush from his lungs in a long, slow exhalation. Prickles of something like fear or shock moved across his scalp. *David*. . . . Telling a joke. Showing off a letter from his kid. Dealing poker. A fat cigar between his teeth. Laughing past the cigar as he knowingly dealt Travis the ace of spades, completing the royal flush which won Travis the game. He'd gifted the card to Travis after the game, depleting and ruining the deck. That was Travis's first ace. It was in his footlocker at home.

"Mr. Moss, or should I say Colonel Moss, gained access to certain information in 1975—information about how his son, David, had died, and about the man who had tracked David's murderers. These records explained how this man went AWOL and tracked down, oh, say, eight or nine of those murderers and then passed judgment on those eight or nine. Killed them. And left an ace of spades beneath each body.

"This man, this Ace of Spades, was in an Army prison hospital at the time. He later was released and received an honorable discharge. All charges were dropped and all paperwork relating to the case was classified. This included the orders—written after the fact—instructing Sergeant Garrick T. Travis to track down and eliminate one Alain Brevard. The paperwork included several ribbons and awards commending Sergeant Travis's work above and beyond the call of duty—paperwork arranged for by a grateful father. David Moss, Sr.

"Ah. I see by your expression that you weren't aware of Mr. Moss's efforts on your behalf. Or of the commendations in your classified records."

The silence built. Travis was numb. He felt as if his past were a violated body under Sayaad's scrutiny. After a moment he blinked, banished his own private ghosts. With a quick gesture, Travis lifted the bottle and finished off the Coors, then tucked the empty deftly into Sayaad's surprised open hand.

"So much for the history lesson. Where does that leave us... Michael?"

"Actually, it's rather simple, Mr. Travis. Our goals are the same. But our public ideologies keep us from taking the same path."

"I disagree totally."

"Oh? To what part?"

"You waltz in here and flaunt the ineptness of the law in my face, while living the good life on illicit drug money"—Travis flung open, stabbing fingers toward Sayaad with his words—"that you get from the lowest pregnant cocaine whore all the way up to the two-faced bureaucrat sitting behind his double oak doors pretending that casual use is chic. A hundred bucks from a pitiful whore deforming her baby with your drugs, or a hundred bucks from a high-class social user, is still a hundred bucks. Our goals are not the same.

"My goal is to eliminate you and people like you."

Sayaad's eyes were steely.

"I believe in Vietnam you accomplished your goal. But, Travis, if you will stop and look at the inept system of justice under which you operate, *that* is why people like myself flourish."

"Bullshit."

"Travis, look at it. Look around you. Look at a world built on a system that no longer works. No one takes responsibility for what they do.

"Your own mayor was implicated on cocaine, and justified his cocaine and alcohol habits by accusing the Justice Department of persecution.

"Cop killers now serve minimum sentences, then get early parole because they were good boys in prison. They stayed out of trouble.

"Rapists of nine-year-old children get sent to be rehabilitated. Then, when released, go on talk shows.

"Even your own police department is out-numbered and out-gunned by underage street thugs, carrying submachine guns and selling dope. Why? Because the men in administrative positions in police departments and government law-enforcement agencies were the street cops of the sixties. They are so afraid of abusing power that they won't use power at all. They are so afraid of creating a 'police state' and getting bad media coverage that they sit on their hands and do nothing.

"I, on the other hand, can think of two rapists who will never brag about what they did to a helpless woman.

They were held accountable for their deeds. They paid the price." He paused.

"It's a downward spiral, Travis. Someone has to do something."

"And you're that someone. You? A drug supplier with ties to the Huntsmen?" Travis wasn't sure why he was objecting. Somehow it all made sense.

"I believe you were the one who pointed out that not everything is as it appears to be... Officer Travis."

Travis answered Sayaad with his eyes in a silent room, the lights of power glittering in a backdrop below them.

Suddenly Nikki stuck her head into the room. "You guys still talking, or can we go dancing? It's been a long time since I've danced with two men."

Travis looked away, glanced back at Sayaad. The green-eyed man smiled, shedding years and cares as he crossed the room to Nikki.

"Remember, Travis, and I quote, dancing is the vertical expression of horizontal desires," Nikki said, laughing.

"I'm sorry Nicole. I'm afraid I can't make it tonight. Pressing business commitments. But you and Travis feel free to go." Sayaad slipped an arm around Nikki, hugged her gently, and glanced back at Travis. Pointedly, he said, "It isn't nice to keep a lady waiting."

Silently, Travis picked up the plastic bag of video cassettes beside the door, helped Nikki on with her fox, and paused. His eyes rested on Sayaad.

"Dinner was excellent. But the conversation sucked."

Later, in the elevator, a seething Nikki turned to Travis. "You know, Trav, you're an ass."

"Yeah. But everyone has to be good at something."

The Next Eleven Days

A judge, unusually eager to provide assistance, had given the go-ahead for wiretaps, listening devices, the works. For eleven frustratingly slow, unproductive days, they got zilch. Brevard/Beauvier was a model businessman, a churchgoer, a philanthropist. He entertained lavishly if quietly, slept with two different businesswomen and a model, and kept impeccable records according to the IRS—even Whizzer was impressed. He ate at places frequented by the elite, and he traveled often and kept to his itinerary. No unscheduled stops. No unidentified visitors. After slightly less than two weeks, Travis felt he was investigating a saint.

Apart from Brevard's sterling qualities, Travis made some headway. They now had a full list of all the Jane Does across the country and around the world. There were sixty-two. Thirteen had been identified. In no case had there been an attempt to bury or hide the body. They had simply been dumped. In every case the body had been located within ten miles of a United States military base. Two or three bodies had been found somewhere in the world, every three to six months for twelve years. In each area a dozen or so bodies would appear. An intense investigation would begin. And the mysterious killer would move on to reappear in a different locale. Interpole was involved. The FBI was involved. All unsuccessfully, because none of these agencies had come up with the key name—Alain Brevard/Amory Beauvier. Somehow, the Huntsmen had unearthed the name. Travis figured he knew how.

There had been four murders in the D.C. area over ten years ago. Then three this year. They had managed to keep it out of the papers. So far.

The only thing that set the D.C. cases apart from the others was the peculiar grid pattern on the bodies and the occasional presence of animal blood. In several cases it appeared the bodies had been placed on a screen after death for up to twelve hours. The screen had star-shaped holes which left star-shaped bruises on the skin of the women. Also, animal blood, identified as beef and fowl, had been dripped onto them in many cases. A dozen meat-packing plants had been searched, but none had star-shaped grid patterns anywhere.

All of the bodies found on United States soil which had been tested for amyl nitrite tested positive. All the victims had eaten a meal within four hours prior to death. All had engaged in sexual contact. One had been a virgin and brutally raped. She was unidentified. Her estimated age—twelve.

Sayaad had provided copies of the snuff films. In one, a girl, no more than thirteen or fourteen years old, had been slashed and then strangled while being raped. The rapist was Brevard's buddy from Nam. The psycho. Dietrick walked out partway through. Travis understood. Randy and Chris were close now; it struck too close to home. Matthews had watched all the films straight through. No emotion. No reaction. Except he now worked on the case on his days off, weekends, nights. He and Travis had taken to following Brevard twenty-four hours a day. And after eleven days, they had nothing.

The drag time was hard on Travis. He stopped eating, drank too much, and dreamed violent dreams. Alain Brevard was slowly driving him insane. He wanted the man dead. Instead, he had to listen to Brevard party, make love, and do business in his courtly formal manner.

But Travis couldn't give up. In his private thoughts Travis fantasized about taking Whizzer's advice and committing legal murder. In his dreams he didn't even care if it was legal. In reality Brevard went unarmed and placed himself in no position to allow Travis access either officially or otherwise. If Brevard was still in the drug trade, he handled no details. He was clean. It made Travis sick. And the rabid animal he kept confined in his mind paced. And waited.

In the last part of the second week Brevard had a slight change in activities. A girl and her English chaperone moved into the Sheraton's finest suite. She looked slightly familiar to Travis, though he couldn't place her. She had dark hair, and flashing black eyes that belied her demure expressions. Saucy eyes. She referred to Brevard as "Uncle Amory," and made several references to his kindness and assistance. Uncle Amory called her Susie.

Dietrick got a bug into her room within twenty-four hours of her first appearance. Unfortunately, the device had its limitations. She liked Pink Floyd and played it around the clock. All conversations were conducted through the raucous music. And Travis still couldn't place her. She smiled in his memory, a different smile than the clean pert smile she turned on her Uncle Amory. In his memory she was lascivious.... He put it aside. She probably just reminded him of someone.

The whole crew set out to discover the identity of Susie no-last-name. Perhaps she was a fledgling actress....

Two days later, a discouraged, exhausted Travis sat in the pouring rain, keeping his part of the twenty-four-hour shift. The car was steamy, and the windows had fogged over repeatedly. Not that there was anything to see. Uncle Amory and little Susie—a real, honest-to-God relative several times removed, not bait, not an actress—sat in a raw-oyster bar owned by a senator's brother, laughing and sipping white wine. Travis made a note to have someone check out the bar's liquor license and remind the owner politely that sixteen-year-olds aren't supposed to drink.

Watching them through his field glasses, he saw Susie lift a mounded cracker to her lips and eat. A dim memory stirred, as he watched, interfering with his concentration, taking him into the past.

Marlow had loved raw oysters. Watching her eat one had been an almost sexual experience. The expression on her face, the way her eyes slitted as her lips closed around the mounded cracker. The way her fingers touched her moving mouth. Her pleasure. Just like Susie. A woman who relished her own sensuality. The pictures swirled and changed, and he saw again his last memory. Only with an effort did Travis wrench from the horror. He was bathed in a cold sweat. Marlow. The memory faded, but images were left burned into his mind. He blinked. Remembered where he was. And why.

Rain pelted against the windows of the car in a rhythmic pulse. A defeated sound. But apt. He was so tired. . . .

The little girl, her bright lips laughing, accepted another oyster, dripping scarlet with sauce. Diamond earrings caught the light. Reflected.

Raw fish. Mentally Travis shuddered in the damp confines of the car. Raw fish. Something twitched, tingling in the back of his mind. It had been there, quietly insistent since Brevard had entered the oyster house. What had he heard about raw fish. . . .

Travis turned on the ignition and eased down the road to the self-service gas station on the corner. Inside was a phone.

Matthews wasn't home. Neither was Dietrick. Of course. Travis resisted the urge to call him at Chris's. He was afraid he'd appear green-eyed and jealous, interrupting over a mild misgiving. He could ask tomorrow about the raw fish. Just the same, he called in to his apartment and left word with Nikki to keep trying Matthews's number with the question. Somehow it seemed important. But not important enough to dial Chris.

Images of Marlow burned against his retinas.

As he hung up the phone, he caught a flash of lights and movement outside. Through the rain, he recognized Brevard's customized BMW, moving down the road.

"Damn."

"I beg your pardon, young man. This is a *Christian* establishment." The tone reprimanded.

"Yes ma'am. Thanks." He barely saw the thin-lipped, gray-haired woman behind the counter as he dashed past into the rain. His car door slammed and the engine roared. Uncle Amory was three blocks ahead. Perfect. Straining forward against the rain and slushing wipers, Travis followed.

The BMW made an easy target, its pace leisurely across D.C.'s well-lit, immaculate capital section. Brevard paused once at Susie's hotel at K and Sixteenth streets. A blur ran under the awning before the car pulled away. The rain diminished as Travis followed Brevard east on K Street, making a left on Vermont Avenue toward Logan Circle. Shortly they entered D.C.'s decrepit industrial and warehouse district. The BMW pulled into a side street, made a right, and cut its lights.

It was a back-street alley, with the obligatory filth, litter, and broken street lamps. The BMW pulled up a ramp and into a dark entryway in an abandoned warehouse. Slowly, lights off, Travis drove by.

"Bingo," he whispered.

CHAPTER 9

SECURITY was non-existent; no cameras faced the street—unless they were expertly camouflaged. Travis circled the block.

The warehouse was probably forty or fifty years old, and obviously unused. At the back were two loading docks with antique boarded-over bay doors and a no-trespassing sign on the service entrance. Its door was in little better condition, but Brevard had just passed in, vehicle and all. Travis was sure the warehouse wasn't on any list of properties owned by Brevard. He wondered if it had once been a meat-packing plant.

Out front was a parked car advertising a security service. A semiretired cop might let him in and give him a chance to reconnoiter.

"Bingo. Bingo. And Bingo!"

On the pad in the passenger seat he noted the address and the time—1900—and a few blocks later turned out into D'Arcy Road. Another pay phone and Nikki still hadn't reached Matthews. Travis gave her the address and time, phoned Whizzer with the same information and a few choice instructions, and drove off.

The raw fish and Susie's smile still bothered him, but

nothing came to mind. He drove on. At least something was happening to relieve the monotony.

By 1930 Travis was back at the warehouse. He parked down the block and waited. In the next fifteen minutes four more vehicles pulled past the no-trespassing sign in the service entrance. Using his field glasses, he got each plate number as it went past. Either security was very good and he would shortly be dead, or Brevard had been at this business so long he'd gotten cocky and lax. Or else nothing was going on.... Travis sighed. The lack of security said it was all innocent. He wouldn't need the backup he'd called for. Not yet. Noting the time—1935—and checking his weapons, Travis left the car, his badge in his hand.

The security guard wasn't an ex-cop, and Travis didn't know him from Adam's house cat. Retired Master Sergeant Bill Harding, his snapping black eyes clear and alert, his salt-and-pepper hair a military quarter-inch long, measured Travis over a hot cup of java. It was so strong it brought tears to Travis's eyes.

Bill grinned. "A mite strong, but what the frig, it's brewed to work away the two o'clock cobwebs. My daughter makes it every night before I come in."

Travis tried to think of something to say that wouldn't include an opinion about the coffee.

"Of course, I had to teach her how to do it right. She likes her coffee ladylike and delicate. You know. That light-brown crap. Now this"—he lifted his mug and swallowed down three large gulps—"is a man's drink. Right, Officer Travis?"

Bill could have been laughing at him, but Travis wasn't sure. Even the walls in the security office wavered as the strong coffee hit his empty stomach. The harsh, bitter taste was like swigging burnt motor oil. Travis tried to drink without making a face.

"Call me Trav."

Bill began World War II coffee anecdotes. Travis ingested pure caffeine and tried to appear interested and patient. Five minutes later, before he could even steer the conversation around to it, he was offered the run of the place.

"I know you're not here to listen to an old soldier ramble"—Travis doubted Bill Harding ever rambled—"and I always cooperate with the law"—Travis had strong doubts about that, too—"so make yourself at home. Here's a floor plan." Bill pulled open a rusty file drawer and pushed a poor photostat at Travis.

"The X's are the time clocks I punch. The dotted line's my rounds. I've got to start one in two minutes."

"What's this in here?" Travis pointed.

"That back part ain't my job." Bill rose and gestured toward the doorway. Thankfully, Travis abandoned his half-empty mug and followed Bill, whose voice echoed hollowly. "That part is used as some kind of advertising office. They have night meetings. Photo sessions, that kind of thing." Bill let his voice wander off. "Like tonight. Funny, 'bout you seeing that suspect lurking near the loading dock." Bill grinned. "Coincidence and all that. You know. The suspect and the photo session . . . both on the same night."

Travis sighed. Bill's heavy-handed comments only added to his caffeine-stretched nerves.

"Yessir. Good thing you're not interested in the back part there. I'd have to run you *off* what with ya not having a warrant. I've got my orders. But since you saw the suspect near the front of the building. . . . You did say you saw the suspect near the front of the building, didn't you?" Bill was grinning.

"Ah? Oh. Sure." Now Travis understood. He had carte

blanche as long as Bill's job wasn't threatened. "Yeah. Right. Near the front. You didn't see him?"

"Nope. Glad you did."

"Is there a door between the front and back parts? So I can stay in the proper area, of course."

"Of course, Officer Travis. One door. Locked, of course."

"Of course."

"Be a shame if your suspect was to jimmy that lock, though, wouldn't it?"

"Real shame. That advertising agency could lose valuable property. I'd have to investigate further if the lock was jimmied. With your permission, of course."

"Of course. Any unlocked door is open to the law. I'll swear to it."

"What was this place anyway?"

"Half a dozen different things."

"Right. I owe you."

"Good. You can pay it off by sharing another cup of java with me before you leave."

Travis groaned. Bill Harding was a cruel man.

At 2015 Travis found the elusive locked door, which was not marked on the floor plan. At 2030, Officer Travis heard a suspicious sound and went through the unlocked door to investigate. There could have been a felony in progress. And since the door had been obviously tampered with, Travis felt he should at least do a quick look-see.

Bill's tacit cooperation enabled Travis to bend a few rules, leave out a few procedures. He hoped Whizzer was making quick time with his instructions. Travis had a feeling he'd need a warrant and backup soon. He checked his watch. At least half an hour before he could expect help.

Travis drew his weapon. His heart was a quick staccato from the caffeine kick, his breath loud in the unexpected silence. No one challenged his presence. Ears straining, he stepped inside. The door closed behind him with a dull click.

He was in a small parking area. There were seven cars. Travis added two license-plate numbers to his list before moving on.

In the far wall there was a door in the center and a dark hallway to the right. Travis tried the door. It opened.

There were no windows, only scant indirect lighting which left his feet in inky blackness. The ceiling, walls, and floor where he stood were covered with a plush, dark carpeting. The walls curved sharply in either direction. He was standing in a curved hallway. It was like a tunnel; he could have been underground.

An unnatural silence throbbed in his ears. Even his breathing, so loud just a moment ago, made no sound. Its echo was instantly absorbed.

Travis's mouth went dry.

The whole complex was soundproofed.

Like a sound studio.

Or a film studio.

Suddenly Travis recalled the significance of the raw oysters. Most of the DC victims' stomach contents had included raw seafood. But Brevard had let Susie off. Hadn't he?

Travis felt sick. Yet, in some primal core an elation was growing. Tonight Alain Brevard would make a new movie. And Travis had just let himself into the long-looked-for studio.

He had half an hour.

Without backup.

Alain Brevard.

A shock of electric heat passed through Travis. Images harsh, blooded, surreal, followed.

Bodies sprawled on plank decking, killed instantly.

Others writhing, dying slowly, gut-shot. Still others missing fingers, whole hands, an eye, left alive, sent back to their master. Witnesses to the creature who hunted him. Each bearing the warning printed on an ace of spades. Two words only. "You're mine."

Nam.

Nights blacker than this cavern, hotter than Hades. Nights when darkness was his only camouflage. When sweat, acrid, oily, rank with fear ran in rivulets. Straining terror. Nights where his only defense was speed, timing, and venom-honed instinct.

Memories of a time when he became someone else. In a place where all the rules were dead and he was alone with an enemy he couldn't find.

When his only companion was hatred and it accompanied him like a dark shadow in the night. Alive. Whispering suggestions, warnings.

Nam.

Memories of a time when hatred began to take shape and substance, to pad beside him almost visible in the mists. When he lost himself in its power. Its purpose. Nemesis.

Alain Brevard.

The years fell away.

The demon within him, so long buried, quivered, reared, and attacked. Travis moved with it down the dark hallway.

Silent, Travis ducked into a recessed door on the inside wall. It too was carpeted.

No witness.

He tried the knob. It was locked. The hallway curved on. Making a circle.

Alain Brevard was here. Alain Brevard was going to commit murder.

The demon howled, its breath hot. Travis's lips stretched with glee.

And so was Travis. Legally.

Moving counterclockwise up the circular hallway, he tried the next door. And the next. Both were locked. He had covered one quarter of the circle. Where was Alain Brevard?

Reason, stunned by the reaction of Nam and death personified, made a weak attempt to reassert control. The demon creature swept it aside, too powerful to notice the inconvenience.

There were two doors now in view. Another on the inside wall, identical to the last three. Evenly spaced. Carpeted. And on the outside wall an odd one. It shimmered softly like polished brass or beaten gold.

Deciding, he crossed the space to the outer wall and tried the shining door. The knob turned easily. Soundlessly.

Procedure forgotten, Travis stepped through. He was standing in a parlor. Pale cream walls, drawn drapery, oriental carpet over bleached heart of pine. Antiques, stuffed chairs. Lamps burning softly. Mirrored tables finely dusted. Travis lifted a few specks with a forefinger. Undoubtedly cocaine. A stocked bar, brandy snifters, cordial glasses, some half full. Exotic labels.

His knee bumped a low table. Its rocking echoed before it stilled. Curios and collectibles, leather-bound books. Travis rested his back against a creamy wall and remembered to breathe. He was drenched in a cold sweat; his legs trembled; the back of his throat tickled.

In this moment of self-awareness, reason seized command. Throwing back his head, he swallowed a taste of raw bile and struggled to control his heart rate. And his hatred. After a long moment, his demon hissed, breathed, and lay quiescent. Waiting.

Sweat dried on his body as the minutes passed. Finally

he was calm. Training now uppermost, Travis checked the door across the room. His footsteps made a strangely loud ambient sound, as if he were in an echo chamber. The door had a security eye which looked out onto the dark hallway and into the vehicle storage area. Fearing alarms, Travis didn't try the door. Instead he checked the windows. The drapery covered painted plaster. They were there only for the ambience, as Chris would have said. He wished to hell he'd dialed Chris's number, to speed up his backup. Deep inside, his demon disagreed. It wanted nothing except Alain Brevard.

Taking a deep breath, Travis went back across the room. Steadying himself he entered the hallway. It was still unoccupied. This time, he remembered to look for security cameras, electric eyes. The hallway appeared clean. He stood a moment, and thought he heard something. Music?

Moving cautiously, Travis crossed from the parlor to the inside wall. The fourth carpeted door was locked. Further on Travis found a fifth door. The feeling of music was stronger but still unidentifiable. He tried the knob. It turned. Standing aside, Travis cracked open the door. Light blared out. It was a storeroom—vacuum cleaners, shelves, Windex and ammonia by the gallon, dozens of used paint cans, gasoline and mineral spirits, sponges, Comet, brooms, a plunger neatly lined the walls. Inside, the music was louder, but the melody and half the rhythm were still obscured. Travis closed the door behind him.

It was 2055. He had traveled one hundred eighty degrees of the circular hallway. No people. No cookies. Travis smiled tightly.

On up the hallway the feeling of music intensified. A heavy disco beat, bass and horns; beneath it, like a cross current, ran a melody innocent and sweet, tripping like a nursery rhyme. Arrhythmic. Like his heart.

A few steps later, the hallway ended. In a cul-de-sac with two doors, he paused. The door that blocked the end of the cavernlike hallway was like the others. Recessed. Carpeted. Locked. The door to his left was different.

Down a short unlit hallway, perhaps five feet, it was marked in the center with an eight-inch silver disk. No doorknob. An electric door. The music throbbed, raced through his veins. Hypnotic. Primeval. His demon stirred.

Suddenly, trapped in the cul-de-sac, doubts began whispering inside his mind. Travis realized the position in which he'd placed himself. His backup had no idea where he was. There was probably no way out. He had no idea what was happening inside. If it was innocent—a simple photo session—he'd blown his cover, the investigation, and his chance to take Brevard.

"Shit." It was 2100—9:00 P.M.

Suddenly something about the music changed minutely, but it raised the hairs on the back of his neck. And then he realized. The melodic nursery-rhyme undercurrent had stopped. Cut off. Been replaced by... screams. Raw, ripping horror. Pain. Disbelief.

Sprinting, Travis raced down the unlit hallway to the electric door. Crashed through. And stopped.

Light so bright it burned, searing into his brain. Instinctively his eyes closed, and the afterimage blinked onto his lids. He squinted against the brightness. The room was like an oven. A steam bath. Heat rolled over him. Above it all was sound, so loud it was rhythmic pain, punctuated with screams and sobbing. All amplified to fever pitch.

Travis fought the pain, the sensual bombardment, and forced his eyes to focus. Wavering in his quickly adjusting vision was a moving mass of bloodied, oiled flesh— twisted, tangled arms and legs, writhing bodies. And beyond, reflected back from a thousand mirrors, his own reflection. Weapon extended.

The bodies separated. In a moment of clarity they became two, the one above raising a glittering, blood-smeared scalpel. Its arm stretched up, the wrist reared back to slash down on the scored flesh whimpering beneath it.

In the mirror beyond, eyes met and the slasher whirled. His body was a fluid, corded machine, lubricated with sweat, oil, and gore. Glistening in the bright lights with blood. Rampant. Teeth bared white; eyes blazing with hysteria and senseless with drugs. Skin rippling, he lunged.

Without Travis's conscious effort his weapon discharged. The shots were almost buried beneath the music. Two round holes appeared in the chest of the charging monster. He stumbled back against the mirrored wall, eyes wide in surprise. He looked down. Blood spurted in its own rhythm. His eyes met Travis's. Laughing, he charged again.

Travis lifted his weapon. Aimed. Fired. The slasher's head snapped back, eyes rolling as if they were trying to follow the bullet's passage through his brain. Slowly, he crumpled. Relaxed. The scalpel still held firm. Seventeen beats of the music. Somehow Travis'd counted.

The girl clawed at the carpet, her blood staining it in rapidly spreading pools. She had lost two fingers on her left hand, and part of one breast, the nipple sheared off. Her face was untouched, but her throat from jaw to breastbone was pouring blood in a steady stream, and her chest and back were crisscrossed with deep lacerations.

Her eyes stared wide, reflected in a thousand mirror images, and her skin was gray with shock. Small mewling movements contorted her lips.

"Shit," Travis said again, the obscenity lost in the throbbing sound.

Holding his weapon to the side, Travis bent and stripped the bed; teddy bears and a china doll went flying. As he bent over the girl he noticed two things. She was shaved smooth all over. And a face was reflected in a dark doorway behind her. Alain Brevard.

Whirling, Travis fired, but the door slammed shut. He fired again and had the satisfaction of seeing a mirror shatter, its pieces held in place like a glass spiderweb.

Quickly, using pieces of torn white sheets, Travis fashioned a tourniquet for the amputated fingers. Down pillows he strapped whole to her chest, and, after placing her on the bare mattress, he raised her legs with sheets and bundled clothing. She was wearing white anklets and baby-doll shoes, and ribbons in her blood-streaked blonde hair. Part of him noted it wasn't Susie. Over her trembling body he placed the coverlet from the bed. Care Bears stared playfully back at him.

CHAPTER 10

FOR the first time Travis noticed the room. He saw dolls, roller skates and ballet shoes, a miniature doll splattered with drying blood. The bed was a four-poster, its high canopy a wisp of frilly lace. A little girl's room was reflected back at him from all around the circular chamber. Against one wall were piled a man's three-piece suit, business shoes, a briefcase.

"Every man's vision of a child nymph." He was glad he couldn't hear the words.

Circling the room, moving in time with the music like some primitive dancer, Travis looked for another electronic panel like the one he'd punched to enter. Repositioning himself, he looked for the place where the door should have been. Nothing. Mirrors and his own face stared back at him, tortured eyes a pale gold-green, devil flecks dancing. The music bruised. Insatiable.

In an instant he exploded, throwing himself kicking, cursing against the walls. Some bounced back. None broke. And there was nothing in the room to throw. Worn, exhausted, he fell against a wall, smearing an oily, bloodied streak.

* * *

The sergeant waited till 2105 before deciding to follow Travis. Even a raw recruit should have finished off the doughnut-shaped studio in half an hour. He himself had reconnoitered it in half that time. Of course, the place had been empty then, but Travis was a pro. Besides, he had a feeling trouble followed that kid like flies after a shit wagon. And Bill was bored as hell.

Grinning, his blood a steady beat in his ears, he entered the dark circular hallway and turned left.

"Always move left. It confounds the enemy," he whispered. Also there were sounds to the right. Doors. Voices. People.

Bill had a knack for getting to the heart of a matter in record time. It was a talent legendary among drill sergeants. And it didn't fail him now. Unerringly, he went straight to the film door. The door hung open a quarter-inch as if someone had left hurriedly and forgotten to push it to. The room was empty. His .38 drawn and ready, Bill entered. And stopped.

Before him was a fully equipped film and sound studio, with cameras both remote-controlled and handheld. TV monitors. All this he'd seen before. But tonight it was all functioning—filming a bloodied, cursing madman around the weird mirrored room.

Travis.

Bill grinned hugely.

A body moved slightly on the bed. A second body would never move again.

After a moment, Travis finally stopped trying to break his face against the walls, and rested against a mirror, the room in sight.

"About time," Bill said. "Fool coulda got his balls shot off." The music was some disgusting disco shit. Bill looked for a way to shut it off. A four-and-a-half-foot black cabinet was topped with a rolling reel-to-reel and several dozen switches. He hit perhaps a dozen, speeding and slowing the music, before he gave up and ripped the reels off. The music died with a broken cry. Bill was an impatient man.

Inside the mirrored room, Travis was turning slowly, his 9mm steady. In the sudden silence Bill could hear Travis's words. From their selection he thought Travis might have made a fair drill sergeant. Only fair. He repeated himself once.

Leaning over, Bill spoke directly into a microphone.

"Mind if I join the party?" Then, "What the frig? Damn."

Travis hadn't responded. The mike was dead. Bill flipped a toggle on the microphone stand.

Inside the macabre, mirrored room Travis turned slowly, steadily, watching for an electronic door to open, or the reflection of one. Hoping he'd know the difference. His ears, deadened by sound for so many minutes, emitted a steady buzz. From the bed the girl called for her mother and bled through her makeshift bandages.

"Whos . . . Whooss."

Someone was blowing into a mike.

"Testing."

Travis spotted a speaker, two cameras, another speaker. But the film room could have been anywhere. There had been enough locked doors.

"Hey, Travis. I blew a perfectly good line on a dead mic. Ain't that the pits?"

Relief made Travis shake. He closed his eyes against the glare. "Bill? Where the hell are you?"

"In a giant jam box about three o'clock."

Travis looked to the right. His own reflection met his gaze, but his shoulders, aching with tension, relaxed somewhat.

"Get us the fuck out of here."

"Tactically speaking, that's a good move. But you tell me how."

"Hell, I don't know. Doors are electronic. You got any switches where you are?"

Bill looked down. And around.

"A few," he said. There were perhaps a thousand.

"Try those."

"Oooookay," Bill said. "Hope you know what you're doing."

For some seconds nothing happened as Travis watched his reflections watching for an attack.

Abruptly the lights went out. In the unexpected darkness Travis lost his balance and went down on one knee. The lights came back on, but this time a hot green glow suffused the room, turning his reflection to instant leprechaun. Then blue. Then a demonic red. Overhead a strobe made his reflection dance as he stood up. The room steadied as the strobe stilled, and was now bathed in a sickly yellow light. He looked jaundiced, his cheeks hollow, his eyes empty sockets. The lights stopped changing, leaving him a specter.

Over the speakers he heard whirrs and clicks. A boom-chack-a-chack-a-boom beat started then stopped.

"Ah, what the frig," Bill said, his voice now electronically modulated to give a long echo, the bass notes predominant.

Suddenly a crash shattered a mirror to Travis's right; its sound expanded, echoing over the speakers. He whirled, dropped, rolled to avoid the massive black form flying into the room. His eyes closed as yellow splinters of glass pricked his skin. The black form bounced, rolled over the slasher's body, and rocked to a halt, wheels spinning. Travis had his weapon aimed at a chair.

A black stick reamed out an even blacker five by six

rectangle. Travis swallowed down coffee flavored gorge and tried to quiet his burning stomach.

"Found it." Bill's voice came over the speakers and closer, from the black hole. He sounded pleased with himself. Travis, if he'd had the time, would willingly have shot the son of a bitch.

Moving quickly, Travis holstered his weapon and lifted the girl. Instantly, her blood soaked through to Travis's skin. It appeared black in the ailing yellow light. He passed her, moaning, through the black hole to Bill.

"What the frig's going on here?"

"Get her out of here and get me my backup. There should be some people on the street by now. Move."

Bill didn't argue. He moved off, carrying his dripping burden, as Travis crawled through into the soft blue light of the control booth. He drew his weapon and moved out after Bill. The cameras were still rolling.

Travis slipped into the hallway, covering Bill as he made his way back through the jimmied door into the deserted warehouse. Behind one of these locked doors Travis knew he'd find a meat locker with a star-shaped grid pattern. The door clicked shut. Travis was alone.

Moving cautiously, Travis traveled up the black hallway. It was even more like a tunnel now, the dim recessed lighting extinguished. The only glow was a dim one just ahead, its source hidden beyond the curvature of the wall.

In the darkness, his private demon growled and placed its steps evenly in the black carpet. Like a cat it paused, sniffed the air. Alain Brevard was just ahead.

Travis's heart beat a bruising cadence in his straining ears. His breath came short. It had been nights as black as this when he'd hunted before. Predatory, he moved toward the light.

The first carpeted door was open. In more ways than

one, Travis had returned to the beginning. Hanging close to the inner wall he pushed open the door.

Beyond was a pie-shaped room, the sharp point blocked off by a full-length window. It looked out onto the yellow-lit mirrored room. In the center of the wedge was a recliner and two tables, both mirrored. Three lines of cocaine, a highball glass, and a half-full pitcher were on one table. On the other were towels. A sink stood in one corner. In the darkness Travis kicked something. A shoe. Socks and a tie hung over a rack. A pile of clothes lay on the floor.

A sickness started deep in his bowels. Someone had watched the filming. Someone had watched a live show. Travis moved out of the dim room into the blackness of the hallway and sucked fresh air with his lungs. It was a moment before he moved again. Deep inside, his demon snarled.

The next carpeted door was open as well. It too looked out on the mirrored room. It too contained discarded clothes, a water pipe, a drink. But instead of a chair there was a deep, down pallet and large pillows. The one-way mirror before them was splattered with blood and solid matter. The body of the slasher sprawled before it.

Travis's sickness grew.

His demon was silent, watching with green-gold cat eyes. It stepped where he stepped.

A third booth had also been used. It was a replica of the first, with its deeply padded armchair. A robe hung on a gold hook. A drink dripped from the mirrored table, its glass overturned. Here the smell of semen was strong.

The smell, like bleach and old wine mixed together, covered him. Travis blinked. Recalled the last time that smell had affected him so. At Chris's. Her body, bleeding and bruised, curled around itself, fetal-like. Accusing. Another victim in a long line of victims wounded because of him. Because of his insufficiencies. His indecision. His weakness.

David. Jack. Marlow. Chris. Some small part of him stronger than the pictures in his mind urged him out of the cubicle into the hallway. That part, cool and decisive, fought the incapacitating memories, the blazing confusion, with icy calm. It dictated. Travis, his mind helpless, followed.

Alain Brevard, if he was still in the building, was somewhere ahead. If he was still in the building, he'd be destroying the evidence. If he'd been listening to the conversation in the mirrored room, Brevard had heard Travis demand his backup. Brevard knew he was a cop. Travis wished he'd taken the camera's film and given it to Bill.

The raw, icy part of him analyzed and accepted all this. Travis, alone in the darkness, slipped to the beaten door that led to the parlor. Searching fingers found it in the dark and opened it slightly. No sound came from the pale-toned room. Empty.

Back across to the inner hallway, the fourth carpeted door opened to a fourth viewing cubicle. Through the mirror/window poured the sickly golden light. And myriad reflections, movement. Alain Brevard. Dousing liquid from a five-gallon container, its color lost in the yellow glow. Spraying it onto carpet, bedding, his slacks were black where the sparkling liquid drenched them. His shoes slipped on the soaked carpet.

Spinning, his feet silent, muffled, Travis sped down the hallway to the cul-de-sac and the electronic door. Pausing, he glanced into the room that blocked the hallway. It was an office. Opulent. Decadent. Dripping and dark with gasoline. The fluid saturated his cloth shoes, soaked through to his feet. Its fumes replaced the scent of semen that clung to him. All this in an instant. The image through the office window was compelling. Demanding.

Alain Brevard sloshed the last of the liquid into the black hole of the control booth, tossing the can in after. Travis bolted the last few steps to the electronic door. It hung open, exposing the circular room. And the slowly closing crack of blackness on the far side.

A second electronic door.

A flash of yellow flame and the door swept shut.

In slow motion Travis watched the match fall to the soaked carpet.

A torch. A bomb.

Whirling, he slammed himself against the wall. The fireball blazed past his face, sucking the oxygen out of the hallway, singeing his hair, his brows, his skin. He was thankful it blazed upward, too high to touch his drenched shoes and the dry carpet where he stood.

The instant the billow of flame receded, Travis moved, tearing back down the hallway, into the darkness. The roar of fresh flames licked hungrily at his path, melting the nylon carpet into a flaming pool.

The air, so fresh only a moment before, was suddenly smoke-filled as the powerful circulation system fed the flames and fanned the smoke. It carried the stench of burning nylon and gasoline and human flesh.

Travis stopped, rested against a wall, and sucked at air that soothed his lungs. Ahead was light. The contained flames brightened the cubicles and spilled out into the smoky hallway. Dancing light in strange patterns swirled slowly.

Behind was the roar of the fire.

Ahead was Alain Brevard.

Travis stepped slowly, his weapon in both hands, his right side scraping the inner wall. He was almost even with the first cubicle when he heard the sound. Liquid, a muffled splash on the carpet.

Through the smoke came an apparition. Alain Brevard.

Lips stretching in a ravening grin, the catlike demon within, the Nam-bred creature of the night, pounced, struggled for control. Won. Travis, standing in smoky shadows, raised his weapon, aimed, waited.

Alain Brevard wiped at his face, dashed wet fingers through his hair, moved closer. His face was suddenly in sharp outline, his shadow massive.

Travis's demon roared. Reason screamed. The conflicting parts of himself maneuvered for control. Like an observer suddenly removed from the rivalry, Travis watched the battle.

The part of him that Nam had birthed spewed out in a putrid rush of steaming ichor. Its name was guilt. The part of himself he hated. Feared. The avenger. The killer. The creature of the night.

Countering it, defensive in posture, was the bright, shining part of himself. The part he'd aspired to. The ideal. Standing on firm principle. On law.

Opposites. Deadly enemies. Implacable. Poised in mortal combat. The final battle engaged.

Travis stepped forward into the light. Alain Brevard looked up. Eyes like black fire burned into Travis.

Bathed in the nacreous light, his skeletal hands wrapped around the weapon, Travis advanced.

Alain Brevard smiled, bent slowly—so slowly—and put down the half-empty can. He raised his hands, fingers splayed. His lips mouthed words that roared in Travis's mind.

"Hello, officer. No resistance. I'll come willingly."

Travis groaned.

Brevard smiled. "It'll all be burned soon anyway. All the physical evidence. Except the girl, and she's of little importance. So you see, I'm ready to be taken in." His voice was flat on the dead air, yet achingly familiar. The slight French tones like old wounds. "You know as well as I it won't be for long," he finished.

Travis trembled, gripped in the collision of opposing forces. Opposing needs. His face in the peculiar light was tormented. Seconds ticked by. The smoke thickened.

Realization dawned in Brevard's eyes; his hands dropped slowly. He tried to smile. The smile became a twitch. He had miscalculated.

Travis pictured the many ways this beast should die, as sweat trickled steadily into his eyes. The battle within had left him frozen. He couldn't even blink away the sting. The heat increased, pressing in. Brevard was speaking. Travis tried to concentrate, to hear the words.

"... It's personal for you ... isn't it? One of my little girls? A sister? A girlfriend?"

Still Travis was silent. Sweat soaked Brevard's shirt, slicked his hair. Something cracked to Brevard's left—mirrors giving with the heat, the sound ominous. Brevard flinched. He had been about to bargain. It was there in his eyes. Brevard still thought he might live out this night.

He wouldn't. The demon in Travis vowed it. Steadied his aim. Brevard licked his thin lips, his tongue black in the strange light.

"I ... What do you want? Money? I've got money. More money than you could ever—"

A crack sounded again, interrupting. Louder this time. The heat roasted dry their sweat. Panic showed in Brevard's eyes. He held out his hands. A gesture of peace. Of pleading. He wavered in the smoke-filled hallway, stepped closer, his throat working convulsively.

"What ... Tell me what ..."

"Nam."

Travis swallowed, hardly recognizing his own voice beneath the searing strain. But Brevard had to know. To remember. To feel. The demon struggled. Spoke.

"Nam. Da Nang. 1973." Travis paused, watching the confusion in the hated face. "David Moss.... Tortured. Killed. His head roped to a dock piling. Jack Delane...his partner. Tortured.... You were called Alain Brevard.

"I searched for you. For months. You got my calling card." Travis stopped. Watched the raw fear clutching at the Frenchman. He too was rooted to one spot, one point in time, his eyes widening with memory.

"An ace of spades and the words, 'You're mine.'"

The words roared, crystallizing the past, the present, into one agonizing moment of time. One instant that was *now*. A pain more blinding than the lights of the mirrored room racked his skull. Suddenly silent, still, the contenders in his mind paused. And in that moment of parched and terrible awareness, they considered one another. Their reality. Their power. Their survival. The near-madness that now gripped their host.

And they chose another way.

Outlines melting, they moved toward one another. Merged. Fused. Became one. Travis's fingers tightened. Squeezed.

Beyond Brevard a flash of blue flame erupted. Exploded. Roared. Raced in. In a split second Alain Brevard was consumed, his hair and clothes a blazing torch, his arms flailing, his scream like an animal impaled. Falling, he kicked over the half-empty can at his feet.

Travis dove past into the smoke-filled parlor, then through the outer door. A moment later he stood trembling in the amazing, impossible coolness and stillness of the street. Muted explosions sounded throughout the building as the flames reached the storeroom.

He fell to the street, nausea rising, lungs burning, soul

exhilarated yet strangely cheated in the final fulfillment. His mind branded with twin images. Alain Brevard burning. And the new monster in his soul. The unknown. The composite.

And Travis knew, as he sucked in painful breaths of cold air, that he'd never be free of the Nam creature. Never free of the killer that stalked the docks in cannibalistic fury. The assassin. The hunter that found whatever it sought. Destroyed whatever it found.

It was a part of him.

Always had been.

He didn't even know if he'd fired.

That night was long. The next days were longer. Paperwork. Red tape. The press. Review boards. Reports. More reports. Somewhere in the long hours he found a moment to visit a hospital for his burns. And Nikki found a reason to move out. She left a note. When he found time he would read it.

The repercussions of the night were still being considered and examined.

Whizzer had the license-plate numbers from the warehouse: three rentals registered to private companies who weren't interested in cooperating with the authorities, two stolen vehicles, and two POVs—privately owned vehicles. One was registered to a colonel's wife and the other to a beautician. The beautician's boyfriend was tentatively confirmed as having been present at the studio. But he wasn't talking. Police were still gathering evidence, but to what end Travis didn't know. No one would say.

Whizzer's sense of humor was the only stable point in Travis's life. Over Travis's desk now hung—framed and signed by a judge—a Death Warrant. Whizzer had dummied up a search warrant and presented it in a mock ceremony attended by all the local cops at Catcher Joe's. At least all the cops still speaking to him.

Matthews was heading the team doing the investigation. Matthews was a busy man. And Matthews was pissed as hell. Travis had screwed up when he hadn't called Dietrick for backup early on. "Travis's pride," he called it. Matthews wasn't sharing shit. Eventually he'd cool down, but for now Dietrick was dry on information.

Dietrick was no help either. Dietrick was getting married; he and Chris were buying a house in Silver Springs. Marriage meant a transfer to a suburban unit and a big desk with a laminated nameplate. It meant a promotion to an easy paper-pushing job where a wife wouldn't forever worry that her husband might get shot. Dietrick had asked Travis to be a groomsman.

Whizzer on the other hand was turning out tons of information and giving it to Travis on the sly. Unfortunately, it was useless. Without the investigation to back it all up, it was meaningless. And Sayaad, who might have illuminated it all, had vanished.

The girl from the studio had lived, but her mind, the doctors warned, might hold little the police could use. Trauma and shock had cleansed it. Most times she was a little girl who cuddled a doll and sang nursery rhymes. For her the night of madness had ceased to exist.

Travis's superiors, however, had excellent recall and insatiable curiosity. They wouldn't let it go. They wanted to know everything.

For a cop the law works backward. One is guilty until proven innocent. For the second time in a matter of weeks Travis was the man of the hour. Guilty. But no one was quite sure of what.

Exhausted, doing without sleep, without downtime, Travis lost weight, lost momentum, made clumsy mistakes. And for once he didn't care. His life had changed irrevocably on the night that Alain Brevard's studio had burned to the ground.

DEATH WARRANT

The old building, once it cooled, was a mound of charred brick and mortar, melted glass, twisted, buckled metal, and pools of the unidentifiable—congealed and sticky or solidified—and human remains. Alain Brevard was dead.

Dental work and fragments of bone were put through the ringer at Connelly's morgue; identified and locked away rather than buried. Brevard was federal evidence. Just about the only evidence the government had.

No bullet was recovered from the remains, but Travis had one round unaccounted for. It hadn't been found.

EPILOGUE

TRAVIS spotted Sayaad at the bar, his long legs crossed negligently against the brass foot rail. The barmaid, dressed in a rich tartan plaid, replenished his drink. Red wine, of course.

As Travis slipped onto the high stool beside Sayaad, their eyes met. He felt a quick shock of déjà vu, but it faded as he failed to place it, and Sayaad smiled.

"A Beam and Coke for my friend."

"Just the Coke. I'm working."

Sayaad raised a brow in polite inquiry. "Oh. Is this official?"

"Is that how you read it?"

"Ah. Enigmatic."

"No shit."

Sayaad smiled and shook his head. "You do have a certain penchant for spoiling the effect."

Travis slurped deeply and loudly on his straw. Sayaad sipped quietly. Amused. Travis, wondering at his constant urge to appear the barbarian before Sayaad, rested his elbows on the bar.

"So."

Sayaad quirked his brow again. Cool. Detached. The

ever-superior European. Except that Travis was certain—almost certain—Sayaad wasn't European.

"I like the news. You like the news?"

Sayaad didn't respond.

"I was listening to the news this morning on my way to work. And you know what? I heard a little something that I found intriguing. You like that word—intriguing? Anyway. It seems some guy named Paul Gaius Southerland"—Travis slurped again, watching for an effect on Sayaad's face—"blew his brains out this morning with an automatic. Messy business."

Sayaad smiled. Was he a little more relaxed than just a moment before?

"It's a presumed suicide... Probable suicide... But not definitely a suicide, if you understand my meaning."

"Oh, it's beginning to come through."

"Yeah?" Travis grinned. "Good. Cause, see, I remembered the name from Whizzer. You remember Whizzer? Skinny guy? Red hair?"

Sayaad was definitely amused. Maybe he liked the dumb cop routine. Maybe he didn't.

"Anyway Whizzer came up with four names from a list of license plates I got the night Alain Brevard said au revoir. Paul Gaius Southerland was one of them. Whizzer gave you the list last night. Or so he tells me this morning. And now all of a sudden he's dead. Southerland. Not Whizzer.

"I find that strange. Do you find that strange?"

"The only thing I find strange is your appalling Columbo imitation."

"Okay. So we'll do it straight. What do you know about Paul Gaius Southerland?"

"Not my target."

Travis paused. The eyes that stared into his were

amused, open, and unquestionably honest. Somehow Travis had expected it.

"Not my target, Travis," Sayaad said again softly.

"Right," Travis said introspectively. "I figured. So... let's talk targets. Brevard was my target. You knew that all along. You aimed the weapon and I fired it for you."

"Are you thanking me?"

"Who was yours?"

Over the airport loudspeakers flight 312, for Rio de Janeiro, was called. Last call. Sayaad tossed a large bill onto the bar and stood.

Travis, still seated, slurped the last drops from his glass. And continued slurping. The waitress looked over, irritated. Travis ignored her, his eyes locked on Sayaad's.

"You're not getting on that plane," he said softly. "I've got a warrant en route."

"I doubt that seriously." Sayaad smiled, his eyes now almost sad. "Come. Walk me to my terminal."

Silently, knowing it was a bad bluff to start with, Travis accompanied Sayaad to the metal detector. There were things he might have said. Steps he might have taken. Instead he said simply, "Your passport. It's issued to Ishmael Sayaad."

"It's real enough."

"The passport or the name?"

Sayaad smiled. "I've been through customs already, so both must have been acceptable."

Travis smiled in return, paused. "Your target?"

Green eyes slitted, Sayaad shook his head slowly. "Who was punished when the CIA assisted with drug runs in Southeast Asia? Who was punished when a plane went down in Central America, killing all aboard? The drug cartels?"

Not seeing the connection, Travis considered. "A riddle? Okay . . . No one?"

"Exactly. However, let us consider the hypothetical."

"Hypothetical."

"Indeed. Suppose there were a hypothetical high military official. A general for instance."

"A general?"

"Since we're being hypothetical."

"Okeydokey."

Sayaad lifted his brows. He did that so well.

"A general," he repeated, "in a position of public trust. A general with the ear of the NSC. And the president. Perhaps the world. Perhaps even Central and South America. Colombia."

"Colombia. You mean the drug cartels. And U.S. involvement with drugs in Vietnam. You're drawing a parallel."

"Hypothetically speaking."

"Yeah. Go on." Travis tried to keep the intense interest out of his voice.

He failed.

"You are aware, aren't you, that Vietnam is located in the Golden Triangle? Called so because of the large amount of heroin and other illicit substances that came through on their way to the West?"

"The Golden Triangle. And a general in the National Security Council."

"Precisely," Sayaad said, as though Travis had discovered some arcane mathematical formula.

"Let us suppose that this hypothetical general was blackmailed regarding certain pornographic material. And that he arranged to use U.S. troops to shield a new drug route that supplies the U.S. And that this same general once helped supply the U.S. troops in South Vietnam with heroin. All with full CIA compliance. Because

Brevard had him so addicted to drugs and blood, he couldn't say no. And because the CIA received valuable intelligence from the sources the general provided.... Hypothetically speaking."

A long moment passed.

"The Huntsmen sent you in to kill a U.S. general who helped open a new drug route. A drug route that... bypassed... Huntsmen controls. Brevard was going solo. And he used this general to...."

"To keep a drug route open. Hypothetically speaking, of course."

"Of course." Travis was quiet. It was too much to take in all at once. Drugs. Porn. And the U.S. government. Travis thought all that crap went out with Hoover's demise or the Carter reorganization.

"What would you think that person's punishment should be?"

Travis had no answer except the one he knew was mirrored in his eyes.

Sayaad flashed a brilliant smile.

Still smiling he turned, dropped his attaché case on the X-ray device, and opened it for inspection. Approved, it went on.

"Oh." Sayaad paused just in front of the metal detector. "This is yours."

He flashed his radiant smile one last time and tossed something golden at Travis. In a quick move Travis caught it—the 9mm round; the symbol of their relationship. It was still warm from Sayaad's hand.

Travis watched as Sayaad boarded the plane. It taxied and lifted into the air.

His fingers smoothed the brass casing. If he hadn't shown up, Sayaad would have ditched the round before the detector, leaving it in the restroom or the lounge. He knew that. Yet the suspicion that Sayaad had expected him was strong. Whizzer had some questions to answer about where he got certain information. Like Sayaad's airline schedule.

Travis needed a drink, regulations be damned. Back in the lounge he took his same seat, smiled half-heartedly at the kilted waitress, and ordered a gin and tonic, no lime.

The TV droned out a soap, and two physically perfect human specimens clutched each other passionately. The waitress brought his drink, flashing a bare thigh at him in the process. He liked to think it was deliberate.

Travis watched the two on the screen rumple the covers and whisper inanities at one another. It was revolting. Tossing a five onto the bar top, he turned to go. A voice held him.

"This is a CBS news bulletin. In an apparent political assassination, Lieutenant Colonel Elwood Denbrant was killed this morning inside the Pentagon."

Travis turned slowly and watched the camera pan the Pentagon's facade.

"According to Pentagon sources, a man who presented a valid ID as a military courier entered through strict Pentagon security, located Colonel Denbrant in his private office, and fired two shots point-blank into his head. The presumed assassin then left the Pentagon. Approximately thirty minutes later Colonel Denbrant was found by one of his aides.

"Military intelligence has already mounted a massive investigation and, according to our sources, expects to apprehend the suspect immediately."

"Too late," Travis whispered. "Too late."

"Colonel Denbrant was special military liaison with the Senate Ways and Means Committee. He was pivotal in Congress's decision to send U.S. Marines to Lebanon, and has had an active interest in Middle Eastern affairs for twelve years. He served as Latin American adviser during the Colombia drug-cartel crisis. He served in Vietnam for two stints and was decorated numerous times."

"Again, Colonel Denbrant has just become the victim of a political assassination inside the Pentagon walls—a Pentagon security breach believed impossible up until now.

"CBS will keep you informed on later developments. We now return you to your regularly scheduled programming."

Travis found a pay phone, made a call, and reported his suspicions and the whereabouts of Sayaad. Not that it would do any good. Brazil had only limited extradition. And by the time local officials could be induced to look for him, Sayaad would be somewhere else—and have become someone else.

Frustrated, yet perversely amused, Travis found his car and drove back to the Law Enforcement Center. He had a report to file with somebody. The feeling of amusement faded. He had a feeling he'd be man of the hour in that somebody's book. And he knew he wouldn't enjoy it one bit.

Once You've Read One
Andrew M. Greeley
You'll Want to Read Them All!

"Greeley spins wondrous romances" (*New York Times*), and his unique ability to touch the heart has made him one of America's most beloved authors. Complete your own Greeley collection with these captivating novels.

- ☐ **LORD OF THE DANCE**
  (A35-752, $5.95, USA) ($6.95, Canada)
- ☐ **LOVE SONG**
  (A35-619, $5.95, USA) ($6.95, Canada)
- ☐ **THE MAGIC CUP**
  (A34-903, $3.95, USA) ($4.95, Canada)
- ☐ **PATIENCE OF A SAINT**
  (A34-682, $4.95, USA) ($5.95, Canada)
- ☐ **RITE OF SPRING**
  (A34-341, $4.95, USA) ($5.95, Canada)
- ☐ **THY BROTHER'S WIFE**
  (A35-765, $5.95, USA) ($6.95, Canada)
- ☐ **VIRGIN AND MARTYR**
  (A32-873, $4.95, USA) ($5.95, Canada)

**Warner Books P.O. Box 690
New York, NY 10019**

Please send me the books I have checked. I enclose a check or money order (not cash), plus 95¢ per order and 95¢ per copy to cover postage and handling,* or bill my ☐ American Express ☐ VISA ☐ MasterCard. (Allow 4-6 weeks for delivery.)

___Please send me your free mail order catalog. (If ordering only the catalog, include a large self-addressed, stamped envelope.)

Card # _____

Signature _____ Exp. Date _____

Name _____

Address _____

City _____ State _____ Zip _____

*New York and California residents add applicable sales tax.

The Irresistible Magic of
Andrew M. Greeley

Bestselling author Andrew M. Greeley, one of America's most gifted storytellers, is truly "an expert on the emotions that make us human" (*Minneapolis Star*). If you've missed any of these spellbinding Greeley titles, here's the perfect chance to catch up!

- ☐ **ANGELS OF SEPTEMBER**
  (A34-428, $4.95, USA) ($5.95, Canada)
- ☐ **ASCENT INTO HELL**
  (A34-949, $4.95, USA) ($5.95, Canada)
- ☐ **THE CARDINAL SINS**
  (A34-208, $4.95, USA) ($6.50, Canada)
- ☐ **HAPPY ARE THE CLEAN OF HEART**
  (A35-722, $4.95, USA) ($5.95, Canada)
- ☐ **HAPPY ARE THE MEEK**
  (A32-706, $3.95, USA) ($4.95, Canada)
- ☐ **HAPPY ARE THOSE WHO THIRST FOR JUSTICE**
  (A34-946, $4.50, USA) ($5.50, Canada)

**Warner Books P.O. Box 690
New York, NY 10019**

Please send me the books I have checked. I enclose a check or money order (not cash), plus 95¢ per order and 95¢ per copy to cover postage and handling,* or bill my ☐ American Express ☐ VISA ☐ MasterCard. (Allow 4-6 weeks for delivery.)

___Please send me your free mail order catalog. (If ordering only the catalog, include a large self-addressed, stamped envelope.)

Card # _____

Signature _____ Exp. Date _____

Name _____

Address _____

City _____ State _____ Zip _____
*New York and California residents add applicable sales tax.

469